THE MURDER AFFAIR

BOOKS BY ALICE CASTLE

A Beth Haldane Mystery

The Murder Mystery

The Murder Museum

The Murder Question

The Murder Plot

The Murder Walk

The Murder Club

The Murder Hour

The Murder Garden

THE MURDER AFFAIR

ALICE CASTLE

bookouture

Published by Bookouture in 2023

An imprint of Storyfire Ltd.
Carmelite House
50 Victoria Embankment
London EC4Y 0DZ

www.bookouture.com

ISBN: 978-1-83790-458-7
eBook ISBN: 978-1-83790-457-0

To Ella and Connie, with love

ONE

Beth Haldane had never felt more uncomfortable. Her toes were being squeezed to death in unaccustomed court shoes, she was wearing slithery ten denier tights instead of her trusty jeans, and she was swamped by a black silk shirt hastily borrowed from her best friend, Katie. Worst of all, her left leg had completely gone to sleep.

Ouch! Suddenly the numb feeling in her calf was replaced by crippling pins and needles. She shifted on the rock-hard pew, but hadn't taken the highly polished wood into account. She shot forward, almost braining herself on the little ledge built into the row in front. Her black-edged order of service went flying and a pile of hymn books fell to the tiled floor with an almighty clatter, echoing all the way to the vaulted ceiling of the church.

There was a loud tut. Her mother, dressed in heavy mourning including a thickly veiled hat that Beth thought preposterous, started telling her off waspishly. Her sharp tones cut right through the organ music burbling away gently in the background. Heads turned all over the church as Wendy really got into her stride.

'For goodness' sake, Beth. I can't take you anywhere, can I? Just sit still, will you? And stop *fidgeting*. You're making a total exhibition of yourself.'

Beth smarted at the injustice. Wendy was the one now drawing attention, as the congregation twittered and nudged each other all around them. But the debacle didn't end there. She peered under her pew, and saw her service sheet had ended up lodged beneath the feet of the woman behind, a well-preserved fifty-something matron. The lady had a wonderful peaches and cream complexion but the red eyes of someone who'd been weeping for days.

Beth gestured apologetically to her, and the woman passed over the now-crumpled leaflet. On the front was a photograph of a devastatingly handsome elderly man, clutching a pipe in his hand. He had the aura of a film star from the golden years of Hollywood, perhaps because the picture was in black and white – or perhaps because of the unmistakably roguish twinkle in his eye. The words *In Loving Memory of Len Broughton* were printed underneath.

Then the lady who'd passed the leaflet glared, as Beth's mother turned to see what was going on now. She apparently had no trouble at all in recognising Wendy Haldane, despite the thick veil. She hissed at her, '*You!* I don't know how you have the effrontery to show your face here.'

'What on earth was that about?' Beth asked her mother in a low voice as they whipped round to face the front. 'What did that lady mean?'

Wendy shushed her and then proceeded to ignore her daughter, busying herself by scrutinising the order of service with the dedication she usually reserved for a winning hand at Bridge. At that moment the organ snapped out of its background mode and started up with a thunderous anthem, and the small, round and balding vicar of St Matthew's shuffled forward and coughed in a vain attempt to get everyone's attention. He opened his mouth to speak, but had to wait until the organist had come to a final, deafening crescendo that seemed to shake the very walls of the ancient church, before he finally said a few words of welcome.

Beth's leg was feeling better now, and she took the opportunity to have another look around. As her mother had insisted they arrive incredibly early, sweeping into a pew only a couple of rows from the altar, Beth hadn't realised quite how full the church was. But it was standing room only. Surely even when she had been pressganged into coming here for Christmas services as a child, it had never been this full? And wasn't it a bit strange that so many of the congregation were women of a certain age – her mother's generation? Funny, also, that so many of them were sitting alone.

'Do you know any of these ladies? Looks like there could be some Bridge Club friends. And look, over there, isn't that Mrs Hill? Your neighbour?' she whispered to Wendy. 'Look, she seems so sad. And goodness, I don't believe it, that's Angela Douglas. Crying!' Beth stared, transfixed, at the sight of the usually poised and elegant head of the College School, Dulwich's fiercely academic girls' academy, sniffing unabashedly into what looked like a black-trimmed handkerchief. Next to her was her deputy, stocky Bernie Troughton, with a face like thunder. Beth caught her eye for a second and looked away hurriedly.

'Beth, do be quiet, the poor vicar is trying to make himself heard,' Wendy said out of the side of her mouth. Beth thought mutinously he'd have a much better chance if he would just speak up a bit. They were virtually at the front, horribly close to poor old Len Broughton's coffin, loaded down with the massive (and in Beth's view totally inappropriate) wreath of scarlet roses that Wendy had insisted on ordering at vast expense from Bartley's in Dulwich Village. Despite this, Beth could hardly hear the Reverend Timothy Bainwright as he mumbled his way through the funeral service. It wasn't all his fault, though. As he started yet another prayer, Beth realised the background noise of weeping, coming from various different corners of the church, really wasn't helping.

She turned to her mother and asked her very quietly, 'What's going on, Mum? Why are all these other ladies crying?'

Wendy hushed her furiously again, then said crossly, 'How should I know? You never liked Len, anyway.'

This was so unfair, and Beth felt she had no choice but to point it out. 'I hardly had a chance to dislike him! I didn't even know you were going out with him until he died. You didn't say one word about it.'

In fact, Wendy had been more than usually aloof for the past couple of months. But this hadn't been, as Beth had hoped, because she'd finally stopped her passive-aggressive games with her only daughter and settled into enjoying her retirement. No, she'd been seeing this Len Broughton instead, gadding about the village like a teenager – until his sudden death.

Wendy took no notice. 'Just because he didn't have a Dulwich accent, and a Dulwich background,' she hissed scathingly. 'I never took you for such a snob, Beth Haldane.'

'I am not a snob! I never met Len, I've no idea what accent he's got – er, had,' Beth started to protest. But then a lady, this time in the row in front of them, turned and fixed Wendy with a peculiarly malevolent stare.

'I don't know how you dare show your face in this church. And now disrupting the service with all this bickering, while I'm trying to remember the love of my life...' the woman hissed, red-rimmed eyes boring into Wendy's.

'The love of *your* life? He was the love of *my* life, I'll have you know,' Wendy shot back at top volume, all her strictures to Beth about silence in church apparently forgotten.

Beth just had time to feel disgruntled on behalf of her poor dad. Surely he, father of Wendy's two lovely children, should have been in pole position? Were his long years of patient servitude now worth nothing? But then there came a high-pitched voice from the other side of the aisle. 'What the hell do you mean?' A trim woman in her late forties shot up. 'Len was my boyfriend!'

All over the church, more women got to their feet and started yelling. If it hadn't been a funeral – and if her mother hadn't been in floods of tears – it would actually have been an amusing 'I'm Spartacus' moment. As it was, Beth watched on, aghast. The vicar, looking thoroughly discombobulated, shifted from foot to foot, wringing his hands. Then there was a flurry of movement as one of the ladies shoved her way out of her pew and rushed up the aisle. For a moment, Beth wondered whether she was going to attack Wendy, or maybe even the poor little reverend, but she didn't pause, flashing straight past Beth and her mother on vertiginously high heels, and throwing herself right on the coffin where it stood by the altar.

Wendy was instantly on her feet. 'Don't you dare squash my roses! And get off my Len.'

It was the signal for general mayhem to break out. At the back of the church, the owner of the village deli thwacked the lady next to her round the head with her black patent clutch bag. Closer to the front, the granny of one of Beth's son's friends picked up an embroidered hassock and hurled it at her neighbour. As Beth looked on in astonishment, a large black cartwheel hat bowled up the central aisle of the church and came to rest against the coffin. Then, to Beth's horror, Wendy started making her way to the end of their pew. Surely she wasn't going to chuck herself into the mêlée? But she was pushed back down by another woman striding up to the altar.

'How dare you shove me like that? What right do you have —' Wendy started.

'I have every right,' the woman said as she turned to face the congregation, standing right in front of the little vicar and blocking him entirely from view. Her tailored black suit was the perfect contrast to the expertly highlighted blonde hair swirling around her shoulders, and the light breaking through the stained glass windows glanced off long diamond earrings and the tears glittering in her eyes, as she announced, at the top of her voice, 'I am Len Broughton's wife.'

TWO

The evening shadows were lengthening by the time Beth settled Wendy back in her pretty little house near College Road. It was just a short walk from St Matthew's Church, scene of the funeral fiasco, but it had taken hours for everyone to be interviewed by the police. Beth privately thought getting the authorities involved had been a waste of time, but the nervous assistant verger had dialled 999 when it looked as though Reverend Bainwright was going down for the third time in a sea of angry middle-aged women, all proclaiming their unbreakable bond with Len Broughton. The arrival of the afternoon keep-fit club members, who held their sessions in the church, not to mention the weekly mother and baby group, meant that the place was still in uproar, with yoga mats and pushchairs being used as impromptu weapons, when Beth finally managed to persuade DC Narinda Khan that there was nothing further Wendy could say to shed light on the affair.

Beth didn't know what was more distressing, having to pull favours with Narinda, her boyfriend Harry York's annoyingly attractive sidekick, or coping with her lovelorn mother, who was still bristling with the need to insist that, despite all evidence to the contrary, she was the only woman in Len Broughton's life.

Beth placed a cup of tea, made in one of her mother's favourite fiddly bone china cups, on a coaster emblazoned with roses that reminded her strongly of the unfortunate wreath. That had last been seen being converted into very expensive pot pourri by a bevy of angry ladies, every one claiming first dibs on Len's affections.

On cue, Wendy sighed gustily. Beth suppressed an equally huge sigh of her own. She was itching to get back home to Pickwick Road, where her twelve-year-old son, Jake, would be shirking his homework and where Colin the Labrador and Magpie the moggy would no doubt be festooned all over the banned sofa. But instead she slumped in the chair opposite Wendy, on the other side of her gas-effect fireplace, and looked across at her. Wendy was shredding a sodden tissue into a horrible mess which, Beth judged with her expert eye, was going to be a total pain to hoover off the carpet.

Beth's relationship with her mother had never been an easy one. She didn't want to judge Wendy too harshly, but she did sometimes wonder whether she had cooked her father to death, presenting him with huge fry-ups every morning and massive steamed puddings every night, until he succumbed to a heart attack far too early. What was more, the family diet changed radically the day after her father's demise, and Wendy had been picking at muesli and salad ever since. Now, looking across at her dispassionately, Beth could see her mother had aged twenty years since this morning.

Wendy's hair had been snow white for years, and went beautifully with her periwinkle blue eyes. But now, even though she was only in her mid-fifties, Beth could see exactly what her mother would look like when she was in her seventh decade, if not her eighth. Her face was drawn, with cruel marionette lines pulling at the contours of her mouth. The events in the church had clearly shocked her to the core.

'Mum, what do you think was going on with Len?' Beth asked her gently.

Wendy, who had been gazing sightlessly out of the window, seemed to drag herself back into the room with some difficulty. 'What was that, dear?'

'Len. I mean, all those women. What on earth was he up to?'

At once, those blue eyes filled with tears again and Beth wished fervently that she'd kept her questions to herself. But, to her surprise, Wendy started to speak.

'He promised me he wasn't seeing anyone else. But I'm beginning to wonder if he wasn't telling me an incy bit of a lie,' quavered Wendy, holding the damp tissue up to her welling eyes. The myriad strings of jet beads around her neck shivered and tinkled with every movement.

Judging by the number of disgruntled well-preserved women in widow's weeds packing out the church, yes, Len had been telling a thumping great whopper. But why were they all so angry? Perhaps there was a bit more to it than just a bunch of lovelorn women. Beth tutted inwardly and pulled out some fresh Kleenex from the box on the wobbly little table between them. All Wendy's furniture was like this particular piece: unnecessarily ornate, useless, and pretty unstable. And it wasn't just the furniture, Beth thought. Then she ticked herself off for being so uncharitable.

'I think you need to prepare yourself for the fact that, yes, Len might have been a bit, erm, parsimonious with the truth,' said Beth gently.

Immediately, Wendy drew herself up to her full height. As this was less even than Beth's own five-foot-not-much, it was not impressive. But it did show Wendy was rallying and coming out of the gloom which had been beginning to worry her daughter.

'I'll have you know, whatever Len might have been, ahem, up to, *I* was the number one lady in his life. He told me that right before he – he – he died,' she wailed, her face crumpling again. Beth wordlessly proffered another handful of tissues and got up to give her mother an awkward hug.

Then she waited for Wendy to get herself under control, while she carried on trying to pat her shoulder comfortingly. As she did so she cast a baleful eye over the room, from the chintz button-back sofa brimming with antique lace cushions too tiny to be comfy, to the decorative plates covering the walls, the shelves of figurines and the innumerable vases of posies. It was such a dainty, not to say overpoweringly feminine, room. Beth only had the black-bordered photo on the order of service to judge by, but handsome, debonair Len Broughton had looked full of vim and vigour. Had he really sat here, puffing on that pipe, pledging eternal love to her mother? Wouldn't he have been a bit of a bull in a china shop in this cluttered, frilly space? And she couldn't help feeling peeved again at the thought that Wendy seemed so much more overset by this death than she had been by her father's, years before.

'What sort of a man was Len Broughton?' she asked her mother when the snuffles had died down and Wendy had been provided with a fresh cup of tea. 'He was smoking in that photo. Surely you can't stand smokers?'

'Oh, cigarettes, no,' shuddered Wendy. 'But a pipe is so manly, don't you think? And his special tobacco always smelled divine. Though he had started smoking a bit too much recently. Oh Beth! If only you could have known Len. You'd have thought he was simply marvellous,' she trilled.

Beth doubted that. She already had a whole raft of misgivings about the very popular Mr Broughton. She kept those quiet, though, merely reminding her mother, 'Well, you could have introduced me. Any time in these last few weeks. Or was it months?'

'Oh, the time just flew by. I feel as though I've known him forever. Or I did,' sniffled Wendy, retreating into her trademark vagueness. This was a sure sign she was trying to cover something up. But what, Beth wondered.

Beth saw tears welling again and immediately wanted to head them off. If she was going to get home at a reasonable hour, she really needed to leave soon, and before she could go, Wendy had to be in a much calmer place. Whatever Beth's disgruntlement about this outpouring for – from her perspective – a total stranger, there was no doubt that the death of this man, and the sudden knowledge of his many other entanglements, had come as a dreadful blow to her mother.

'What about that woman who was saying she was Len's wife? Did you know he was married?'

'Well of course I didn't, Beth. You can't possibly imagine I'd get involved with someone who was spoken for? I'm sure that woman is nothing but a... a... deranged fantasist.'

Beth shrugged. She hadn't thought her mother was going to get involved with anyone at all, married or not. Perhaps she'd been naïve. Wendy had been widowed for years. And, by the look of things, she'd totally got over Beth's late dad.

'Well, she was pretty convinced that she was his wife.' Beth didn't say so to Wendy, but the woman had stuck to her guns, right through her questioning with Narinda Khan.

Beth just happened to have been behind a handy pillar outside the sacristy when the DC had been trying to extract the meat of the issue from the self-styled Mrs Broughton. After all, it wasn't often that you saw pitched battle break out between the matrons of Dulwich. A little light bitching over the dinner tables of the village was to be expected, perhaps. One-upwomanship about the prospects of children or grandchildren was almost a given. Catty remarks about the success, or otherwise, of other people's interior design schemes could be waved away. But full-on hair pulling, tripping people up, slapping them with dusty copies of *Hymns Ancient and Modern* and screeching in church were shenanigans that had never been witnessed in Dulwich before, Beth was willing to bet.

'But did you actually recognise her? The woman claiming to be Len's wife?' Beth persisted gently.

'Oh, well of course I did,' Wendy snapped, as if goaded just that bit too far by her daughter's wilful ignorance. 'Everyone knows Margery Brinkwell.'

Beth was taken aback. 'And you know her, too?'

'Not as well as Len, apparently,' Wendy said with another tremulous sniff. Beth watched anxiously but her mother's eyes didn't brim over this time. Indeed, thinking about her love rival seemed to be drying up her rivers of tears every bit as successfully as Beth could have hoped. 'That woman has a lot to answer for.'

'So she didn't use Len's surname, then?'

Wendy rolled her eyes. 'Obviously not.'

'And they didn't live together?'

'No,' said Wendy shortly. 'Of course they didn't. Len has... had... a divine little cottage in Calton Avenue. And that Margery Brinkwell lives on a broomstick somewhere.'

'Brinkwell, Brinkwell... Now that I think about it, the name is familiar,' Beth said. 'Is she something to do with the Wyatt Estate?'

A spasm, almost of pain, crossed Wendy's face. 'She is indeed. Well, she is now. She used to be one of those nurse managers at King's College Hospital – you know, the type that bosses everyone about. But that wasn't good enough for her and now she bullies everyone at the Wyatt Estate instead.'

The Wyatt Estate was the body that administered the fortune of disgraced swashbuckler Sir Thomas Wyatt. Wyatt, who had founded the school Beth's son Jake attended, had made it big in the sixteen-somethings and his wealth was even more ginormous now, as the land his schools, church and almshouses stood on had steadily increased in value over the centuries. Much of the housing stock around Dulwich Village, including Beth's own Pickwick Road, was built on Estate land and Beth and her neighbours had to pay a peppercorn rent for it every year, which Beth at least bitterly resented, thanks to her in-depth knowledge of Wyatt's abhorrent crimes as a slave trader. Beth dimly remembered seeing the name Brinkwell on the list of trustees... and now she came to think of it, had even once had her pointed out at a swanky do at Wyatt's Museum of Art that her best friend Katie had dragged her to.

'So she kept her maiden name. And you really hadn't ever heard a whisper about her and Len?'

'Clearly not,' Wendy said shortly. 'But I suppose, looking back on it now, nothing would surprise me about *Margery Brinkwell*. That's why I think she was probably the one who murdered Len.'

Beth, who'd been wondering again if now might be a good moment to extract herself, as Wendy seemed to have got past her crying jag at last, was brought up short. 'Murdered him?'

'Yes, darling. I haven't wanted to say anything before. Well, you know me, I hate to make a fuss,' Wendy said, dabbing eyes that were modestly downcast. 'But now the funeral's out of the way, I feel I can speak at last. And the more I think about it, the surer I am that something... terrible happened to Len. I bet it was that Brinkwell woman behind it. But I want you to find out for certain.'

THREE

Wendy said 'that Brinkwell woman' with such animus that for a moment Beth felt sorry for her. It wasn't pleasant being in her mother's bad books. And the idea that Len Broughton had been murdered was surely absurd. Wasn't it?

'What on earth makes you think he might have been, erm, done away with?' Beth asked her mother.

'People don't just drop down dead for no reason, Beth. I think he was murdered. And if he was, it had to be Margery. I'd stake my children's lives on that.'

'Hang on a minute! Can we keep my life out of it, please? You can swear on Josh's if you want to,' Beth said. She was very fond of her older brother but, as usual, he was away photographing a war in a difficult corner of the globe. What he didn't know wouldn't hurt him. 'Just tell me what on earth makes you suspect that it wasn't a natural death.'

'Well, for one thing, it was so sudden. Len was absolutely fine, on our – his – last evening. I dropped him off at his place after a meal at our usual Thursday restaurant – that new Italian trattoria, so romantic – and I distinctly saw that woman loitering around the house even though she doesn't live there, as I told you. Normally he would have come back home with me,' Wendy said coyly. 'But he said he wasn't well and had a bit of work to do.'

'So he was ill?' Beth pounced.

'Really, Beth. You can be a bit peaky without dying. Anyway, when I saw her, *Margery*, naturally I just thought he'd had some sort of scheduling clash – he worked in planning at the council, you see, and as Margery is with the Estate, well of course they'd have to have meetings from time to time...'

'But surely not in the evening? And at his house? It doesn't sound very, um, professional.'

'Yes, thank you, Beth,' Wendy said tersely. 'Obviously I know that now. But at the time I thought nothing of it. I trusted him implicitly. Anyway, the next thing I knew, he was...' She collapsed in tears again before finally getting the word out as one long continuous wail, 'Deeeaaaad.'

Beth reached for the tissues again but the box was empty. She got up and searched the tiny galley kitchen, but although the cupboards revealed enough tins of low-fat soup to take her mother easily through a brace of nuclear winters, there were no more boxes of Kleenex. She went to the downstairs loo, looking askance at the artful bouquets of dried lavender and knick-knacks clustered everywhere, and pinched a roll of loo paper. She handed it to her mum.

Even though her eyes were swimming, Wendy spotted the substitution immediately and was not amused. 'Oh Beth, really,' she protested weakly, then started weeping again.

Beth sat back down and resigned herself to her fate. She sent Jake, now in Year 8, a quick text exhorting him to complete all homework after having a quick snack but before even glancing at a screen. Harry had also sent her a WhatsApp and she suppressed a loving smile, responding simply with a row of hearts.

'Well, if you can't spare me any of your attention, Beth, you might as well go, you've obviously got far more important things to do than listen to your poor, heartbroken mother,' Wendy snapped.

Beth bit her lip, put her phone face down on the arm of her chair, and then gave her mother her best poker face.

'OK then, Mum, is it just because Margery Brinkwell was hanging round Len's house that you think she murdered him? Or is there more to it than that?'

Wendy rearranged her necklaces crossly, the beads jangling as she tried in vain to untangle them. She gave up with a sigh. 'Well of course there's more to it. I mean, what was she doing there, for a start?'

'Mum, she was married to the guy. You heard her. It sounds like she had a right to go there, even if she didn't live there permanently,' Beth pointed out gently. 'Did you spend much time at his house?'

'No,' said Wendy. 'In fact, we always came here. But that's no excuse for her to be lurking around. None at all.'

Beth was beginning to feel that sneaking sympathy for Margery Brinkwell again. If Len had been unwell – and as he had been pronounced dead not that long afterwards, this seemed like a given – was the woman hanging around because she could see he wasn't on top form? Perhaps it was odd Len hadn't wanted Wendy to stay. But then, he was being pretty sneaky about the whole already-married thing. And, if he was feeling off-colour, perhaps he just needed a rest. While Beth loved her mother dearly, she could not, hand on heart, say she was always relaxing company. Even when you weren't mortally ill.

Beth wasn't sure how much of this to say. She wanted to keep things realistic – but hopefully not tip Wendy over the edge again. She thought rapidly. Was there anything which would distract her mother from her tears, and these strange accusations? Maybe if Beth could get some more information about what Len Broughton was really like? If there was any truth at all to the idea that he had been murdered, this might well shine a light on motive. After all, the character of the murder victim often helped to suggest why they'd met their fate. In this case, if there was any chance that her mother was right, then Beth would lay an outside bet on the fact that Len's death had something to do with him being an incorrigible womaniser. Wendy's first words did nothing to dispel the notion.

'If only you'd met Len properly, Beth. Then you'd have known exactly how charming he was.' Wendy sighed, a faraway look in her eye. 'Everybody loved him. He just had this... wonderful way about him. And he always knew what to say to people, and when. That's an art, you know. Something you'd do well to cultivate.'

Beth tried not to react to the implied rebuke. Wendy was continually giving Beth helpful hints on where she was going wrong with her life. Unfortunately, it always made her want to veer off even further in the direction her mother was counselling her against. And being a massive flirt, at the very least, didn't seem the best way for her to get things done.

'Have you ever thought that Len might have been a bit too charming for his own good?' she said very quietly, before hastening on to less contentious matters. 'I know what, Mum, tell me how you met him for the first time.'

'Oh! Oh yes...' Instantly Wendy was all a-twitter at the happy memories. 'Well, of course I'd known him a little bit for years, because of all his good works on the council.'

'Aha,' said Beth. 'So that's where you crossed paths.' Wendy had been in a war of attrition with her next-door neighbour, Mrs Hill, for years now. The initial row had been over Mrs Hill's carp, which gave Wendy 'the willies'. Then Mrs Hill had struck back (more effectively, it had to be said) with a denunciation of Wendy for harbouring Japanese knotweed in her back garden, and had promptly got the authorities involved.

'Yes, Len asked me to explain what was going on. So I went to the meeting and, well, there was a little twinkle in his eye that I have to admit I did find rather...'

Beth had to break in here. It was too cringeworthy. 'But they said you had to get rid of all of the knotweed, or risk a huge fine?'

'Well, criminal prosecution, actually. Apparently, if knotweed gets off private land and into public areas, it's a big hoo-ha. What a lot of fuss for a little plant. But Len was so sweet, explaining it all. And then lovely Joshy was wonderful, getting rid of it.'

Now Beth really ground her teeth. Her commitment-shy brother had indeed been dragooned into coming home to help out with the weed expulsion, as Wendy hadn't wanted to employ expensive experts, but it had been Beth and Harry who had organised and carried out most of the work, with Josh sauntering in at the last minute to put a match to the bonfire that Beth, Harry and Jake had laboriously made according to council guidelines at the furthest edge of Wendy's garden.

'Anyway,' said Beth quickly, before Wendy could expound any further on what a total hero Josh had been. 'That was the start of it, was it?'

Wendy now squirmed a little in her seat. 'Well, not exactly. Because I'd heard on the Bridge grapevine that Len was close to a couple of the lady members...'

'So you knew he had a bit of a reputation? Even before you got together?'

'A "reputation", Beth! That's such an old-fashioned way to put it. I never knew you were such a Puritan,' Wendy scoffed.

'That's funny, because you brought me up to be one,' Beth countered, and then immediately felt terrible when Wendy got all teary again. 'Come on, Mum, go on with the story. So how did you and Len finally get together?'

Again Wendy lost her peevish look and her eyes became

unfocused, looking back on the recent past with every sign of rapture. 'Oh, it was one of those wonderful moments of serendipity. I was just popping into the library to get the latest book on Bridge technique. Not that I need to swot up, you understand, but it doesn't do any harm to be au fait with the latest trends, does it?'

Beth, whose own brush with Bridge a while ago had put her off the game for life, merely smiled encouragingly.

'Well, Len was in the library, talking to the chief librarian. He was so good at doing the rounds of all the local resources, making sure everyone was happy.' She shook her head sadly.

'Was this chief librarian by any chance an attractive woman of about your age?' Beth asked.

'Cheryl Brandreth might be younger than me by a whisker but I couldn't possibly comment on whether she's attractive or not,' Wendy replied in the smug tones of someone sure she was winning that particular beauty contest. 'Anyway, he wasn't talking to her for long. Because as soon as I came in, I had a little mishap with the books I was taking back. I dropped them by the entrance. Well, those plastic covers they put on library books are so slippery, aren't they? And before I knew it, Len had come over and was helping me pick everything up. He was such a gentleman,' Wendy sighed reminiscently, and tailed off into a rapturous silence.

'Well?' said Beth restlessly. 'What happened next?' She was more conscious than ever of time ticking on. She'd have to get the supper started soon, and sort out Jake's swimming kit for the next day. She had a horrible feeling she hadn't fished it out of the washing machine that morning.

'We got chatting. Len just had such a gift for making you feel at ease. And, of course, he had those matinée idol looks. He saw that I was giving back some books on cookery for one and he said what a terrible shame it was to be on one's own, how he had never quite got used to being a widower...'

'Not surprising, given that his wife is still alive,' Beth couldn't help remarking.

Wendy sighed gustily. 'If you aren't going to be supportive, I'm not sure I can continue.' Her mouth set into a determined little line that Beth was all too familiar with.

'It's not that, Mum. I'm really sad about what's happened. But it looks like Len was playing you, doesn't it? And not just you. A whole bunch of people, if the congregation in that church was anything to go by.'

'I disagree entirely. Len might have had the odd bit of fun here and there. He was a very attractive man. I can't deny women were drawn to him. But I was his one true love. I know that, because he said so.' Wendy pressed the fragment of loo roll to her eyes.

'Look, I know you're terribly upset, Mum. But do you think there's a possibility that he said the exact same thing to all the other ladies as well?'

Wendy took a deep breath and said in her firmest voice, 'No I don't, Beth. Absolutely not. We were everything to each other. In fact, we were s-s-soulmates. And that's why I owe it to him to find out exactly what happened to him, and why. Obviously, I'm in no state to have the police milling about, it would simply be much too upsetting. But you'll look into it for me, won't you, Beth? For your old mother? And of course you've got lovely Harry to help you out. After all, that's how you've done so well with your other cases.'

Wendy said this with her usual soft-spoken lilt and her head tilted gently to one side. Beth put her teacup down with such a thump on its delicate bone china coaster that for a second she was sure she must have cracked it in two. Thank heavens, it was fine. That was more than could be said for her blood pressure, though. Where did her mother get off? Harry was the last person who'd help her solve crimes and if Wendy didn't know that... But there was no point getting cross. Wendy would only cry again, and she'd be sobbing even more if Beth left her to make unwarranted accusations of murder against upstanding members of the community like Margery Brinkwell. She could get arrested for less.

There was nothing for it, Beth would just have to tackle this Len Broughton business herself.

FOUR

At home later that evening, Beth did her best to concentrate on the Finnish noir on TV. She was in her favourite place in the world, on the sofa with Harry. Magpie was sitting right next to them, pretending she wasn't breaking one of the cardinal rules of the house, and Colin was lying on the floor across her toes, wishing he was. Jake was tucked up in bed with his light off.

Yet despite all the essential elements being in place, she couldn't concentrate on the events in the snow-strewn town being terrorised by a dastardly serial killer. She was still grinding her teeth at her mother's infuriating comments about Harry solving her cases for her. If only! She'd told her mother often enough that Harry wouldn't discuss a thing with her, let alone present her with solutions when she asked. And now her mother expected her to wrap up this business in seconds flat. She sympathised deeply with her poor mum, she was clearly in bits about Len. But this was going to be no easy matter.

Could Len really have been murdered? Or was Wendy letting her imagination – and her dislike of Margery Brinkwell – get the better of her? And was Beth really being snobby about the whole idea of her mother and Len?

Facing the fact that Wendy had had a relationship – even if it had been necessarily short-lived – was quite difficult for Beth. She'd somehow imagined that her mother would always be contented with her status as a widow. As far as Beth knew (and she shuddered slightly at the thought) Wendy had never even flirted with a man. But maybe she was wrong. Maybe Wendy had been sizing up all the available single men at Bridge and at innumerable village dinner parties for years, and Len was the first one who'd somehow made the grade.

Beth wasn't really sure why Wendy felt her resistance to Len was down to snobbery. She'd never met the man (until that very day, and he'd hardly been in a position to make much of an impression – although admittedly his coffin was extremely shiny). What she did know was that he was a whiz with the ladies. Most of the womenfolk of Dulwich seemed convinced he was in love with them. He must have been doing something to encourage them, mustn't he? So the signs were that, if Beth had reservations about Len, they were probably entirely justified.

She was a bit picky about some things, Beth conceded, as the plucky Finnish detective kicked down the door of a dodgy-looking outbuilding in the frozen wastes outside Helsinki. But she was sure that, if Len had lived, reduced his number of girl-friends to one, and done something about the excess wife as well, she would have welcomed him into the family. There had definitely been something about him, even in that photo on the order of service. Maybe it had been the cravat. Or the pipe. Or that roguish glint in his eye. Those chiselled looks, and that beguiling smile, seemed to invite you to share a special secret. Beth could see how attractive that could be – even when the secret was a marriage and umpteen other love interests.

It was not easy, once someone was dead and gone, to get their full measure. Wendy was obviously biased, and as she'd got it firmly stuck in her head that Beth was against Len, it was no use going to her for a properly dispassionate character sketch of the man. She needed to find someone else who knew Len well, who could say what he had really been like. From the number of weeping, furious ladies in the church, there were plenty of possible informants out there, but would they be capable of giving balanced opinions? In the meantime, Beth decided she'd use the resources already at her disposal.

'So, Len Broughton. What kind of a bloke was he, do you think?' she asked Harry airily.

Harry didn't even take his eyes off the screen. He just grunted and said, 'Hmm. I suppose this means you're going to poke around in that, now?'

Beth winced. If only her mother could hear this. Then she'd know how much help her daughter got. She tried again. 'So you admit there's something there? Something that doesn't add up about his death?'

On screen, the hero detective was now grappling with a sinister figure in a dark hoody, waving some kind of pointy Finnish agricultural implement that looked as though it could do plenty of mischief. 'Uh? What? No, just a regular heart attack. Circumstances were a bit unusual, I suppose.'

'In what way?' said Beth, passing Harry the bowl of crisps. If she kept him topped up with snacks, he might not notice her trying to ferret information out of him.

Harry took a large handful and gave Beth a measured look. 'Don't think I can't see through what you're doing. But as no one's raised any doubts about the death, it doesn't do any harm to tell you, I suppose. He died in his office. Found by a security guard.'

'His office? Not his home?'

'Definitely the office. At about eleven o'clock at night. When he'd been in bed with one of his, ah, ladies, only a couple of hours before.'

Ugh, thought Beth with a shudder. She hoped that meant

Margery Brinkwell, not her mother. Though Wendy would not be pleased, if she got wind of this. Maybe Len had just gone to his place of work for a bit of a rest from all the women. Given what Beth had so far gathered about his hectic love life, it made sense. But hadn't Wendy said he wasn't feeling well? That's why he'd gone to his place and not hers. 'Did he also have a bed in his office, then?' Beth said.

'Nope,' said Harry laconically.

'I wonder why he would get up and go into work, that late at night?' Beth frowned.

'Search me,' said Harry. 'Any more of those crisps?'

Beth, who'd only just put the bowl back on the floor, realised her mistake too late. The crisps had been within a couple of inches of the ever-questing nose of Colin, and the bowl was not only suddenly empty but looked as though it had been thoroughly licked clean. Colin met her eye guiltily for a second and then whined.

'Well, don't blame me if you've got a tummy ache, Col, serves you right,' said Beth, levering herself out of the sofa's fond embrace and padding off to the kitchen in her fluffy socks to scrub out the bowl and get another bag of crisps. All the way there and back, though, she was deep in thought.

What could have lured a sick Len Broughton into his office so late at night? What – or should that be, who? Or had he just pretended to feel ill as an excuse to get rid of Wendy? Whatever had gone on, one thing was for sure. If Len had gone to his office for a rendezvous, his last meeting had not gone at all well. Indeed, it had proved fatal.

FIVE

Beth had always had wistful, unrealistic dreams about doing things together with Wendy, enjoying the sort of cosy relationship mums and daughters had in books and on screen. She should have remembered to be careful what she wished for. Because Wendy, previously much too busy with her hectic Bridge schedule, had now freed up acres of time and was available at the drop of a hat to discuss Beth's progress. Or rather, the lack of it.

'So what exactly have you achieved, so far?' Wendy said, pressing a tissue to her red nose the next day and running a disapproving eye down Beth's small frame, clad, as ever, in a ratty grey jumper, jeans and scuffed pixie boots. 'You could at least have got the mud off your shoes before we came in here,' she added as an aside.

Beth drew her feet under her and tried to ignore the tell-tale trail of clumps dotting the formerly pristine floor of Mariella's, the village's latest in-café. 'It's not my fault if it gets a bit boggy underfoot in the park these days, is it? Poor old Colin needs his exercise. I told you I'd have to meet you after his walkies.' Beth stirred her cappuccino a bit too briskly and the clouds of fluffy foam disappeared into the coffee. A bit like her mood, going rapidly downhill under her mother's merciless scrutiny. But wait a minute, she wasn't fourteen and without a voice any more. She sat up a bit straighter in her creaking rattan chair and fixed her mother with a determined look.

'Actually, I am making some progress on Len. Did you know, for instance, that he died in his office, at around eleven p.m.?'

'Yes, I'd heard that,' said Wendy.

'Why on earth didn't you mention that to me, then?' Beth said sharply. 'I thought he was with Margery Brinkwell. Isn't that why you suspected her?'

'That's one of the reasons,' said Wendy darkly, blotting her eyes with her tissue.

'I see. And did you know he went to the office after having a visit, um, from one of his girlfriends?'

'Well yes, I knew that too. As the "girlfriend" was me.'

'Oh. You didn't say. In fact, I thought you said Margery Brinkwell was outside his house after your dinner date. And you left him there?'

'I was sparing your blushes, Beth. There was no "dinner date". We didn't actually have a meal at all. We went to my house, if you must know, and, well...'

'OK, OK, I get the picture,' Beth said, only just resisting the temptation to put her hands over her ears, and wash out her imagination with extra-strong detergent.

'Then I left him at his house, as I said. And I'll have you know I wasn't just one of his girlfriends,' Wendy continued. 'He always said I was the – the – light of his life.' Her voice was quavering now and she snapped open her handbag to find a fresh tissue, and lifted it to her swimming eyes.

Crikey, this is going well, thought Beth. Then her mother spoke up again.

'In fact, you could say I was actually his fiancée.' She put the hand not clutching a tissue to her breast in a dramatic gesture. 'A few days before that last night, right outside his house, he asked me to do him the honour of making him the happiest man alive.'

Beth's jaw dropped. 'And you didn't think to mention that to me?'

'It was too raw,' said Wendy, starting to cry again. 'I was going to tell you, of course, but I was adjusting to his loss. And you didn't take it very well when I said I had a boyfriend. I thought you'd be even more peeved if I said he was my fiancé,' she added, dabbing her eyes.

There was some justice in this, Beth acknowledged, pressing her thumb and forefinger to the bridge of her nose, where a sudden headache threatened to bloom. The news that her mother's secret relationship had been so serious was difficult to swallow. 'It's certainly a lot to take in. I don't think your engagement would have gone down brilliantly with Len's actual wife, either. He might not have been the "happiest man alive" when she got to hear about it.'

In fact, thought Beth, it gave Mrs Broughton, aka Margery Brinkwell, quite a strong motive for murder – one which she'd need to look into.

Wendy, meanwhile, was now outraged. 'Beth Haldane! I don't know how you can be so unfeeling. If your father could see how hard you've become...'

'I doubt even Dad would back you up in your plan to become a bigamist,' Beth couldn't resist saying drily, though she knew it wasn't going to land well.

Sure enough, Wendy got shakily to her feet. 'Well, if all you're going to do is insult your aged mother...'

'Oh Mum,' Beth started, but luckily she was interrupted by a waitress, bringing over their order of two brownies. By common accord this marked a ceasefire. Wendy sat herself down again, and they were soon enjoying a bit of blessed silence as they got on the outside of the squidgy cakes. They did both love their chocolate. At least they that much in common, Beth thought wryly. Though that was probably the long and the short of it.

'Listen, Mum,' Beth began again when her plate bore nothing but crumbs and even Wendy's was half finished. 'This investigation you want me to do is bound to be painful. I'm not sure you should put yourself through it. But that's fine, I can let it go. The police would probably make a better job of it.'

Interviewing a whole bunch of lovelorn women, all of whom would probably react like Wendy to a bit of gentle questioning, was going to be no fun, Beth thought to herself. But Wendy had other ideas.

'Well, normally I'd agree with you. But they sent a little constable round this morning before I came here to meet you, because they found my texts to Len on his phone. When I said it was murder, this boy – honestly, they get younger every day – just patted my hand and told me I'd had a shock, as though I was making it all up,' said Wendy, in outraged tones.

Beth felt more than a sneaking sympathy with the PC. She could imagine how well that had gone down. But then Wendy leant forward confidingly.

'The other thing is, as well as not believing a word I've said, the police are hardly discreet. I don't want my business bandied about the whole of the village,' Wendy said, shooting a furtive glance at their nearest neighbours in the café, a brace of mummies with jammy toddlers in high chairs, who were well out of earshot and were, in any case, at the phase of motherhood where nothing is more fascinating than the contents of your own child prodigy's nappy.

'I suppose not,' Beth shrugged. 'Does that mean my investigation is still on?' she asked, hoping she didn't sound as unenthusiastic as she felt.

'Well, if you wouldn't mind, dear,' said Wendy. But

although the words sounded conciliatory enough, the tone was perfunctory. Beth's mother had just dumped a difficult and complex problem in her daughter's lap, and clearly expected her to sort it out – pronto. 'And the sooner my name is cleared the better,' Wendy added for good measure. 'In fact, I'd like it all smoothed out in time for the Bridge Club tournament.'

SIX

Beth raised an eyebrow at her mother. 'What do you mean? When is this tournament?'

Wendy started reorganising her innumerable necklaces. 'It's in a couple of weeks, so you have plenty of time,' she said dismissively.

'Two weeks? Are you kidding?' Beth blew out her cheeks. 'And why is it so important that things are sorted out before then anyway?'

'Oh for goodness' sake, Beth, I would have thought that was perfectly obvious,' sniffed Wendy. Then, when Beth continued to stare at her, baffled, she finally relented. 'Well, if I have to spell it out... there have been one or two murmurs in the club.'

'Murmurs?'

Wendy's hands went to fiddle with her necklaces again, then she seemed to think better of it. 'If you must know, a few of the other members may have thought they had some sort of claim on Len... Nonsense, of course, but I don't want any unpleasantness lingering. The tournament is such a big event for us. I don't want my special day ruined by any nasty talk.'

Beth couldn't help smiling. '*Your* special day? So you're going to win?'

'Would it be such a surprise if I did?' Wendy said, all wounded dignity. 'Of course I've no idea who'll play better on the day. But I don't want there to be any kind of *atmosphere*.'

Beth sighed. For once, she understood. It was never fun to be gossiped about. And the more Wendy threw herself into her Bridge, the faster she'd recover from this whole Len business. Meanwhile, her mother's beloved club, stuffed as it was with ladies of a certain age, could be a repository of potential suspects. That was if this really was a murder at all. The police constable might have a point.

Just then, the doors of the café swung open and a large group of women came in including, Beth saw with a frisson of dread, her nemesis, uber-mummy and terror of the Dulwich playgrounds, Belinda McKenzie. Belinda was about to sweep past Beth's table without acknowledging her – par for the course these days since various friends of Belinda's had come to grief during Beth's previous investigations – when she spotted Wendy. Immediately, Belinda swivelled on her high-heeled boots and swooped down on Beth's mother to give her the regulation kiss on both cheeks. Her handbag swung off her shoulder and crashed onto the table, coming within a whisker of knocking Beth's cooling cappuccino all over her. She yanked the cup away just in time.

'Mrs Haldane! Wendy! *So* marvellous to see you. I was sorry to hear about Len's death. Now tell me, do I have this right? He was your... boyfriend, wasn't he? Or was he, um, your... fiancé?'

At once there was an outbreak of giggling behind Belinda, where a group of her usual acolytes and cronies was clustered. Beth's hackles rose. She'd only just heard about the engagement herself, so it was infuriating that Belinda was up to speed with the gossip already. And look at the two-faced way she was pretending to cosy up to Wendy, while laughing at her up her sleeve. Well, the Haldane women might not be as close as either could wish, but they were family. Beth would stick up for her mum any day of the week against the likes of Belinda. Whatever she had initially felt about the whole Len business, she was now in – one hundred and ten per cent.

Wendy, however, had not smelt the very large rodent currently at their table. She was simpering away to Belinda, blissfully unaware of the other woman's hidden agenda. 'That's right, Belinda. He was such a lovely man, as I'm sure you know. You do know all the right people in Dulwich, dear.'

'I like to think I do, Mrs H,' Belinda said. 'But strangely I don't think I ever met Len Broughton. Now isn't that odd?'

Wendy didn't notice the sting in the tail of this statement, but just lifted her tissue to her eyes. 'So tragic, now you never will.'

'Tragic? Yes, it absolutely is,' Belinda said, raising her eyebrows – as far as she was able – to the coterie behind her, who burst into titters again. 'But I won't keep you, I'm sure you must have so much to do. There's an awful lot of admin when someone dies, isn't there? That's what my mother found after my father passed away. So much responsibility, being next of kin.'

Beth took this to mean that Belinda knew perfectly well Wendy had no formal relationship with Len Broughton at all, and the paperwork – and everything else – would be dealt with by Len Broughton's widow, not by Wendy. Belinda shot Beth a significant glance even as she gave Wendy a last, deeply patronising, pat on the shoulder and sauntered off, to take control of the largest and most central table in the café. As soon as she and her friends sat down, a fresh gale of laughter broke out.

Beth, gathering up her own much less impressive handbag and drinking down the dregs of her chilly coffee, hissed to Wendy, 'Let's get out of here.'

Wendy smiled benignly in Belinda's direction, completely oblivious to any undercurrents the conversation might have had. Then she waved Beth away. 'You go, dear, if you're in such a rush. I'll just finish my drink. And do report back to me when you've finally made some progress. I don't want to have to keep chasing you all the time. I do have a lot to do, you know.'

You don't, thought Beth. And you've got less on your plate than you had a week ago, when Len Broughton was sauntering around the village breaking hearts. You won't be spending time trying to look good for him or cooking him suet puddings, as you did for Dad. Or, perish the thought, going on 'dates'.

But, while her mother was not bowed down with winding up her 'fiancé's' estate, she was still in mourning. She'd obviously felt deeply about the man, reprobate though he appeared to be. Beth had to cut poor Wendy a little slack. She kissed her mother's pale cheek and left the café, glad to get out into the fresh air again and away from the suffocating atmosphere Belinda McKenzie always seemed to bring in her wake.

They were in the thick of autumn now, with piles of leaves here and there despite the best efforts of the street cleaners. The air had that peaty tang that carries a threat of winter to come. But there were bright baskets of purple and yellow pansies hanging from the streetlights and some of the shops had started filling their windows with Halloween decorations. Beth wrapped her cosy old jacket around herself more securely, and was just wondering whether to head to Wyatt's to do a smidgeon of work, or whether going home for a cup of tea curled on the sofa with Magpie and mulling over her new murder case might be a much nicer option, when someone called her name.

She turned, and the day suddenly got better. There was Katie, her best friend in the world. They'd had a bit of a blip recently, when Beth's friend Adua was killed and she'd suggested Katie's cleaner might have had blood on her

Marigolds. But Beth had taken it all back, Katie had forgiven her, and they were now on the best of terms again.

'Fancy seeing you here,' said Katie, who for once was without her dreadful dog, Teddy. Teddy kept being kicked out of obedience classes, which put immense stress on Katie. She liked things to go well. She had a lovely kind husband, a great twelve-year-old son, Jake's partner in crime Charlie, and an incredibly stylish home. Then she had acquired Teddy. As far as Beth was concerned, the dog was the devil incarnate, lightly disguised as a cockapoo.

'No Teddy today?' Beth asked nervously, half-expecting the pooch to leap out from behind a lamppost and scare the bejesus out of her.

Instantly a guilty look dimmed the perpetual sunshine of Katie's blonde good looks. 'Don't judge me, Beth,' she said in a low voice. 'But I've... I've got a dog-walker.'

Inwardly, Beth was turning cartwheels of joy at the realisation that Katie was going to be a lot freer in future. But she tried to look mildly concerned instead of ecstatically happy. 'Oh, um, really?' she ventured.

'Yes, I feel awful about it, but... got time for a coffee?'

Beth's hardwired reaction to this phrase was an instant yes, but today she was acutely aware that Wendy was still inside Mariella's, no doubt expecting her daughter to have dropped everything to sleuth away on her behalf. 'Absolutely, but do you mind if we go to Jane's? Um, well, Belinda's in there.'

Katie gave Beth an old-fashioned look. 'You shouldn't have to skulk around trying to avoid her, you know, Beth. Particularly as she's constantly striding around the village. In the end it's going to mean you can't even set foot outside your own front door.'

Beth, who secretly thought that might be quite nice, nodded away. 'You're right, but I just can't face her at the moment. Plus, well, Mum's in there, too, and she's just given me a huge job to do. She will be furious if she sees I'm slacking and not getting right down to it.'

'Oh, I'd love to see Wendy – but of course, Beth, let's go to Jane's if that's easier for you,' said Katie immediately. Beth smiled gratefully and they walked the few paces that separated the great rival cafés that vied for the not inconsiderable coffee business of Dulwich Village. As Mariella's was currently winning the battle for hearts and pockets, there was a nice table going at Jane's and Beth subsided gratefully. Anyone would think she'd put in a hard day's work already, not glided from one café to another while shirking her actual job. She had a bit of a twinge about all the filing that was going to be building up in the Archive Institute. But she'd deal with it all tomorrow, really she would. The priority now was to get Katie up to speed on Len Broughton.

'Oh my God, I cannot believe all that! I almost wish I'd been there at the funeral to see the fight,' said Katie five minutes later, eyes alight. Then she realised what she'd said. 'Of course, it must have been absolutely terrible for poor Wendy, though.'

Beth just shook her head. 'Honestly, I couldn't believe it when Mum said she had a *boyfriend*,' she said, all but choking on the very word. 'And then, almost in the next breath, announced he was dead. Before I'd even had time to meet him.'

'Well, I don't suppose he did it on purpose, Beth,' Katie said reasonably.

'That's the thing, though. That's why Mum's given me this massive job to do. She's only gone and convinced herself Len was murdered.'

Katie drew back, horrified. But then she spoke slowly, feeling her way. 'I wonder if he was? I mean... I know it sounds mad. But given everything that's happened here lately, and since the whole church was packed with his other girlfriends...'

'I'm beginning to think the same. The police don't seem interested, Belinda is laughing at Mum behind her back... me looking into it is her only chance, really.' Beth wrinkled her nose.

'Well, I suppose there are probably enough people around who'd want him dead. If he'd suddenly taken up in a really big way with Wendy, maybe he was about to dump all his other, er, side chicks, I think they call them? They might not have liked that. And didn't you just say he also had an actual wife?'

'Yes, Margery Brinkwell.'

'Oooh, that's a great name for a murderer, isn't it? I bet she did it. I mean, she must have the biggest motive of anyone,' said Katie.

Beth widened her eyes. She'd thought her friend was going to say what she usually did when something like this cropped up, and tell Beth firmly she ought to leave it all to Harry to solve. But no, she'd leapt straight in – even though Beth privately thought deciding the widow was the chief suspect was a bit of a cliché. She smiled at her friend. 'I can't believe this. Sounds like someone might be getting back into the detective business!'

Katie giggled, then quickly clapped a hand to her mouth. 'I shouldn't be laughing! These are real people and their lives. It's not just a puzzle for us to solve.'

'That's true, except that one of the worst affected people – Wendy – has made me promise to do my best to unravel it all, before her blessed Bridge tournament,' said Beth.

'In that case...' Katie was toying with her spoon, clattering it in the saucer of her cup. Then she looked up. 'Well, would you consider having a bit of help with this one? I mean, we did look into that whole thing before, didn't we?'

Beth was stunned into a momentary silence. Yes, Katie had helped her sort out a particularly gruesome killing that had taken place on Peckham Rye. But she had then made it plain that she had far too much on her plate to carry on sleuthing.

'I thought...? But yes, of course, if you'd like to, that would be amazing. Have you got time, though?'

Katie sighed. 'Well, part of me wants to keep Charlie in cotton wool forever, you know. But he's at the age now where he really resents me keeping such a close eye on him. He needs his freedom.'

Beth almost dropped her cup in surprise. 'Really?'

'Well, actually, no, I don't think that. But Michael does,' Katie admitted. 'He's told me to back off. And Teddy's with the dog-walker, which Michael thinks will settle him down too... Honestly, it's as if Michael thinks all our problems can be solved by just taking me out of the equation. So I'm going to take him at his word. See how he likes it if he doesn't have any clean socks because I'm too busy tailing Mrs Broughton around Waitrose!'

'Waitrose? Don't tell me it's finally happened?' Beth knew that Katie, like most village residents, was yearning for the posh supermarket chain to set up anywhere in their vicinity.

'No. No, it hasn't,' said Katie, momentarily downcast. 'But I can dream, can't I? All right, I'll be following her around the Dog Kennel Hill Sainsbury's – but the principle's the same.'

'Yes, yes, it is,' said Beth, secretly wondering how long it would be until Michael reversed a lot of his recent pronouncements on what Katie should and shouldn't be doing. Investigating potential killers was much more perilous even than being towed around Dulwich Park by that little menace Teddy. 'This is really exciting. I think we should have a toast,' she added, raising her cappuccino.

Katie clinked Beth's cup with her own. 'What shall we drink to, then?'

'To Wendy's murderous affair – and all who sail in her,' Beth intoned, and they both laughed as they sipped their drinks. And then Beth caught the eye of a well-preserved woman of a certain age, glaring at her from the back of the coffee shop, and she put her cup down so quickly that coffee sloshed everywhere. Was she one of the women who'd been at the church? She certainly looked angry enough. And if Len really had been killed, as Wendy insisted, that meant there was still a murderer on the loose in Dulwich – maybe even in this café. Suddenly things didn't seem so funny after all.

SEVEN

The next day, Beth was idly standing with her hands in the sink, looking out at her little back garden. Proudly in the spot once occupied by the sagging posts of Jake's old football goal was her shoffice. This had originally been positioned in the corner by the fence separating her property from that of her neighbours, the Bentincks. Since recent grim events which were all too fresh in her memory, it had been repainted, repositioned – almost exorcised – but still Beth couldn't set foot in it. Luckily, Harry had no such scruples and it was now stuffed to the gunnels with his vast collection of Golden Age whodunits.

The garden itself had also had a long-overdue makeover, and the dreadful scrubby lawn and dead and dying shrubs which had fringed it since Beth had moved in had been swept away, in favour of a Mediterranean-style multi-level patio of creamy stone with large flowerbeds planted with easy stuff that even Beth couldn't kill, like hydrangeas and bulbs. There was still space for Magpie to scratch around and uproot what she could, and Colin wasn't averse to trying to eat things when she wasn't watching.

Altogether, it was a huge improvement – so why was Beth

frowning so deeply as she scrubbed at the breakfast dishes? She didn't like to admit it, even to herself, but this quest her mother had dumped in her lap had got her stumped already. In some ways, it reminded her of her first investigation, as there were just so many potential suspects. Every woman of a certain age at the funeral was a person of interest, and presumably – from what she was beginning to gather about Len Broughton's non-stop love life – there would be a fair few who were too upset about his demise to be seen in public yet.

How on earth was she going to get her finger on the pulse of the forty- and fifty-something ladies of Dulwich? If it had just been Wendy and her close friends involved, Beth could have done a one-stop interrogation session at the Bridge Club, which met at least twice a week in magnificent Belair House, a beautiful Georgian wedding cake of a mansion just up the road from Wyatt's Museum of Art. But not all Len's women were into Bridge. Wendy didn't enjoy having to identify her many love rivals, but she'd said darkly that he always talked about what a sociable time he had in his job at the council. Everything Beth knew about local politics could be written on the back of one of her fanciest earrings, and as she didn't have any of those, she was basically totally ignorant. She was going to have to get up to speed, and quickly.

She was gazing out blankly, weighed down by the thought of all this, when she caught sight of her own reflection in the glass of the kitchen window. The pane was pretty dusty – despite her OCD habits, she hadn't got round to cleaning it this week – but when she pushed her fringe out of the way, she could see that her eyebrows were looking haphazard, even for her. And, when she looked down at her hands, her nails were bitten to the quick and her cuticles – whatever those actually were – were probably in shreds. With a grin, Beth decided it was high time for some expert intervention.

This wasn't her usual response to anything that could be

described as 'pampering'. As far as she was concerned, the idea of 'me time' treats like bubble baths, spa days, massages and facials was hell. But she was always willing to step out of her comfort zone for an investigation. Because where did wealthy middle-aged women in the village gather, like bees to honey?

Beth turned away from the window, wreathed in smiles, and got straight on the phone to Katie. 'Um, I'm going to ask you a question I wouldn't normally come out with, but just try and go with me on this. Does your bikini line need waxing?' she blurted, as soon as her friend picked up.

'Oh, er, well, Beth, that's quite—'

'Because I think it does, and I think we both need to book some urgent sessions at Green's.'

'The beauty salon in the village? But why? I mean, Michael might get a bit of a shock if I made any radical changes at this point, and I wouldn't have thought that Harry...'

'No, Katie, just think about it. We need access to lots of middle-aged women in a hurry. And that's where they all hang out. Listening to whale music and getting their nails done.'

'Oh, that's a little bit of a caricature, isn't it, Beth? I mean, I know it's not really your sort of thing.' Katie carefully avoided any judgement of her friend's scruffy appearance. 'But, well, I'm all for having a nice facial every now and then.'

'It won't just be a treatment, though, will it, Katie? We can pick up all the inside gossip there. And hopefully get some gen on Len.'

'Oh! Oh I see. Yep, book us in. Can't wait. If we find anything out, it'll be a bonus. But Beth – just for a manicure or something. I'm not up for a wax.'

'Course not, Katie. I draw the very painful line at that.' Beth giggled.

'Good,' Katie said.

But Beth didn't think it was so good when she looked up the price list online before making their appointments. It turned out she could barely afford to look at a pedicure, let alone step her snaggle toes inside the salon and get one.

For a moment she felt quite uncomfortable. But then she told herself off. This was a potential way forward, a means of cutting down the large number of middle-aged ladies who might, just possibly, have had a hand in shuffling Len Broughton off this mortal coil. And if it succeeded in finding the person who had made her mother so unhappy, it was surely worth every penny. So Beth secured two short-notice slots, at eye-watering expense, for hand and nail treatments that very afternoon.

Maybe Wendy would even reimburse them for the mani-pedis? A part of her knew this was extremely wishful thinking. But still, the waiting room at Green's was bound to be a fertile hunting ground. Well, at this price, it had better be.

EIGHT

It was ridiculous, Beth knew, but she'd decided to spruce herself up a bit for the appointment at Green's. So, at 4 p.m. on the dot, there she was in her cleanest pair of jeans, having spent a good ten minutes that afternoon brushing mud off her boots in the garden, under the eye of a perplexed Colin. Nothing wrong with that stuff, he seemed to be telling her with every huff and wheeze. In fact, in his view, the only problem was there wasn't enough mud – which they could put right now if she'd just take him to the park?

She'd had to close the door on his sorrowful Labrador face, having scrawled a hasty note to Jake telling him to do his homework before going within a centimetre of the games console in the sitting room.

Now she was sitting bolt upright in a chair in the waiting room of Green's, looking around her beadily, while a supremely relaxed Katie flipped through a glossy magazine with every appearance of absorption, as though she did this every day of the week. Which, of course, she easily could. But Katie, though a lot better groomed than Beth, was nothing if not practical.

Nail, hair and eyelash extensions were not compatible with a life lived mostly upside down, exhorting other women to improve their downward dogs – and certainly they were diametrically opposed to looking after the dreadful Teddy, who was always trying to drag his long-suffering mistress through a hedge backwards.

The beauty parlour waiting room was plush and womb-like, with pink velvet chairs, darker rose walls and lots of pretty potted orchids. A serenely beautiful girl on reception spoke in a quiet, sweetly low voice every time the telephone tinkled. But it was the other women waiting who took up most of Beth's attention.

One was a cosy, plumpish matron of around sixty, with a frizz of greying hair that puffed out around her head like a halo. She had on a smock top and battered jeans, and her short nails were ringed in black. If she'd met her in the street, Beth would not have said she was the type to be a salon devotee. Had to be in for a manicure, Beth decided.

A couple of seats along was a girl in her late twenties, who looked every inch a yummy mummy on an afternoon off. Her silky blonde hair appeared freshly ironed, and there were diamonds winking from her ears, while the third finger of her left hand was so heavily encrusted with them it was a wonder she could lift it. All the outward signs of wealth she was displaying caused an ignoble worm of jealousy to writhe in Beth's bosom. This woman had a husband who hadn't died on her, but lavished her regularly with jewellery. Her children were in expensive schools, and would be until they were spewed out into an expensive university. Her car probably left Beth's for dust at traffic lights.

But this was ridiculous, thought Beth sternly. Who knew what went on behind closed doors? Her husband might be still alive, but he could be horrible. At least James had been a lovely man. And now Beth had Harry – sweet, warm and funny as well as bossy. Her set-up might not be totally conventional any more, but they were happy. She needed to lose her terrible prejudices, she decided. Just then, the woman looked up and gave Beth an acid glance, perhaps having felt her scrutiny. Beth looked away quickly.

Sitting directly opposite them was a lady with mid-length soft brown hair in gentle waves. In many ways, her outfit was similar to Beth's habitual jeans and jumper combo. But the lady's jeans were miraculously well-fitting and sculpted her enviable figure, while the sweater draped as only the finest cashmere can. Her handbag and shoes were shiny brown patent. Her face, then, when she turned to stare at Beth for a second, came as a shock – her cheeks were hollowed with age. She was seventy-nine if she was a day. She wasn't going quietly into her eighth decade, however. She had the shiny unlined forehead of the Botox frequent flyer and unnaturally pouting lips. Her expertly kohled eyes widened when she saw Beth. She leant forward a little and beckoned to her. Beth obligingly craned in.

'Excuse me,' she said in a high-pitched voice. 'Is your mother... Wendy Haldane?'

Beth smiled. 'Yes, she is,' she replied with an automatic smile. But she should have known better. As things stood in Dulwich, Wendy was more or less at daggers drawn with half the females over the age of forty. From the way the lady withdrew and looked at Beth down her nose, she realised this might well be another one of Len's cast-offs. 'Um, you must be very sad about the death of Len Broughton,' Beth offered, turning her expression to suitable mournfulness.

The effect was immediate. The lady's eyes teared up and she snapped open her bag to reach for a tissue. Before she could find one, Katie had reached across the little seating area with one of her own, and a sympathetic smile.

'This must all have been so terrible for you,' Katie ventured. Silently, Beth blessed her.

Instantly the woman's hackles went down as she sniffed into the tissue and admitted that yes, it had been the most ghastly business. 'Poor Len. He relied on me so much.'

Then, to Beth's surprise, the round little matron on the other side piped up. 'I don't see why he needed you. I'm the one he loved!'

'Well, dear, let's just say I supported him, shall we?' said the well-heeled older lady smugly.

'I'll have you know that I helped him out, too,' the other woman replied.

Beth and Katie looked at each other. Neither could quite believe things were going so well – or so badly, depending on which side of the Len divide you were on. As they watched, fascinated, the situation in the waiting room deteriorated as the ladies laid into each other. The lovely girl on reception whipped round in alarm, unable to make herself heard on the phone now that voices were raised in anger. For, to the surprise of all, the young blonde had also chimed in and claimed Len Broughton as the love of her life.

My goodness, Len was a busy bee, thought Beth. How on earth could he have taken in so many women? And what did they mean about 'support'?

Katie was doing her best to pour oil on troubled waters, but the volume was rising and the receptionist was frowning, getting to her feet. Beth decided she had to step in.

'Ladies, ladies. Len wouldn't want you all to be upsetting yourselves like this, would he?' she shouted above the hubbub. To her relief, the angry voices died down a bit, though it was probably just to check whether Beth too was going to announce herself as one of Len's girls. She realised she only had a short window to make an impact on these women, before they started wrangling again. 'Listen, as you might all have heard, there are questions being asked about the way that poor Len died.' Well, Wendy was certainly asking questions, that was for sure. Anyway, it had the desired effect, distracting the women from bickering – but unfortunately they just started on Beth instead.

'What?'

'You can't be serious!'

'Who's said that? And why?'

Beth put up her hand to forestall any more questions. 'I can't go into it all now. But we do need to get an idea of who was where on the night poor Len died. I wonder, do any of you remember exactly what you were doing that evening?'

For a second, there was complete silence, and Beth was worried that the women would simply tell her to get lost and carry on shouting at each other. But she had reckoned without the competitive spirit that lurked at the heart of many Dulwich residents. Each of these women had worked hard to get where they were, either by scoring in business or in marriage. Now they all wanted to win at the alibi game.

'Well, I was at choir practice,' Mrs Wavy Brown Hair leapt in first, stealing a march on her younger rivals. 'We went on so late that night, till past ten. And then there were drinks in the Dirty Dog afterwards.'

Beth nodded. The Dirty Dog was the nickname given to the Greyhound, the pub in the village Never much of a drinker, Beth avoided the place even more assiduously on a Friday night as the tenors from the Wyatt's Choral Society were notorious for getting tanked up, and the sopranos were no better.

'I didn't get home until after eleven thirty. My husband wasn't amused, he'd already gone up to bed,' Mrs WBH remembered.

At this, the grey-haired lady broke in. 'Your husband? And did he know about you carrying on with my boyfriend?' The question was inflammatory – but it was asked in perfectly matter-of-fact tones.

'*Your* boyfriend?' said the young blonde with a shake of her perfect locks and a derisory laugh.

'And what about *your* husband? Does he know?' the middle-aged lady asked her in turn, again with that strange tone of polite curiosity.

'Well, really! How dare you, and what business is it of yours anyway?'

Beth and Katie looked at each other. This was rapidly getting out of hand again. Then a white-coated therapist popped her head out of one of the rooms at the back of the salon. At first Beth was taken aback. She'd almost forgotten they were all there to get treatments done. But then she realised her window to get some alibis sorted was closing right before her very eyes. She turned quickly to the younger woman.

'You won't have any trouble remembering what you were up to that night, I bet,' she said, as encouragingly as she could.

'Of course not,' the woman snapped. 'I was at my Bridge classes with a group of friends and... also with my husband,' she finished more quietly. 'In the Rosendale. We're doing a special course, you know, before the tournament. Then we all had dinner after the session. We were there till just about closing time.' The Rosendale was a nice gastro pub, but a fair walk from the village, and it shut every night at 11 p.m. 'I chose it because I knew Len wouldn't see me there. He – he got jealous,' she said, starting to sob.

The lady with the grey halo was the only one of the trio who hadn't yet burst into tears. As the receptionist and the therapist watched, horrified, she started laughing hysterically instead. 'Oh, this is so absurd. Len didn't have a jealous bone in his body. He would have loved all this. He revelled in his power over women.'

'Ridiculous!' said the older lady. 'And anyway, he always told me I was the only one.'

'And you believed him.' The grey-haired woman was now bent double with laughter.

'Well, if it's all so funny,' said the blonde, sniffing. 'Why don't you tell us where you were that evening?'

'Oh, that's easy,' she said, with tears of mirth rolling down her cheeks. 'I was with Len.'

NINE

Beth wasn't sure if the woman understood quite what she had said. But silence fell on the little gathering. The receptionist and the therapist looked at each other in mute horror. The salon manager had popped out to the dentist that afternoon, assuring them it was going to be a lovely easy afternoon, and fuss and bother of this magnitude was definitely above both their pay grades.

Beth sighed and decided she had no choice but to step in again. She got down to business. 'If you could just give me your name and address,' she said in a matter-of-fact voice. To her surprise, the lady did just that.

'Harriet French. I live in Burbage Road. Much too busy with my allotment to have time for singing or playing games like these two,' she said, seemingly oblivious to the vicious glances she was getting. 'But I have nothing against other earthy pleasures. And,' she added defiantly, looking round the tiny waiting room, 'I have nothing to hide.'

'Len must have left you at some point that night, though,' Beth pointed out. 'After all, he was at his house at about nine thirty and he was found dead... elsewhere, at eleven.'

The others murmured their agreement, but Harriet French just shrugged. 'Well, I didn't say he stayed long. Just long enough. And I'm a deep sleeper. Especially after, you know, a very... special moment,' she added with a reminiscent smile which caused the older lady to crumple the tissue in her hand viciously.

This timeframe didn't fit very well with what Beth already knew, about Len having spent time earlier with Wendy, and she suddenly wondered if Harriet was just doing her best to wind up her rivals. If so, it was working a treat.

'You could have followed Len to wherever it was that he died, and bumped him off there,' said the blonde angrily. 'My name is Venetia Porter and I, um, actually live in Camberwell Grove,' she said, a mite defensively.

The other two women sat up a bit straighter at that. Beth was willing to bet that, with the unique snobbery of the Dulwich resident, they were both now feeling quite superior to someone who lived outside its hallowed borders.

'I'm Simone de Waal, and I live just opposite here, in the house next to the graveyard,' said the older lady with a touch of pride. Beth immediately gave an involuntary shiver. She knew the house well, and it was stunning – a huge Georgian mansion. But it just happened to be right next to one of the last-known plague pits in London and, even worse, Beth's friend Adua had recently been murdered right there, behind the controversial electricals recycling bin. The fact that the bin had now been removed, due to public pressure, didn't make things any better in Beth's eyes. If it had never been there at all, it wouldn't have proved such a convenient spot for a wily murderer bent on secreting a body. Maybe her friend would be alive to this day. It was unlikely, though, as Adua had turned out to be a bit of a blackmailer in her spare time. A very dangerous occupation. Beth sighed.

Simone de Waal seemed to be expecting lots of admiring

comments on her good fortune in living in such a splendid spot. Well, she'd be waiting a long time. Venetia looked put out that her Camberwell home (lovely though it no doubt was) had been upstaged so successfully, while Harriet French seemed not to give a damn. She was still wreathed in smiles, lost, it seemed, in remembering her last, extremely satisfactory, encounter with Len with a cat-got-the-cream smugness about her that was quite insufferable. Again, Beth wondered where Margery Brinkwell and her mother fitted in with this encounter. Hadn't they both insisted in their ways that they, too, had had 'special nights' with Len on his fateful last evening? If Wendy hadn't kept banging on about murder, Beth would have been sure the man had died from simple exhaustion.

'Well, if that's all, we really should get on with your treatments, ladies,' said the girl in the white jacket nervously with a glance at the clock on the wall. The hand was inching inexorably round the rose-adorned face and they needed to get on.

'I'm first, I believe,' said Simone in a lordly way, getting up with a touch of difficulty that hinted at well-concealed joint stiffness, but then sweeping out behind the therapist.

'What are we supposed to do? Wait here like lemons? Or are you going to interrogate us some more?' Venetia said scathingly to Beth.

Beth opened her mouth for another question – might as well while the going was good – when another therapist came through from the back of the parlour. 'Hi,' she said to the receptionist. 'Just back from my break. Now, who's with me?' she smiled brightly, apparently oblivious to the very odd atmosphere in the little waiting room.

Before the ladies could tussle again, the receptionist nodded towards Venetia, who got up with a shake of her blonde tresses and followed her to a treatment room.

'Just us, then,' said Harriet French unnecessarily. Katie smiled but Beth couldn't resist plunging in again.

'So were you surprised, by the turnout at the funeral? Did you know you weren't the only one, erm, having a relationship with Len?'

'Well really, dear, I don't know where you've been hiding all this time,' said Harriet French with that little amused gleam in her eye that was so irritating. 'Is it possible that you don't know?'

'Don't know what?' Beth knew she sounded grumpy, but she didn't care.

'Well, two things, I suppose. One, that Len had a very good reason for wanting, ahem, the support of as many women as possible.'

'Okaaay,' said Beth. 'And what's the second thing?'

Harriet French got to her feet as another white-coated girl appeared and signalled to her. 'Why, that Dulwich is a flourishing centre of polyamory, that's all,' she said nonchalantly over her shoulder.

TEN

Beth and Katie sat motionless in the little pink waiting room, digesting Harriet French's bombshell. They looked at each other. Katie was the first to speak.

'Beth?' she said tentatively.

'Yes?' Beth replied absently, still in shock.

'What actually is polyamory?'

Beth was silent for a second, then plunged in. 'I think it must just be the latest modern way of saying everyone's sleeping around and monogamy's for old farts.'

'Old farts like me,' said Katie.

'And me,' Beth said with a shrug, and they both burst out laughing. The receptionist glanced over at them as though she was going to remonstrate, but then little dimples peeped out and she smiled too. Just then the phone rang and she switched back to hushed mode as she listened intently and keyed another appointment into her laptop.

'Do you really think Harriet French is right? That Dulwich is a hotbed of, well, bed-hopping?'

'There's a lot of beds in that sentence,' said Beth, then she shrugged. 'I mean, honestly, I wouldn't have a clue. All I can say is that it certainly isn't going on in Pickwick Road. As far as I know. And that's the thing – you just can't be sure what happens in other people's relationships, can you?'

'You really can't,' said Katie. 'Mind you, I wouldn't be surprised about some people...'

'Care to name any names?' asked Beth, but Katie shook her head. Beth did wonder if she was thinking about Belinda McKenzie, who was Katie's near neighbour in Court Lane. If Belinda was having any odd parties, then Katie would be well placed to see the comings and goings, as it were. But Beth shook the idea away. She had enough on her plate with Len Broughton's love life without delving into any other murky pools.

'I suppose polyamory might explain the number of girlfriends who turned up at the church, at least,' Beth said. "But it wouldn't fit the fact that they were all so cross. I think it's supposed to be a consensual thing. I wonder what the other factor was that Harriet was hinting at.'

A thought seemed to strike Katie. 'Do you think your mother knows? About Len and, um, this whole polyamory business?'

Beth clapped a hand to her mouth. 'Oh my God! No, I can't believe that for a second. She really believes she was his fiancée. Despite all the evidence to the contrary, including a fully paid-up wife. It would absolutely kill Mum to know Len was into anything like that.'

Their talk was broken up as a treatment room door opened. Then Simone de Waal wafted past them, looking even more polished than before, if that was possible. Beth wondered what on earth she had had done. Everything had looked perfect before she went in. Maybe she'd just had her shoes buffed so they shone even more brightly? Or maybe it was more Botox, which might explain why she hadn't acknowledged them.

The therapist ushered Mrs de Waal out and then turned to Beth and Katie. 'Now then, ladies. Who's first?'

Beth immediately deferred to Katie and her friend followed the girl with a smile. In truth, Beth wasn't much looking forward to her own manicure. It was going to be such a waste of time – and money. What with digging away in the archives, keeping on top of the new garden, sorting out the pets and all the cleaning she felt she had to do, fancy new nails would only last a few hours. She made a decision.

'I'm so sorry,' she said to the lovely – and very patient – receptionist. 'I've just had a text, bit of an emergency. I need to rush off,' she said apologetically, mentally crossing her fingers.

'Of course, of course,' said the nice girl. Beth was pretty sure she didn't believe her story, but after the time they'd had at the salon this afternoon, they could probably all do with a bit of a rest once Harriet French and Katie were finished.

Beth sauntered out into the crisp autumnal air, tart as a green apple, thinking she'd never been so pleased to get out of a room before. All right, it was a very swanky place and she was sure all the treatments were excellent if they were your thing – but now she was feeling that bubble of delight which comes when something you haven't been looking forward to is unexpectedly cancelled. Dulwich Village was sparkling in the last of the afternoon sun. She smiled happily at the display outside Bartley's the florist, a real harvest festival of glowing orange and yellow chrysanthemums.

Now she'd be back home in time to see that Jake got down to his work properly, and she could even squeeze in a quick saunter round the block with Colin. She texted Katie to let her know she'd chickened out, hoping her friend would find it funny rather than annoying, and pottered the short distance back home.

It had been a very odd interlude, at the beauticians. But at least they could rule some groups out – the choir lot, assuming they had all gone to the pub after their session that fateful night. And the Bridge classes group, if everyone had eaten at the

Rosendale after their lesson. Harriet French had no alibi for the crucial time, hinting only that she'd been curled up in her own bed in a state of post-coital bliss. But she seemed to have genuinely enjoyed her time with Len, and obviously placed on him far fewer burdens of expectation than many of his women friends, who seemed a disgruntled bunch. She'd been perfectly happy with a dalliance, rather than an engagement like Wendy. She had no motive for the killing, as far as Beth could see.

But could Harriet just have a very good poker face? Beth had been fooled once before by a talented actor who had skilfully misdirected her suspicions – she wasn't going to have the wool pulled over her eyes so easily this time.

Something about the woman's short, grimy nails – nearly as bad as Beth's own – and the fact that she had an allotment suddenly made her think. If Wendy was right that there was something fishy about Len's death (and granted, it was a big 'if') Beth knew from Harry's massive library of old whodunits that plants were a rich source of toxins. Nightshade, yew berries, foxgloves – they sprouted all over the place and were potentially lethal. Could Harriet have brewed something up that had seen Len off? But she'd seemed the only one of the trio who'd been perfectly happy with the way her relationship was going. So she didn't have a motive. Or was it that Beth just hadn't found it yet?

* * *

Beth was having another of her favourite evenings, at home on her sofa with Harry on one side of her and Magpie on the other. Jake had gone upstairs ages ago and Colin was sniffing hopefully at an empty fish and chip bag from Olley's. Beth knew she'd have to get up and shove it into the outside bin soon, or there was a real danger the old Lab would eat it whole and leave her with the consequences.

They didn't often get takeaways these days as they were trying to retrench, after the expense of the garden refurbishment and shoffice purchase, but Beth had splashed out with the money she reckoned she'd saved on her manicure earlier. It was the kind of financial reasoning that often had the family teetering on the edge of penury – but it was very hard to argue with the deliciousness of Olley's chips.

Beth was licking her fingers and sighing when her phone rang. It wasn't by her side, nor under Harry's large warm arm, or even under Magpie's fluffy tummy. Beth got up and finally unearthed it under a pile of whodunits over by the telly. Honestly, those were all supposed to be in the shoffice now, she thought to herself, shooting her boyfriend a cross glance. But he was impervious. Episode two of the Finnish detective show, which had started so promisingly, was so complex that even Harry couldn't pretend to be following and he had fallen asleep.

It was Katie ringing, so Beth pressed the button to answer and took herself into the kitchen so as not to disturb Harry's soft snores. 'Hi, so sorry about disappearing like that... um, I think I might be allergic to manicures...'

Katie laughed. 'No worries. I'm surprised you lasted as long as you did. I'm sure it was only because we were getting all that good gossip. Just don't be jealous when you see my nails, they're fabulous.'

'Promise,' said Beth, thinking that one was going to be very easy to keep.

'But I didn't ring about that, it's the disco. You know we have to be there. And I've said we'll help out with a few decorations too.'

'Oh, Katie, you didn't! You know what I'm like at that sort of thing...'

'Just for the food table that we'll be manning.'

Beth groaned aloud, then Katie spoke again. 'Now Beth

Haldane, don't you dare bail on me on this one. Or I really will be cross.'

Beth took this light-hearted threat more seriously now than she might have done a month or two ago, before she and Katie had fallen out. All right, so Beth had suggested Katie's cleaner might be guilty of murder. But what was a little accusation between friends?

Quite a lot, as it turned out. Beth's unfortunate comment, completely wide of the mark, was just one of the stresses that had pushed Katie into an uncharacteristically tetchy frame of mind. Dreadful Teddy the cockapoo had been another factor, as well as the horrible news that both her son, Charlie, and Beth's Jake, had fallen victim to a school bully. It had been a tough few weeks. Even though they were over it now, Beth was still trying to treat Katie with a lot more consideration than normal.

'No, no, of course I'll do my bit. You can rely on me,' she said quickly. 'It's just... well, I can't pretend I'm exactly looking forward to the whole disco thing.'

'It's not supposed to be fun for us. But it's the boys' first chance to really interact with girls, you know, so it's important.'

'Well, girls aren't an alien species, they spent years at the Village Primary and that was mixed,' Beth began, then hastily tacked on, 'But yes, you're so right, we want to make sure this goes well.'

'In view of all that awful stuff with Gregory King, I'd say it's essential,' Katie said firmly.

Beth privately wasn't so sure. Gregory King, a nasty piece of work in Year 9, had tried to manipulate Charlie and Jake into filming each other kissing girls from the College School – against the girls' will. Jake had been so anxious that he'd lost a lot of sleep, and then started dropping off in class, and Charlie had been really upset, too. But the plan had been scuppered and, to Beth and Katie's relief, the King boy had been suspended from Wyatt's School.

In view of the disappearance of the villain of the piece, Beth was all for letting the boys get on with their first disco without their parents breathing down their necks. But Katie, who had struggled with IVF for years before having Charlie, was finding letting go tricky, though her son was now a tall lad of almost thirteen. When Beth had seen him the weekend before, she had been pretty sure he was getting his first pimple. Neither he nor Jake were going to enjoy having their mums wrecking any street cred they might possess at their first big night out. But she sighed inwardly and accepted her lot.

'OK. So, remind me, what sort of decorations again?'

With a rendezvous scheduled to discuss themes, and no washing-up to do for once, Beth pattered off to get Colin's lead for his final nightly turn round the block. When she wandered back into the sitting room, he was sitting bolt upright, alerted by the soft jingle of the clip. Harry was still asleep, but to her surprise Beth couldn't see Magpie anywhere. Oh well, must have whizzed outside via the catflap when she wasn't looking, she decided. She picked up the Olley's bag to drop in the outside bin, but as she did so, the cat shot out, a last bit of fried fish clamped in her mouth.

'Honestly, Maggers, you're as bad as Colin these days,' she said as the cat pranced away, unrepentant.

Though it was cold out on the street, Beth rather enjoyed these short walks with Colin, once she'd hastened past the house next door with its forlorn For Sale sign. The place, which used to be full to bursting with the vibrant Bentinck clan, was now dark and empty, almost as if it had withdrawn from the life of the street in shame and sorrow at what had gone on within its four walls. She slowed down when she reached the cheerier windows of the Christie-Smith house, with its distinctive topiary hedge which reminded Beth of a tiara, and right down to the Kendalls' house at the end, before turning and coming back on the other side of the road, as was her habit. That way

Colin got the maximum number of smells for his money, sampling the fascinating calling cards of other dogs. They were just turning back into Beth's little front garden when her phone shrilled.

She fished it out and looked at it in surprise. The only person who usually rang her this late was Harry, with fulsome apologies as some terrible case or other took up all his concentration. But Harry was snoozing in the sitting room. Ah, it was Wendy. But that was very odd. By this time of night, she would normally have been asleep for several hours.

'Mum? Everything OK?' said Beth a little anxiously.

There was silence for an ominous few moments, and Beth was getting seriously alarmed by the time Wendy finally burst into speech. 'Oh Beth, have you got anywhere yet? Have you found out who killed my Le-Le-Len?' She ended on a full-blown wail and Beth realised she was in floods of tears.

'Mum, do you want me to come round?'

There was another perplexing silence from the other end and then an outbreak of sniffing. Beth, who had asked the question fully expecting – and hoping – to get the answer no, was now stuck. She really didn't want to have to visit her mother this evening; it was cold and dark and Colin, who was standing patiently looking up at her, was obviously yearning for his comfy basket in the kitchen. But she couldn't leave her mother in distress.

Ten minutes later, Beth parked outside her mother's little house. She had left Colin at home, blissfully curled up with one of his favourite chew toys. She had tucked a rug over Harry, still stretched out on the sofa but now with Magpie cuddled up next to him like a hot water bottle. There was not a peep out of Jake.

Somewhat reluctantly, she cracked open the car door and the night air rushed in. Gosh, it was quite chilly. She wrapped her scarf more tightly round her neck, while she couldn't help thinking it was a little unreasonable that her mother had summoned her, so late, to cope with her emotional crisis. Wendy had been briskly unsympathetic when Beth had had her own meltdown moments as a teenager, over this boy or that, or more often over the sad death of her beloved father. And she hadn't really been much better when James had died, perpetually comparing it to her own widowhood with the strong implication that everything had been much worse for her. Beth had long ago realised it was best to soldier on alone, instead of hoping for comfort. Her mother just wasn't very motherly. But, Beth thought wearily, that didn't mean she had to be the same.

She got out of the car and walked as quickly as she could up the path, and opened the door with her own key. 'Mum? Where are you?'

The house was quiet and still. In the gloom, Beth saw all the ghostly outlines of the figurines her mother was addicted to, clustered on shelves in the hall, like bystanders shocked into silence by some disaster. And there was no sign of her mother at all.

She opened the sitting room door. The chair by the fireside where Wendy always sat was empty. There were used tissues mounded up here and there, and a couple of empty teacups left on the army of dinky side-tables that always tripped the unwary. There was no point looking in the dining room, surely. No one had sat in that gloomy place for years, since her father's death.

Beth made her way down the passage, made narrower by the shelves of knick-knacks. She was getting more worried by the second. She headed towards the silent kitchen. But the light here was off too. Where in heaven's name was Wendy?

ELEVEN

Beth snapped on the fluorescent light, and there was an angry buzzing for a second before it burst into action. And there, at last, sitting in a high-backed chair with her back to the door, was her mother.

'Oh my God, Mum. Don't do that to me again,' said Beth, striding forward.

Wendy was clutching a tissue in her tiny hand, her head angled towards the dark garden. She looked, for all the world, like the French Lieutenant's woman washed up in suburban Dulwich. 'What, dear?' she quavered vaguely.

With an inner tut, Beth picked up the kettle and turned the tap on full. The noise of rushing water and clattering teacups woke her mother out of her reverie.

'Well really, Beth. You do make the most awful racket.' But at the end of the sentence, there was a little sob.

Beth went over to her mother's side, and put an arm round her. 'What's up, Mum? What's all this about?'

'How can you ask me that, Beth? You know what it's about. It's my L-L-Len...' Wendy tailed off soggily, then blew her nose loudly in the disintegrating tissue. Beth silently handed her a handful of fresh ones and scooped the used tissues away to fling into the bin. She filled the kettle and got out some of her mother's least twiddly mugs.

'A cup of tea will make you feel much better,' she said bracingly.

'Honestly, Beth, have you forgotten my insomnia? I won't sleep a wink if you make me drink caffeinated tea at this time of night,' said Wendy, reacting as though Beth was trying to poison her.

Beth silently flicked the teabag out of one cup, rattled around in another cupboard, found a dusty box of peppermint infusion and sloshed boiling water into both mugs. By this time, her own private yearning was for something a lot stronger than tea. But she pushed the mug in front of her mother, who cupped her hands around it and seemed to draw a little strength from the warmth.

'Listen, Mum, I'll just nip upstairs, shall I, and bring you a cardigan or something? You can't sit here in this thin dressing gown. You'll catch your death...'

Of course, it was quite the wrong thing to say. Instantly, Wendy was off again, torrents of tears pouring down her cheeks. 'Death! It's all around me. How can my Len have died? He was in the prime of life, so fit, so vigorous.'

He certainly had been vigorous. Beth didn't quite want to think about how much energy he had poured into that love life. Even though she was now committed to investigating the mystery, it wasn't impossible that Len had simply, ah, overextended himself. Wendy's talk of skulduggery could be mere wishful thinking.

'Len was older than you, Mum. I mean, that's not ancient, obviously,' she said quickly. 'But he wasn't twenty-one, let's put it that way.'

'From your perspective, that might be past it, Beth. But from where I'm sitting, Len had so much more to give.'

Yes, thought Beth. And the trouble was, he was giving it to everybody. But it was absolutely no use saying that. 'If you don't want a cardigan, how about I get you one of your scarves from the hall?'

Wendy assented to this and Beth trudged off to harvest one from the hooks near the front door. Her mother always had these in profusion, as well as the innumerable beaded necklaces she insisted on draping around herself so she tinkled like a wind charm. Maybe Len had found it attractive? Though as Beth was beginning to discover, he didn't really seem that fussy. It seemed to have been a case of any port in a storm, and since there hadn't been a storm for ages, it was just any port. She was going to have a job to persuade her mother that Len had not been the knight in shining armour of her imaginings. And perhaps it was kinder not to try.

Looping the woolliest possible scarf over her mother's thin shoulders, Beth couldn't help wondering about Wendy. This relationship with Len, ill-starred as it had been, was at least a sign that Wendy might be emerging from the cocoon of selfish preoccupation she'd hidden in since Beth's father's death. And asking her daughter to investigate the circumstances of Len's demise had been a rare – very rare – example of Wendy showing an interest in someone other than herself.

The trouble was, it was so hard to know where to begin. Although it appeared the choir and the Bridge contingent had alibis, if Beth knew Len – and she was beginning to feel as though she did – there would be plenty of other women out there at the time of his death who were unaccounted for. Plus the satisfied customers from his assignations on that night, Margery Brinkwell and Harriet French. And, if she were to be believed, Wendy as well. Yeesh.

And wasn't Beth overlooking another very large group of people who had a strong motive to rid the world of Len Broughton? For, if the wronged ladies of Dulwich had an axe to grind about this Lothario's behaviour, how much more incensed must their cuckolded husbands be?

As she sat in the kitchen with Wendy, patting her hand and watching her slowly sip her peppermint tea, Beth realised this really could be her most difficult case yet. Everywhere she turned, more people came out of the woodwork with a strong motive for seeing Len Broughton dead. And she had to get it all sorted out in time for her mother's beloved Bridge tournament in less than a fortnight's time, so that everyone could concentrate on their cards, not the gossip about Wendy.

If he had still been alive that night, Beth realised she might have been strongly tempted to kill him herself.

TWELVE

There was nothing like a heavenly cappuccino in the morning to make the world seem like a better place, and Beth took her first sip and sighed with pleasure at her friend Katie. The serene surroundings also served as balm for her jittery soul. Mariella's café was a porcelain figurine-free zone – though Beth personally would also have trimmed down the foliage a bit, she decided, as she brushed a bit of a dangling spider plant out of her hair.

'You don't know how badly I needed this. I was up half the night with Wendy. God, she's in such a state.' Beth shook her head.

'Poor thing, she must be so devastated. Um, and I've heard about a few... other women?' Katie, dressed from head to toe in the finest yoga gear Sweaty Betty could purvey, instinctively lowered her voice.

'You might as well say it loud and proud. I don't think there's a soul in Dulwich Village at this point who's unaware of Wendy's status as just one of Len Broughton's massive harem,' Beth said bitterly. 'And no, it doesn't seem to have made a jot of difference. She's still completely in denial about all the others. And she's convinced Margery Brinkwell killed him.'

'Do you think we should just cross-question Margery and see if we can take her off the list?' said Katie earnestly.

'Ordinarily I would do that straight away, but I think my mother is just blaming her out of jealousy. In any case, I think it's more likely to have been one of the women he spent time with, ahem, indoors that evening. Margery was just hanging around his house, and then he went to the office, so I don't think she had as much opportunity as some of the others. I vote we shelve her for the moment and concentrate on all the rest. It's not like there's a shortage. And we need to find out the cause of death, too. Harry said it was a heart attack, but if Mum's right it can't have been, it must have just looked like one.'

Katie looked thoughtful. 'I'm surprised we haven't heard more on that. There's usually such poisonous gossip flying around here.'

As if to illustrate her point, at that exact moment Belinda McKenzie sashayed into the café and stared straight at Beth. Striding forward in what had to be yet another pair of brand spanking new boots, this time over-the-knee numbers in buttery suede which surely must have cost Barty McKenzie dearly, Belinda came to a stop in front of Beth and Katie's booth.

'So, I hear your mother is *still* going about saying she's Len Broughton's wife-to-be,' Belinda announced loudly. 'Despite me kindly dropping her a hint the other day...' She didn't even need to snigger herself; the little gaggle of wannabe yummy mummies who always trailed around after her were happy to oblige.

Beth winced, but before she could speak, Katie held up a hand. Belinda had made a mistake. Though open about her loathing of Beth, she usually attacked her when Katie was elsewhere. This time she was having a go right in front of her. Katie was the most popular yoga instructor in the area, and one of the nicest people you could meet, but she was no pushover. She now had an unusually martial look in her eye.

'How's your shoffice reconstruction going, Belinda?' Katie asked. Her tone of voice was sweet and innocent, but the effect was immediate. The pack of mums behind Belinda fell silent. The shoffice was a very sore point indeed with the McKenzies. It had been the size of the Albert Hall, a massive studio-cum-gym-cum-screening-room that had been the envy of all, until one of its turrets had fallen off, nearly killing Belinda's favourite dog. Then Barty had been found in a compromising position with the au pair in its cavernous interior – but that was another story.

'Oh! Oh. Fine, thank you,' Belinda mumbled, and she tottered away to her usual table, pausing only to give Beth a passing glance which stripped all the remaining foam off her cappuccino.

'God, thank you,' said Beth, touching her friend's arm in gratitude. 'Saved my life. Again. You are wonderful, you know.'

'All in a day's work,' said Katie airily, but Beth knew from her slightly pink cheeks she was pleased at the compliment. 'In fact, talking of helping, I was going to mention something to you about that...' she added more tentatively.

Immediately, Beth stiffened slightly, her habitual reaction to anything that might put her on the spot. But she told herself to relax. This was Katie, not her mother or Belinda. It wouldn't be anything awful.

'It's about the Year 8 disco,' Katie went on.

Oh God, thought Beth. It *is* awful after all. 'I thought we had that all sorted out now,' said Beth a little defensively. 'I've got it in my diary. And I've promised I'll help out with the decorations...'

'Yes, yes, you swore you would,' Katie reminded her eagerly.

'But do you really think it's a good idea, us going?' said Beth.

'I mean, they're big boys now... nearly teenagers. Won't they just be furious if they see us there?'

'Well, Charlie won't. He knows I'm going, after what happened. And he's fine with it.' Katie's normally smiley mouth was set in a firm line.

Beth sighed to herself. If Charlie was reconciled to his mother going, that meant Jake was expecting Beth to turn up too. He'd probably complain, when she confirmed to him this was the case. But that would be for form's sake. It looked as though there was really no dodging the ordeal.

'I'm not quite sure why you think it's going to be so dreadful, anyway, Beth,' said Katie, putting her cup down after a sip. 'There will be lots of other parents. It'll probably be a laugh.'

A laugh, Beth thought hollowly. She'd dreaded school discos enough when she'd been a participant. Trying to look her best, yet knowing the 'popular' (tall, blonde) girls would get all the dances and she was forever doomed to be a despised wallflower, had been tough in her teenage years. Now spending yet more hours as a spare part, sipping lukewarm wine out of one of those awful thin plastic cups while spying on her son – who might well be finding out for himself just how uncool he was – did not sound like any kind of *laugh*.

But a bargain was a bargain. 'I've said I'll go with you. And I will. But obviously I'm going now to sue you for breach of promise if it doesn't turn out to be wild fun,' said Beth, trying to make light of her reluctance.

'Sounds like it should be your mother with the breach of promise suit,' said Katie.

'Well, I don't suppose she'll get far, as the groom is dead,' Beth said flatly.

Katie gave her a sympathetic look. 'Anyway, Beth, you never know, you might well be able to do some investigating at the disco.'

'Really? How's that going to work?' Beth sounded every bit as sceptical as she felt.

'Well, like I say there are bound to be lots of other parents going, and teachers... and maybe some of them know more about the whole Len Broughton situation. Actually, some of the older teachers might even have dated him themselves.'

This was a startling idea, but Beth conceded Katie might well have a point. 'Why not, I suppose? As he seems to have been giving a turn to literally every woman in the district. Honestly, trust my mum to get involved with such a shyster.'

'Poor Wendy. But she certainly wasn't the only one taken in.'

'I know, I know. I shouldn't be so hard on her. She's really taking it so badly. I suppose it's her first foray into dating for, what, two decades? And it's been an abysmal failure by anyone's reckoning.'

They both thought about it for a second, Beth from the perspective of someone who'd been saved from making her own dating mistakes by fate, in the shape of DI Harry York, and Katie, from the lofty heights of the safely married.

Beth stirred her cappuccino slowly. 'Maybe you're right, Katie. Maybe the disco will give me another opportunity to rule some people out. At the moment we've got virtually the entire female population of Dulwich in the frame. Not to mention their angry husbands.'

'I'll be helping you out with the investigation every step of the way this time, remember,' said Katie brightly. 'We're bound to get through the suspects really fast, no matter how many there are. We'll definitely get it all sorted in time for that Bridge tournament thingy your mother is so keen on.'

In truth, Katie's previous involvement in the dog-walking case had been something of a mixed blessing. She had turned out to be quite a stickler for doing things by the book, whereas Beth was now used to flying by the seat of her not uncapacious pants most of the time. But it was always great to spend time with Katie. Beth felt a sudden flush of gratitude. 'Thank you so much, Katie. How are things going with Teddy, by the way?'

'With Sophie the dog-walker taking him to the park before and after school, he's a lot more manageable. And Charlie is quite self-sufficient these days, I agree with Michael really,' she added thoughtfully.

Beth nodded as neutrally as she could. She had always given Jake a bit more leeway than Charlie got, though this was due to her own inability to juggle her freelance work, demanding pets, Wyatt's job, addiction to manic house-cleaning and a continuing inability to get on top of the cooking, rather than any conscious decision to respect his boundaries.

'Well, that's brilliant. Here's hoping we sort this one out in super-quick time,' said Beth.

Belinda, who had sauntered over, apparently to look at the cake display on the counter near them, even though she had not been seen to ingest carbs or sugar since her daughter Allegra's first birthday party thirteen years ago, immediately whipped round and bustled up to their table. 'Ooh, you seem cheery, Katie. What's it all about? Beth, is that policeman of yours finally making an honest woman of you?'

Beth just about managed to suppress the anatomically impossible suggestion she felt like yelling at Belinda, and bent over her cappuccino instead. It had only taken the blasted woman a few minutes to recover from Katie's clever put-down earlier. Honestly, she had a hide that would put the most weather-beaten old rhino to shame. Belinda switched her glance to Katie and cooed in much gentler tones, 'Come on now, Katie. It's not neighbourly to have secrets. Do tell.'

Katie just winked at her and, with a smile of ineffable sunniness, said, 'Wouldn't you like to know?'

Belinda laughed along, but Beth could see from the way her knuckles tightened on the handle of her huge handbag that she was pretty furious. She hoped Katie's second brave attempt of the day to take Belinda's heat hadn't made her a horrible enemy. As Beth knew all too well, having Belinda on your case was exhausting. But before things could get even more uncomfortable, Belinda's little swarm of mummy friends started drifting over to see what was going on. All they had in common was a slavish devotion to their leader, and they had been left on their own a mite too long. A second later, Belinda had shepherded them back to their table, this time without a backward glance.

Katie leant forward. 'I do hope Belinda's not going to be difficult this term.'

'When isn't she, though?' sighed Beth. But she was resigned to the situation. Her strange standoff with Belinda had been going on for so long at this point that she was almost used to it. 'Seriously, it doesn't even bother me that much any more.'

'I can't believe that,' said Katie with a shake of her head. 'But anyway, we've got more important things to think about. Now then. What's our first step with this investigation? After all, if Len was really murdered, then there's a killer loose in Dulwich Village. And I think we should probably get on with finding them. Don't you?'

THIRTEEN

Beth thought about Katie's brave words later that afternoon as she finally settled down to do a spot of work in the Wyatt's School Archive Institute. It hadn't really occurred to her, until Katie had said it, but of course by this point the killer must be thinking they had got away with it. They'd certainly want to keep it that way. So they might well start picking off anyone making a fuss about the death of Dulwich's answer to Casanova. And who was making more of a fuss than Beth's own mother, Wendy?

Beth hated the idea that her mother might be at risk. She quickly dialled Wendy's number but the answering machine kicked in. For a second, she panicked. Then she realised that Wendy was bound to be playing Bridge. She'd call her later, just to check how she was getting on. It hadn't been many days since the funeral and there had been little sign so far of Wendy's tears drying up, but if she was now feeling well enough to go to her Bridge Club then that was really good progress.

She hoped Wendy was not airing her suspicions with all and sundry over the Bridge tables, though. Dulwich was a hotbed of scurrilous talk at the best of times. Beth knew this from her own street. If a visitor parked in a resident's bay in Pickwick Road, then everyone was up in arms for days, and the culprit who'd allowed this appalling transgression would be under no illusions about how badly they'd behaved. Throw in a real scandal, like love rat Len's epic cheating, and then a murder on top of that, and people would be talking of nothing else at their drinks parties for months on end. Would Wendy be able to resist cashing in on her moment of infamy, as Len's most determined girlfriend and apparently bigamous fiancée?

The more Beth thought about it, the more worried she got. All right, she had other, pressing concerns which should have claimed her attention. She needed to think about how she was going to handle the disco business, for example.

She was sure Jake would be hoping against hope that she'd think better of coming as the fateful evening neared. She needed to brace him for the fact that she would definitely be hiding behind a pillar gawping at him as he made his debut in mixed company. Not because she wanted to, but because she'd made that unholy pact with Katie. Poor boy.

As well as sorting out some sort of disco decorations (and what on earth would those be?) she also needed to get to grips with updating the interior of her own home, following the garden revamp. Her tins of magnolia paint, though they had now been moved all the way from the hall into the tiny study, were busily going rusty. She had a huge folder of freelance work that she ought to be plodding through. And there was always her actual job, here at the Archive Institute. She looked around distractedly at her towering in-tray.

But it was no good. As usual, the latest mystery to beset the area was uppermost in her mind. She picked up her phone again and dialled Katie.

'Katie, listen, I think Mum's gone to the Bridge Club – yes, yes I know that's a good thing, but what if she's telling everyone everything she knows about Len's final days? And saying he was murdered? And what if, you know, the *wrong person* just happens to be listening? Oh, would you? Thanks so much, Katie. I'll see you outside Belair House as soon as you can get there, then.'

With no more ado, Beth gathered up her handbag and coat, and rushed out of the door of her office. A second later, she was back, poking her head round and saying to the empty room, 'Sorry! I'll be back to sort you out soon, I promise.' Ridiculous, but she felt better once she'd done it. Then she was scampering out of the grand school gates and charging up the road leading to the beautiful stately building which housed Wendy's Bridge Club.

Beth and Katie had tangled with the Bridge Club members once before, investigating the suspicious death of Wendy's long-suffering partner. They had enjoyed a certain amount of leeway and had been tolerated by Deirdre McBride, the director of the club. But that had been then. As she held her sides and panted after her gallop, waiting for Katie, Beth suddenly wondered whether they would even be allowed in this time. Still, nothing ventured, nothing gained... A minute later, Katie appeared, a lot less out of breath and looking as svelte as ever in her running gear, even though she'd had a lot further to come. Beth tried furtively to unstick her fringe from her forehead as they sauntered past reception without being challenged and made their way up the stairs.

'They must think we're Bridge Club members,' Katie said under her breath.

'I'm not sure that's very flattering,' puffed Beth. 'The average age must be about one hundred and fifty.'

They were both still giggling when they rounded the corner and bumped straight into Deirdre MacBride, standing at the top of the stairs. She looked them up and down before speaking.

'I wondered who was making all that noise. You realise the

Bridge Club is in session? It's not long till the tournament now, after all.'

Beth had forgotten how seriously the members took things. Bridge was just a game, but in Dulwich you could be forgiven for thinking it was a religion. They played in hushed silence, and there were all kinds of arcane rules that Deirdre was only too happy to impose if anyone put a foot out of line.

'I'm sorry, Deirdre, but as you know, my mother's been having a very difficult time of late...' Beth began.

Immediately, and a little to Beth and Katie's surprise, Deirdre MacBride's uncompromisingly plain face seemed to soften slightly. The layer of powder on her cheeks cracked as she gave a sympathetic smile. 'Ah yes, poor Wendy. She's suffered quite a loss...'

Beth nodded, and would have spoken up, but Deirdre hadn't finished.

'...As have several other of our members. In fact, a lot of our ladies have turned up in black recently. And I don't think it's a coincidence.'

Beth gave a meaningful look at Deirdre's own black wool jacket and skirt and the older woman bridled a little and swept into the ballroom where the Bridge session was taking place. Beth raised her eyebrows at Katie, and they followed.

The room was full, but was as silent as a church – and an awful lot quieter than St Matthew's, where Len Broughton's funeral service had been conducted so rambunctiously. Despite the air of profound concentration, a few heads turned to watch as Beth and Katie followed in Deirdre's wake and made their way to Wendy's usual table, by one of the large windows that gave onto Belair Park. 'Oh dear. The waterworks have started again,' said Deirdre in a low voice. 'Well, I suppose you could take her away with you?'

Beth looked at Wendy, who hadn't even registered her

daughter's presence. She had her head buried in a tissue. 'Has she been like this the whole time?' Beth asked.

'No, she was fine earlier. And she's dummy at the moment.' Luckily, Beth knew enough about Bridge to realise this wasn't a terrible insult, it just meant Wendy wasn't an active player this time round. 'So it's fine, really. But I'm not sure she can play the next hand...' For once, Deirdre MacBride looked quite human, her glance full of compassion for poor Wendy. Beth was definitely wondering now. Deirdre couldn't be yet another of Len's playthings. Could she?

'Um... did you know Len yourself?' she ventured. At once, Deirdre shot Beth a glance. Beth felt Katie stirring beside her, and hoped she wouldn't pipe up to say that was an unfair question. It probably was... but it was one they needed the answer to.

'What have you heard?' Deirdre hissed. She looked all around the room, as if to check whether anyone was listening, but they were all glued to their cards.

'Oh... not much,' Beth said cagily. 'It's just that Len seems to have been quite... free with his favours. And you, well. Forgive me, Deirdre, but you do look like his type.'

This was a total lie; if the past few days had taught Beth anything, it was that Len really wasn't that fussed. Tall, short, thin, nuts like her own mother – no one seemed to have been safe from his attentions. Deirdre was definitely on the fierce side, and if Beth had been Len she wouldn't have gone there in a million years, but then Beth definitely wasn't Len. It was as though someone had told him to take a selection of the broadest spectrum of ladies Dulwich had to offer, and make them all his slaves.

And, to Beth's dawning astonishment, it appeared she had struck lucky. If she wasn't mistaken, that was a girlish blush now breaking through Deirdre's face powder. It sat very oddly with her prickly tweedy jacket and her air of no-nonsense command.

But it told its own story. Deirdre must be one of this willing number.

'It was just a moment of madness, you understand. Well, three weeks. He just swept me off my feet,' Deirdre said in a sing-song tone they had never heard her use before. Then her face changed. 'And I had reason enough to regret it,' she added darkly.

Just then there was a sob from the table, where Wendy appeared to have run out of tissues and was searching fruitlessly in her handbag for more. Beth wondered if she had heard what Deirdre had just confessed to – or whether she was overwhelmed with memories of her own.

'I'm sorry, Deirdre, I'm going to have to take Mum away with me now. But perhaps we could meet up later to discuss Len?'

'Oh. Oh, I don't know about that,' said Deirdre, snapping back into her usual sergeant-major mode.

'Wouldn't it be a relief to get it all off your chest?' Katie said soothingly. Thank goodness, it was just the right tactic. Deirdre seemed to struggle with herself for a moment, then she caved in.

'Oh, all right then,' she said. 'I suppose I could fit a quick drink in, say four o'clock at the Dirty Dog?'

Beth, while inwardly goggling at the idea of Deirdre starting drinking at 4 p.m. on a weekday, nodded enthusiastically. 'Brilliant. See you there.'

With that, she and Katie went over to help Wendy up, with Beth pressing a wodge of clean tissues into her mother's hand. 'Sorry about this,' she mouthed to the other three Bridge players at the table. Normally, she felt they'd be furious at this inconvenient interruption to their game. But, given the scene Wendy had been on the verge of making, they were all just very relieved to have her hauled away.

'See you next time,' Wendy quavered damply as she collected up her innumerable scarves and adjusted her necklaces. Beth picked up her bag and Katie took her coat. Deirdre patted her quite fondly on the shoulder as the little trio made their way out of the ballroom.

Once they were outside, but not yet down the stairs, there was an outbreak of chatter from the ballroom, but then the tinkle of Deirdre's trusty director's bell was heard demanding silence and a renewal of that level of concentration necessary in Dulwich to outwit one's neighbours – at Bridge, if at nothing else.

'Are you OK, Mum?' Beth asked Wendy as they finally got outside the building.

Wendy sniffed once or twice but straightened her shoulders and looked defiantly at her daughter. 'What? Yes, yes, of course I am. I'm fine. I really don't know what all the fuss is about. Honestly, you do get yourself in a stew about things, Beth.'

Beth looked at Wendy, sparks coming out of her ears. But before she could let rip, Katie butted in.

'What do you say to a nice cup of tea at home, Wendy? It's quite nippy standing out here, isn't it?'

Immediately, Wendy relaxed and gave Katie a watery smile. 'What a good idea, dear. Let's do that.' She allowed Katie to take her arm and the pair sauntered off together down the gravel drive.

Not for the first time, Beth was left thinking how much better Katie would be at filling the difficult role of Wendy's daughter. Beth had been making a hash of it for years, and could really do with some time off for good behaviour. But just then, Wendy turned round. 'Do come along, Beth. It'll be nice to get into the warm. This cold gets right into my bones. I'm not as young as I was, you know.'

Don't I know it, thought Beth crossly. And it's only thanks to Katie that you're going to get any older.

FOURTEEN

Immediately Beth was brought up short. The way Wendy twisted her age to her own advantage was maddening. Sometimes she clamoured for compliments on her youthfulness, sometimes she insisted on the deference due to decrepitude. But whichever way she was playing it, and however infuriating the switcheroo often was, she was Beth's mother, and her daughter loved her. Even if it sometimes required deep breaths and tightly clenched fists to remind herself of this fact.

Beth picked up her pace over the last of the gravel, and soon they had made the short journey to Wendy's place.

As soon as Wendy was installed by her fireside with a cup of tea and a plate of intricately iced biscuits, and Beth had shut the front door on her, she let out a giant breath. 'Thanks, Katie. You're so good with Mum. I don't know how you do it.'

'That's easy.' Katie smiled. 'People aren't nearly so annoying when you have absolutely no DNA in common.'

It was a point Beth mulled over later that day, as Harry sent her a perfunctory text saying he was going to be late, and Jake WhatsApped her to say there was a rugby practice he'd forgotten about so he wouldn't be back till after six. Beth was on the way to getting riled, when she suddenly remembered her date with Deirdre MacBride in the Greyhound. She gave Katie a quick ring to see if she was going to join them, but she sheepishly admitted she was 'helping Charlie with his trigonometry'. This was bad news for Beth, as it meant a) there was Maths homework, of the type she hadn't even understood when she'd been at school herself, so had no hope of assisting Jake with, and b) he was out at rugby anyway, and would probably be too tired to do it when he got back, mud-splattered and hungry, so that was another assignment that risked being dashed off in seconds flat tomorrow morning.

Oh well, thought Beth, as she stood in front of the slightly-too-high hall mirror just before four that afternoon and did her best to perk up her appearance with a dried-up mascara wand. Maths probably wouldn't be Jake's subject anyway. If only gaming and sloth were on the national curriculum, he'd be winning all the prizes at Speech Day. She picked up her shoulder bag and locked the door on Colin's hopeful muzzle. 'No doggies at the pub, Col. I'll take you out later,' she said to try and reassure him. But as she turned to go, she heard a heart-wrenching sigh from the old Labrador. Today hadn't been a lot of fun for Colin. Tomorrow she'd make it up to him, take him to the park for a proper run around.

Beth strolled to the village, past the little parade of rather silly shops selling overpriced silk dresses, expensive diffusers and the sort of fancy guest soaps no one ever used. She squared her shoulders as she prepared to push at the pub door, with its nineteenth-century etched glass and polished brass handles. The Greyhound was an old coaching inn, from the days when Dulwich was mostly open fields, a mere stage on everyone's journey to the capital. Once, carriages had driven right under its archway into a courtyard beyond, where ostlers would rub down the horses for their push on into central London. Now the only horsepower in evidence was from the vast SUVs stacked up outside, jostling for parking space amidst the double yellow lines of the village. The pub's façade was dotted with window boxes filled with cascades of nasturtiums. They were edible, Beth suddenly remembered, which reminded her of her earlier thought about poisonous plants. Could Len have eaten something which had produced heart attack symptoms? She made a mental note to keep the idea in mind.

Beth wasn't much of a boozer at the best of times, and going to a pub alone was not her favourite thing. She always hated to stand out, and she imagined the sort of cliques that filled the Greyhound on a weekday afternoon would not be kindred spirits. But when she looked around, the place was quiet enough. There were a few clusters of people at the old oak tables, but no one seemed at all alarming. Apart from Deirdre MacBride, who raised an arm and waved at her from a corner seat by the window.

Beth wandered over to join her. 'Can I get you anything?' she asked politely. But Deirdre just indicated her almost full pint glass. Beth blinked at it for a second, then realised the mannish drink fitted with Deirdre's bristly tweeds and sergeant-majorish way with a whistle – and made her romance with Len all the more poignant.

Beth went over to the bar. She was a bit stumped about what to order. She didn't love beer or lager. Nor did she fancy a glass of wine right now. Tea seemed a bit of a cop-out, if they even served it... In the end, she went for a glass of fizzy mineral water with ice and a slice, and hoped that Deirdre would think it was a gin and tonic.

When she was sitting back down opposite Deirdre, she raised her glass to clink it with the older woman's. 'To, er...' She stopped in confusion.

'To Len Broughton,' Deirdre supplied, her mouth a straight line.

Beth blessed her inwardly. She'd been wondering how on

earth to get started on this ticklish topic without the emollient presence of Katie. But Deirdre had presented her with an open goal.

'How are you feeling now about... all that?' Beth said diffidently. She wanted to unlock the floodgates – but at the same time was hoping against hope that Deirdre wouldn't break down. It was hard enough dealing with Wendy's apparently unstoppable tears.

But Deirdre was made of sterner stuff than Wendy. She merely swallowed once or twice and blinked away her emotions, before answering in a gravelly voice: 'It's been hard, I grant you. But Len and I were over a while ago. That's given me the distance I needed to become... philosophical.'

'I see,' said Beth, who wasn't entirely sure that she did. 'Was it a long, um, relationship?' Deirdre had said earlier it had been three weeks – but Beth wondered whether that was true.

Deirdre was silent for a while and Beth worried that she'd gone too far. But it seemed the older woman was just choosing her words. 'Not long in time, but in depth... certainly.'

'Goodness,' was all that Beth could muster in response. She was beginning to look on Len with newfound respect. He had certainly made quite an impression, and on the unlikeliest people. 'And did you know that he was... still married?'

Deirdre's eyes hardened a bit at this. 'Certainly not. It goes without saying I would never have got involved, had I been aware of that fact. Len was... I'm not going to say a liar, but he was certainly economical with the truth when it suited him. I discussed my late husband, and he gave me to understand, somehow, that he was in the same boat. But I now realise that wasn't true.'

'Do you know his wife, Margery Brinkwell?'

Deirdre gave her a level look. 'I think most people in Dulwich know Margery, particularly those who live on Wyatt's Estate property like me.'

'Why do you think she kept their relationship a secret?'

Deirdre mulled for a moment. 'I've pondered this myself... I think it was all over years ago, and they just never got divorced. And she was probably embarrassed about the, er, other women and suchlike.'

It sounded plausible, thought Beth. 'Do you think she could have had anything to do with his death?' she ventured more tentatively. She didn't really want to go throwing accusations around... but the woman had to be a suspect.

'Margery? No. The very idea is ridiculous. I have no great affection for the woman, but only because she – or the Wyatt Estate – refused me permission to double-glaze the windows at the front of my house. I had no idea she had any kind of connection to Len.'

This confirmed Beth's view that Wendy was wide of the mark on Margery Brinkwell, so she turned the conversation. 'Were you surprised that my mother says he had asked her to marry him? Did he, er, ask everyone?' Beth twisted a little nervously as she asked this. She wasn't sure it was going to go down at all well. But she had to try and find out what on earth Len Broughton had been up to, and whether this had been his usual modus operandi.

Deirdre thought for a moment. 'There were some signs... he was wistful about us being a couple, he asked me if I thought we'd always be together. I think if I'd reacted to any of those things in a more favourable way, he might have, well, popped the question. But I probably wasn't very receptive,' she added.

Looking at Deirdre's large square face, which had received a fresh dusting of powder since she'd last seen her, Beth was surprised Len had ever dared speak to her, let alone sweet-talk her. Her prickly tweed jacket perfectly mirrored her attitude, Beth would have thought. But she was clearly wrong.

'I enjoyed his company. And it was refreshing, after so many years alone, following Hugo's death. My husband, you know.' Deirdre looked down at the scrubbed oak table and fiddled with a beer mat. 'No more solo holidays, someone to sit with in restaurants. Company, really. But even if it meant having a plus-one again after all this time, I couldn't see Len filling Hugo's shoes. It would have been wrong to carry on, just so I didn't have to be sitting on my tod.'

It looked as if Len had tapped into a deep well of loneliness that lurked, unsuspected, under Deirdre's bristly jacket. Beth felt a wave of commiseration sweep over her. She knew how it felt to be alone, having weathered years of isolation after James's death, before Harry had appeared on the scene. It wasn't easy, in a world designed, like Noah's Ark, for those who went through life two by two.

'Good for you, not compromising. If you knew your feelings weren't strong enough. And of course it's saved you a lot of trouble now, as he was actually married all along. Does that seem in character, the fact that he lied to you?'

'And to half of the rest of the village as well? I'm afraid it does. That's one of the things that stopped me "committing", as I think people say nowadays. At first it was very small things, like his whereabouts on any given evening. He could be very vague. And then if I did manage to pin him down and he said he was at an event or something, it would turn out that it had been cancelled that evening. He was very plausible, but underneath that he was... slippery.'

Poor Len, Beth thought. Running so many inquisitive women must have been a nightmare. Not that she had any sympathy, but as someone who regularly found they were out of milk, she couldn't help admiring the logistics required to keep so many, much more demanding, balls in the air. He had also been brave enough taking Deirdre on. But having to face cross-questioning from her on his whereabouts would have crushed a less wily man. Beth wondered whether he had actually been relieved when she had let him down gently.

'Did you have any inkling that he was seeing, well, so many others?' It was another difficult question, but aside from tearing a strip off her beer mat, Deirdre didn't show any outward signs of discomfort.

'I knew he had an eye for a pretty girl,' Deirdre said, with a suspicion of colour in her cheeks again, and Beth realised with a shock she meant herself. 'But I didn't know how far he was taking it. He was the type to look very appreciatively at every waitress, if you know what I mean.'

Beth did know, and avoided men who couldn't help casting an eye over others in her presence. It would do nothing for her self-esteem if a partner spent a lot of time mentally auditioning her successor. Thank goodness Harry seemed oblivious to most other women – including his too-pretty-by-half sidekick, Narinda Khan. She nodded encouragingly. 'When did you suspect it went further than just looking? If you ever did.'

Deirdre sighed. 'I suppose it was at an event at Wyatt's Museum of Art,' she mused. 'You know they have drinks evenings?'

Beth nodded. She loved going to these with Katie, enjoying the thrill of being in her favourite gallery after closing time, champagne glass in hand, trying not to bolt the sophisticated canapés too fast, rubbing shoulders with the great and good of the area.

'People usually behave pretty well at those dos, don't they?' Beth frowned, trying to remember any untoward happenings, but all that came back to her was a happy blur of fizz and chat. Katie knew everyone who was anyone. After helping a lot of them achieve a serene tree pose in clinging Lycra, they could hardly stand on ceremony with her after-hours. And those she hadn't taught yoga to, she'd hobnobbed with over dinners with Michael. In a way, it was a little surprising she didn't seem to know Len Broughton. But what Deirdre said next perhaps explained that little mystery.

'There was one unfortunate evening – I think it was the opening of the Rembrandt exhibition a few years ago.'

Beth remembered the occasion well – it had been quite a feather in the museum's cap to gather a respectable number of the Old Master paintings to complement the jewel in its own collection, Rembrandt's *Girl at a Window*.

'What happened?' she prompted gently.

'Um,' said Deirdre, looking at Beth a little nervously and sinking about an inch of her drink in one go. 'It was pretty embarrassing, really. We'd gone together. He'd picked me up from my house, you know, in Dovercourt Road.' Dovercourt was a lovely street, very close to Pickwick Road but, in Beth's considered view, not quite as nice. 'And we walked together. It was rather romantic. It was a lovely summer's evening. The stars were out... he bought me a little bunch of roses.' Deirdre sighed a gusty sigh.

Beth looked at her in surprise. She would have said that no-nonsense, downright bossy Deirdre was the last woman alive to be swept away by all the old hearts and flowers clichés. But it seemed she had a very soft gooey centre beneath that bristly jacket. Len was clearly a charmer, not to say a bounder. These must be the very tactics he'd used on her own mother. Beth all but gnashed her teeth at the thought, then forced herself back to Deirdre and her sorry tale.

'We were having such a super time to start with, just sipping our drinks, mingling... I always loved being on Len's arm. He was a fine figure of a man, you know. So tall. Commanding... Always with his pipe. *So* distinguished.'

Funny, thought Beth. Those were the exact same words often used to describe Deirdre herself – apart from the pipe of course. Did everyone search for their own mirror image? But no. She and Harry could hardly be more different. Apart from him being a good foot (probably a foot and a half) taller than Beth, he was so focused on his work, and so vague about their life together. For a second, she wondered when he'd be finished that evening, then realised she hadn't been listening when he'd told her that morning. She'd been going over everything she had to do today instead. Then she shook herself mentally and concentrated.

'That all sounds so nice, but what happened to, well, break the spell, if I can put it like that?'

Deirdre started pleating the beer mat, which was by now in quite a state. 'I suppose I became aware... you know when someone is staring at you? You just feel a tingle. I turned round, and this woman was glaring at me as though she hated my guts. It gave me quite a turn.'

'Did it? Was it... Harriet French, by any chance?'

'The gardener? No!' said Deirdre. 'This was someone short, a bit gingery... She didn't really look like a Dulwich type, if you know what I mean?'

Beth digested this. The description rang a faint bell... but she just couldn't quite think why. She'd have to come back to it later.

'But how did you get from this person staring at you, to knowing that Len had, you know, done the dirty?'

Deirdre rolled her eyes a bit at Beth's phrase but continued heavily. 'Well, she didn't leave me in much doubt. As soon as Len went off to the bar to get us some top-ups – he was such a gentleman about things like that – she moved in and grabbed my arm. She pulled me outside into the cloakroom. And then she told me everything.'

Beth, by now, was on the edge of her seat. She took a sip of her water, to try to look a little less avid, but the bubbles went up her nose and she sneezed.

'Bless you,' said Deirdre gruffly. 'Anyway. It was such a shock.'

There was a silence, until Beth realised that was as much as

Deirdre was going to volunteer. 'Wait, you mean it was a shock he'd been having another relationship on the side?'

'Not so much that. It was more... the money angle.'

'The money angle?'

'Yes. It turned out he'd done it to her too.'

Beth almost didn't want to ask the question. But of course she had to. 'What did he do, Deirdre?'

Deirdre looked down at the table, and swept the remnants of the beer mat into a soggy heap. 'They really should clear these tables,' she grumbled quietly.

'Deirdre?' Beth said again.

The other woman's head shot up. 'Oh, all right then, if you must know. He was borrowing money from me. And from all the rest of them. And when I say borrowing... I'm not sure there was any intention of paying anyone back.'

Beth was stunned. 'You mean... he was doing it for the money?'

Deirdre was now looking impatient. 'Yes, of course. Didn't you realise? That's what it was all about. That's why he romanced so many women. He was fleecing us. All of us. Trying to get money... for his habit.'

FIFTEEN

Beth sat back so abruptly she almost gave herself whiplash. 'Money? For his habit? You mean he was some sort of drug addict?' She pictured that eulogy photo again. Len hadn't looked raddled or cadaverous or anything else you might associate with persistent abuse. Even as she conjured it up in her mind's eye, his image gave her a naughty wink, and he waved his pipe seductively at her. She shut her mind in annoyance.

'Honestly, Beth. No. Of course it wasn't drugs. It was worse than that, really.'

'Christ! What on earth was it, then?'

'It was... horses,' Deirdre mumbled.

Addicted to horses? Beth's brow furrowed for a second. What did Deirdre mean? Then the penny dropped. 'Oh. Racing. Gambling.'

'Yes. And don't say it like it's a tiny thing. He got through fortunes. Not his own, though I suppose he must have wasted that first. But all those women in the church, at Bridge, the choir too, I bet not one of them went out with him without parting with at least a few thousand.'

'A few thousand!'

'Yes, Beth. And that's probably something you should be asking your own mother about.'

Oh my God, thought Beth. Deirdre was right. Could her mother, would she, have lent or given this dreadful Len money, to waste on gambling? She couldn't possibly have known that's what he wanted the money for, Beth was sure of that. 'Good grief. I'll have to go and ask her, you're right. But listen, did he get money out of you too?'

'Of course.' Deirdre shrugged. 'Obviously, I'm usually a no-nonsense kind of girl,' she looked down self-deprecatingly. 'But Len seemed to get right under my skin. And when he begged me for just a pittance, said it was for a sure thing, well, one look from those eyes... I just couldn't say no. I suppose I shouldn't have been surprised when the "sure thing" fell at the first fence, but there was always another... It sounds silly now, but he was so persuasive. He was a handsome devil, all right. The way he looked at me, the way he made me feel. It was actually worth it. For a while, anyway. What's money, after all, compared with a bit of fun? That's what he always used to say.'

Beth shook her head, hoping Deirdre would take it as sympathy. In fact she was seething at the way Len had manipulated her, and presumably others too. What did his losses matter, indeed, when he wasn't footing the bill?

Deirdre seemed to have come to terms with it. Or she was wealthy enough not to mind. But Wendy, now, that was a different story. Beth knew her mother had been left comfortably off by her father, who'd carefully insured himself up to the hilt to protect his loved ones. But he'd died so long ago, now. And prices were rising, the cost of living was biting, inflation was taking off like a rocket... Wendy, in common with many women of her generation, had never worked. So nothing had been coming in, while plenty had been going out, not least to fund the purchase of the endless stream of scarves and beads and porcelain gee-gaws she loved. How much money had she actually got left? Had Wendy done something really stupid, which might leave her facing impoverishment in her old age?

Beth felt the cold clutch of dread. She had enough difficulty making ends meet herself, half the time – although the position had been eased by her job at Wyatt's and the fact that Harry was pulling in a decent salary and helping to keep the little household afloat. But having had more than her fair share of money worries made her certain she didn't want Wendy to fret in the same way. She would hate to see her mother struggle – and though Beth wasn't now as poor as she had once been, she wasn't really in a position to bail her mother out. This could be very serious indeed.

She swigged down the rest of her mineral water, and thanked Deirdre profusely for the terrible news. At least she now knew what she was dealing with. And it did explain the sheer number of women Len had romanced – and their rage levels – not to mention providing a very clear motive for someone to bump him off. It wasn't so much a question of his libido any more, as his out-and-out greed.

Beth left Deirdre finishing off the last of her drink, seemingly quite cheered up by getting the truth about Len off her chest, and made to rush out into the darkening streets of Dulwich. But, as she approached the etched glass doors, she saw someone out of the corner of her eye, on the other side of the large pub – someone trying to make themselves inconspicuous in an alcove...

Beth stepped boldly over. 'Margery, er, Mrs Broughton, er, Brinkwell, I recognise you from the, um, church service,' she said, omitting to mention that Margery had been trying to yank chunks of her mother's hair out at the time. 'Nice to meet you properly. I'm Beth Haldane.'

'I know who you are,' said Margery Brinkwell. Her rather beautiful aristocratic face was aloof, as though she had caught a whiff of something nasty but was too well brought up to mention it. When Beth remained smiley and drew closer, she spoke again. 'I'm amazed you have the cheek to approach me, after what your mother did.'

It was the wrong tack to use with Beth. 'As far as I can see, all my mother did was get taken in by your husband. If she'd known you were married to Len, she obviously would never have had anything to do with him.'

'So you say,' said Margery, shaking her head. This caused her long diamond earrings to shimmer, and Beth peered, fascinated. 'I don't know what on earth you think you're looking at,' Margery added tersely.

Beth hesitated for a second, and then decided it was a case of nothing ventured, nothing gained. I really must get that printed on a T-shirt, she thought to herself. She slipped into the seat opposite Margery. 'I think we've got off on completely the wrong foot. Surely we all want the same thing? We want to find out what happened to your husband?'

'Nothing happened to my husband, Ms Haldane. It's very sad, and of course I'm heartbroken,' Margery said, staring into the middle distance for a second before speaking again, a harrowed expression on her face. 'But he was a heavy smoker who was a bit too fond of a rich meal, and a lot too fond of the looser sort of ladies, as we both know. Anyway, you're being disingenuous. What you really want is for people to stop whispering about Wendy.'

'I don't think there are any rumours about my mother,' Beth denied stoutly.

'Oh, come on. Everyone is saying that she knew he was married, and was trying desperately to get rid of the competition – me. But whatever scheme she had in mind rebounded, and Len ended up dead instead.'

Beth blinked. She'd had no idea that people were suggesting Len's death had been a botched attempt by her mother to kill

Margery. All the more reason for her to buckle down and solve this mystery as fast as she could. 'All I can do is assure you that Wendy would never in a million years do such a thing. She hasn't a murderous bone in her body.'

'But she's been very quick to say it was a suspicious death, which isn't helpful. It just makes it all the more tragic for me. There is no shortage of suspects and now we all find ourselves in a very difficult position. Whereas I know he died from natural causes. Perhaps you can use your influence to get her to lay the whole matter to rest. Poor Len, how he would hate all this.'

Margery took a small sip of her white wine, her eyes full of sorrow, and Beth suddenly wondered what she was doing here, drinking alone in the afternoon. It didn't seem like the sort of thing that the stately Ms Brinkwell would approve of, let alone do.

'Are you waiting for someone?' Beth asked.

'A friend has just left, if you must know. Harriet French, do you know her?'

Harriet French, how interesting, thought Beth. The grubby-fingered gardener from the beauty parlour who'd said she'd had a tryst with Len on the evening of his death, bringing his tally of conquests that night to three. 'I met her recently, by chance,' Beth conceded.

'A perfectly pleasant woman. Her allotment is an absolute picture every summer, amazing blooms. She has such a display of climbing roses, interspersed with jasmine and nicotiana, it's quite spectacular. I have to take an interest as part of my work for the Estate, as the allotments are on Wyatt land. But she's a habitual liar,' said Margery, offhandedly. 'She's been saying some things about Len, on the last day of his life... quite ridiculous.' She sounded cross, but in a mild way, as though her library book was a day overdue. Not as though Harriet French was telling all and sundry that

Margery's husband had been canoodling with her, in his final hours.

'Speaking of, er, Len's last day,' Beth said a little nervously. 'I just wondered whether you and Len had had plans that night? I mean, it seemed unusual for him to have gone to his office so late...'

Margery tutted. 'Is there anyone in this place who doesn't know his timetable? Oh, but wait, I forgot. You're the one who has that little hobby, don't you? Detecting, or something?'

Beth looked down at her hands, and then ploughed on. 'It would be great to know what you were doing while Len was in his office that night. Just to clear things up,' she said, hoping her tone made the request sound perfectly normal.

Margery looked at her for a second, as though considering whether to refuse to answer, or even flounce off. Then, with a sigh, she spoke. 'So, you have the temerity to ask for my alibi, do you? You obviously believe your poor mother's ramblings. Oh well, what harm does it do to tell you? Of course I didn't go to his office with him at eleven p.m., why on earth would I have done? I stayed in my own home.'

'Not Len's place? Was there anyone else there with you?'

'No. I was in bed, and asleep. We were never blessed with children, so the house was empty.' Margery then took another sip of her drink, and looked at her watch. 'Now, it's been interesting, but I really must call a halt to this little interrogation. I hope I've put your mind at rest.'

Beth nodded numbly. She wasn't entirely sure what she'd been expecting, but Margery had been more forthcoming than she would have thought possible. She remained seated while the woman gathered her things and left the pub. Still, the encounter had left an odd taste in her mouth. It was, she realised, because Margery seemed genuinely sad about Len Broughton's death. And Beth had believed her when she said she'd been innocently at her home when Len had died in his office. In fact, Beth had probably been right all along in thinking that, once Wendy had made the awful discovery that Len already had a wife, her unreasoning hatred of Margery had seriously distorted her thinking.

Her instinct was to run immediately to Wendy's house and have it out with her. But as she knew from years of experience, that was very unlikely to be a useful step. Wendy would immediately take refuge in tears – if she wasn't already crying, her default mode since Len's death. And then she would refuse to speak to her daughter.

No, Beth needed to go home and regroup. Give this matter some proper thought. She also wanted to see if Jake was back from rugby practice yet. And she had to give some consideration to their supper. While all that was going on, she could work out a strategy for tackling Wendy tomorrow, when she was feeling a little calmer.

That was her plan. But as usual, Beth's life didn't conform one bit to the nice, neat strategies she liked to evolve. As soon as she got home, she knew something was up.

For a start, Jake was back, but he was downstairs, not up in his room working at the trigonometry homework, or even pretending to do so. He was going through the washing basket in the kitchen, scattering items behind him as he searched frantically for something. Colin was helping him by barking a lot, and even Magpie was sitting on the kitchen table, eyeing him carefully. Beth, who had been pretty convinced her son didn't even know where the linen basket was, looked on in astonishment.

'Um. Something missing?' she said drily.

'Oh. Didn't hear you come in, Mum. Yep, I was just, er, seeing if you'd washed that sweatshirt of mine... you know, the new one.'

Beth had been surprised two weeks ago when Jake insisted she buy him this, and asked for a pair of jeans too, from the same big-name brand. It was the first time ever he'd expressed any interest whatsoever in anything he was wearing. In fact, it would have been a total bolt from the blue – if she hadn't known from Katie that Charlie had also suddenly demanded new jeans. It was all to do with that perishing Year 8 disco.

Beth waded through a fortnight's worth of dirty washing strewn on the floor, and started stuffing things back into the basket. 'I don't think it's in here, hon. Have you looked through your floordrobe?'

Jake shuffled from foot to foot. He was now taller than her, she realised with a jolt. She was officially the shortest person in the house. Just then, Colin wagged past and she realised she still had a few inches on the pets. She'd just have to be sure she didn't overfeed them in case they had the temerity to grow.

'Oh, no. Haven't looked. I'd better go and do that.' Jake thudded out of the kitchen and up the stairs, as Beth shoved a load of the washing into the machine. Might as well try and get through some of this backlog before it took over the whole house. She'd got a little behind with the chores while listening to her mother's woes in the last few days.

'Found it!' came a slightly muffled voice from upstairs.

'OK, chuck it down. And while you're at it, clear up everything from your floor and hang it up properly, please.'

The only response was the closing of Jake's door. She hoped, in his bid to unhear her last command, he'd actually turn to his homework and get on with that. She walked out into the hall. Jake had duly flung the sweatshirt downstairs, and it was now starfished on the bannisters.

While the machine rumbled through its cycle, Beth started to worry about her mother again. She wondered if this was one of the few occasions when she could activate her brother, Josh. Although her senior by a couple of years, Josh was so carefree and footloose that he always seemed at least a decade younger than Beth, particularly now that she had the surprisingly grown-up tally of a stable relationship, an almost teenage boy and two pets on her hands. Josh was still at the casual-girlfriend phase, a plateau which, in his case, she fully expected to last forever. As long as he didn't turn into a Len in later life, she thought to herself.

She rang his number, not at all surprised when the dialling tone had that strange echoing quality which gives away the fact that the recipient is abroad.

At the point when Beth was giving up hope of getting an answer, there was a click and a voice said, 'Yello?'

'Josh!'

'Sis. Good to hear from you. What's up?'

'Can't I just be ringing to see how my big brother is?' Beth said.

'You can... but you aren't. I know what a stress-head you are, don't forget. Tell me the worst.'

'It's Mum,' Beth sighed. 'She's fallen in love...'

'Oh, that Len bloke.'

Immediately, Beth felt fierce indignation. How come her mother had told Josh about her 'engagement', and not her? It wasn't as if he was even in the country. But then she realised she was being ridiculous. It hardly mattered that she had been out of the loop. She was now firmly in the thick of things, and would infinitely prefer it if Josh could take some of the load off her shoulders.

'The thing is... he's died. And he was married to someone else, anyway.'

Down the phone line there was a pause, and then a low whistle. 'Blimey,' said Josh. 'A rotter, then.'

'Looks like it. Oh, and Mum thinks he was murdered.'

'Well, then, that's much more your line than mine,' said Josh airily. Beth knew, just from that tone, that he was already mentally disengaging from the whole business, putting it in the 'Beth' pigeonhole and turning over all responsibility to her.

'But no, wait a minute, Josh. Mum is really cut up about this. Crying all the time. I had to take her home from Bridge today. And she's got the tournament coming up soon.'

'Poor love. It must be a shock. She sounded quite sold on him,' Josh said, but the airiness hadn't vanished. Beth kicked herself. She should have known a weeping woman was no inducement for Josh to come home. He spent his whole life dumping girlfriends the moment they started becoming emotional.

'It's not just that. It turns out Len might have been a wrong'un in other ways.'

Now she had piqued his curiosity. He sounded a little less drawling, and a bit more alert, then he came back with a question. 'What do you mean, sis?'

'He was a big gambler. And it seems he was taking large sums of money off most of his girlfriends. And there were a lot. So many I'm having trouble even identifying them all.'

'Sounds like a ton of dough.' Josh was now sounding quite thoughtful. Beth knew he wouldn't be worried for himself. He was handsomely paid as a freelance war photographer, fearlessly poking his camera lens into the world's hellholes to put foul deeds on record. But his footloose life depended on his mother being financially stable and reasonably content with her lot. If Wendy were suddenly in need of more support, even Josh would probably not be able to resist her calls for him to spend more time in the UK.

'It might be about time I popped back for a week or two,' he said slowly. 'Haven't beaten that lad of yours at football for far too long.'

Beth laughed – but thought Josh might get a bit more of a run for his money this time. Jake had been a foot shorter last time Josh had been over, when they'd still had the old mini-goal-posts up in the back garden. Now Jake was playing rugby several times a week, even threatening to be quite good at it, and the garden had had its revamp. 'He'll look forward to that. Will you be bringing Rose?' she asked. His latest girlfriend had seemed radically different from those that had gone before, not least because Josh gave every appearance of doting on her.

'Nah, threw me over, didn't she?' Was that a lovelorn note in Josh's voice, Beth wondered. If so, her brother would be well placed to comfort Wendy in her hour of need.

'I'm really sorry to hear that, Josh. She was lovely.'

'Yeah. Julie-Ann'll be coming, though.'

'Oh. OK, great,' said Beth, wondering when she'd ever learn. Julie-Ann must be his latest. Expecting Josh to have developed proper deep feelings about a woman was as ridiculous as thinking Belinda McKenzie was going to grow a heart. It simply was not going to happen. 'Mum is going to be thrilled to see you. And so am I.'

Beth put the phone down. With Josh around, hopefully cheering her mother up, Beth would have one less thing on her plate. And she could turn all her attention (every bit not taken up by, say, her job at Wyatt's) to solving this Len business as quickly as possible. If she knew one thing about murderers, it was that they rarely stuck at just the one killing. There was always someone who started to represent an awkward loose end, that just needed tidying up. With her own OCD tendencies, she knew how nigglesome that must feel – though of course she stopped short of murdering people.

However thoroughly Len might have deserved his fate (and with every passing day Beth saw more reasons to bump him off) it was terrifying having a killer lurking in the shadows. And this time, it felt closer to home than ever. Because one of the dangliest, loosest ends in this whole business was none other than her own mother.

SIXTEEN

Beth thought later that she should have known, as soon as Harry texted her saying he'd be late home that evening, that something was up. She just had that instant feeling something really bad had happened.

As it was, it wasn't until she was rushing down the road towards Wyatt's School the next morning that she first became aware of how serious it was.

True, there had been a few times lately when the centre of Dulwich had been festooned with crime scene tape and had played host to a distressingly large collection of police vehicles. Not so long ago, it had heralded the killing of her friend Adua. A few weeks ago there had been yet another fuss and Beth's heart had been in her mouth, thinking she could hardly stand any more, and it had turned out to be nothing more than a swirl or two of naughty schoolboy graffiti on the large wooden planters that now blocked off Court Lane as part of Southwark Council's controversial Low Traffic Neighbourhood scheme. So this time she wasn't sure if she should trust her own instincts, as she passed the white police cars with their garish blue and yellow trim.

But there it was. The sure sign of dark deeds, a white SOCO tent shivering in the autumnal breeze. Beth had recently had one of these in her own back garden for far too long. Immediately she started wondering how she could possibly get some information on what was going on. Could it really be another killing? And if so, who was the victim?

She was just scanning the faces of the white-suited officers pottering about importantly, to see if she knew any of them, when she was hailed by someone on the other side of the road.

'Oi, Beth!'

There was no mistaking that foghorn voice, issuing from a tiny round body in a white puffa coat. Beth crossed over and gave her friend Nina a big hug. As usual her auburn curls were flying this way and that and her impish expression made her look like a wilful cherub. 'You could almost pass for a SOCO in that jacket. Fancy diving in there and seeing what's up?'

Nina chortled. 'Love that, wuncha? Nah, more than my life's verse. They'd be hauling me off down the gaol and you'd be stuck feeding Wilf his five a day.'

Beth smiled down at little Wilf, who was clutching his mum's hand. She knew full well any five a day the lad got his chops around were likely to be his favourite fish fingers, thanks to his zero tolerance attitude to vegetables.

'In you go, hon,' said Nina, ushering Wilf through the gates of the Village Primary. Then she turned to Beth and said the magic words. 'Time for a coffee?'

Beth sighed with pleasure. 'Definitely. And it's on me if you've got any info about what's going on there.' She gestured back towards the police activity.

'Chapter and worse,' said Nina, tapping her nose, and Beth took her arm. They made their way to Mariella's, but there was already a queue streaming out of the doorway and down the street.

'God, everyone wants to sit down and have a gossip today,'

said Beth, exasperated even though she was champing for exactly the same thing. There was nothing for it. Beth led Nina on to her own favourite place, the Aurora, which was a little further round the corner. Nina's face was a picture. Like Katie, she was no fan of this rather grim little café, with its substandard coffee, sticking front door and wobbly chairs. But it did have one thing going for it – you could always, *always* get a seat. This morning was no exception, and as the waitress was unashamedly wearing earpods and could hardly hear even their coffee orders, Beth had high hopes that they would be able to chat without being overheard.

'So, what's the word on the street?' she said, once the lukewarm cups had been slopped in front of them and the waitress had stomped off to the back room behind the counter.

'You'll never guess,' Nina started promisingly. Beth leant in, hoping she wasn't getting too excited over nothing. Nina was partial to winding her up over this sort of thing. But for once, her friend came up with the goods immediately. 'It's only a blinking murder. All the mums are saying it's someone else who worked for the council.'

'Oh my goodness, really?' It sounded as though Beth's worst fears of last night had come to pass. This could be the sort of loose end that had got the murderer reaching for their sharpest pair of scissors. And it seemed that thread had been inexorably cut. 'So, do you think it was someone who worked directly with Len Broughton?'

Nina shrugged. 'No one's sure, babe. But they're all saying it's a woman, from the council, and looks like she was offed last night. Maybe she was one of the idiots who installed those stupid flowerbeds in the first place. Everyone hates them.'

Beth shook her head. How awful. 'But is there any connection to Len? I mean, they worked in the same place...'

Nina shrugged. 'He wasn't in his office very often. From what I hear,' she went on.

Well, mused Beth. He hardly had time. So many affairs on the go, so much money being cadged out of those poor women... but wait a minute, that was a thought.

'What did he actually do at the council?' Beth asked, kicking herself for not having asked this question before.

'He was in charge of housing, wasn't he? You know, planning and stuff.'

Beth fell silent. This would have confirmed all her father's worst prejudices about local councils. He'd always been of the opinion that such departments were woefully corrupt, with backhanders being exchanged to allow unsuitable people to build, with little reference to what was best for the area. His own particular bugbear had been the rash of conservatories that had been built in the 1970s and 1980s, which had mostly rotted or fallen down at this stage. Beth now knew that wasn't necessarily because of council skulduggery, as it owed a lot to a feud between the main two firms of builders operating in Dulwich. But if Len was a housing officer, and also always in dire need of money to fund his gambling habit, would he really have been able to turn his nose up at the occasional bribe? From all that she'd heard about the man and his morals, she didn't think so.

'So, do you know the poor woman who died, then?'

Nina jogged her cup with her elbow and coffee streamed everywhere. 'Me? No, why would I know her?' she said, as Beth scrabbled around in her bag for tissues. Once she'd stemmed the flood, Beth looked up at Nina again. Her friend was peering out of the window, an abstracted expression on her usually dimpled face. Even her curls seemed a little more subdued than usual.

'Everything OK, Nina?' Beth asked.

'Course. Yeah, yeah. Well, I've lost my phone. But don't worry, it'll turn up like a bad peseta. And I was just thinking about... you know.'

'What?'

'Well, they're saying she was strangled. Right in one of those blinking flowerbeds.'

'The LTN boxes, you mean?' The massive wooden planters had been filled with a mixture of gorgeous vibrant plants over the summer, which had been going a bit droopy as the autumn advanced. 'What a place for someone to choose.'

'I know, right? The allotment society is going to be up in arms,' said Nina, still thoughtful. The society had taken it upon itself to maintain the boxes, once it became clear that the council wasn't going to be as assiduous about deadheading petunias as the good folk of Dulwich expected.

'Well yes,' admitted Beth. 'But also – that's quite a horrible place to die. And an awful way for it to happen as well.'

'Yeah,' said Nina shortly, stirring what remained of her drink. The waitress, naturally, hadn't ventured out to clear up, or take away any of the sodden tissues. 'Sucks, doesn't it?'

'It really does.' Beth shook her head. 'Are people saying it's connected to Len's death? I mean, it must be, mustn't it?' she was saying, just as the door jangled as someone tried to open it. They obviously didn't know the trick, which was to shove hard enough to almost knock the glass out of the door. But, after a short struggle, they fell into the café, and then to her astonishment Beth saw the newcomer was Harry.

He brushed himself down, nodded to Nina, and turned to Beth with a big smile.

'Well, Beth. I would say what brings you here, but I imagine you two are finding plenty to keep you busy this morning,' he said with a dry chuckle.

'Caught red-handed,' said Beth impishly. 'But it's not illegal to have a coffee in Dulwich Village, is it? If it is, you'll have to put almost the entire population behind bars.'

Harry laughed at that. 'So, I suppose you're going to ask me a whole lot of questions I can't answer?'

'Well, now that you mention it... But seriously, we were

about to go,' Beth said, suddenly remembering that annoying comment of her mother's, suggesting Harry solved all her crimes for her. It just wasn't true – but anyone seeing them here like this would probably think Wendy was right. Besides, she had a ton of other things she should have been giving her time to, not least her job at the Wyatt's Archive Institute.

But Nina's eyebrows shot up. 'I was gonna say, the refuels are on you, Harry.'

As was quite usual, Beth could see Harry inwardly digest and translate Nina-ese and then bumble over to the counter to do her bidding. Beth shifted uncomfortably in her seat. But then Nina leant across to her.

'Relax. You got a right to have a drink, girl.'

Nina had a point. For goodness' sake, this was just a short break in her hectic schedule, Beth told herself, crossing her fingers. Harry came back just then, picked up a chair from one of the other tables and swung it over as though it weighed no more than a feather. It then groaned a little as he settled his six-foot-four bulk on it. Next, he fixed both women with a broad smile. 'Lovely to see you both out and about. Brightens up my day!'

'Yes, things look a bit grim out there. I suppose all that's going to keep you busy,' Beth said, gesturing vaguely in the direction of the SOCO tent.

'So, got any leads, mate?' Nina asked him point-blank.

At this, he chuckled again, and tipped his chair back a little, almost causing the waitress, who'd been coming up behind him, to drop the cappuccinos she was carrying. As it was Harry who had caused the kerfuffle, she didn't say a thing, merely simpering at him flirtatiously as she carefully positioned his cup. Nina's she plonked down unceremoniously and there was no sign of Beth's at all.

'Um, I think it was three of those?' Beth said mildly.

'Coming up,' said the girl over her shoulder as she stomped back to the kitchen area.

'I see service here has improved hugely,' Harry said with a grin, meeting Beth's eyes and holding them. They'd had one of their earliest encounters in this very café, and the recollection made Beth's insides go a bit fluttery. A lot had happened since that day, but it was lovely that Harry remembered. She couldn't help smiling back reminiscently for a moment.

'God's sake, you two. Get a room, why don't you,' said Nina, and Beth tried to hide a blush behind her fringe. Harry coughed and took a sip of his coffee before he spoke again.

'Now then, ladies, if I know you at all, I'd say you have a million more questions right now.'

Instantly, Nina piped up. 'If you'd just confirm the cause of death, that'd help. And the time, I 'spect that would be useful.'

Harry now gave Beth a completely different look, and the flames that had burnt brightly only a few moments ago were doused. It was quite unfair, thought Beth, as it had been Nina asking.

'I can't tell you stuff I don't know myself yet, can I?' he said. 'And now I'm afraid I should be getting on. Maybe you should be, too?' he added more gently. Then he picked up his cup and slurped the contents, wincing at its bitterness, before bending down to plant a kiss on the top of Beth's head. He smiled briefly at Nina, and the next moment he'd wrenched the door open again and sauntered out into the fresh autumn day.

Both Nina and Beth were left looking after him, though Beth was willing to bet their thoughts were quite different.

'I'll say this for him, he knows how to make an entrance and an exit, your geezer,' said Nina, watching through the window as Harry marched down the road. No prizes for guessing he was off to the SOCO tent to get answers to the questions Beth was so interested in.

'Do you think we're just wasting our time with all this?'

Beth asked Nina urgently. 'Should we just get on with our lives?'

For a second, Nina was silent. 'What would you do if I told you yes, would it make any difference?'

Beth knew she shouldn't be surprised at her friend's perceptiveness. There was little, short of a Sherman tank, that could deflect her once she'd got the bit between her teeth. But it seemed self-evident that she had to be involved. Her own mother was at the centre of this business, for good or ill. And now that there appeared to have been two murders committed, the need to put a stop to the whole business was even more pressing than it had been before. She looked at Nina and shrugged. For a second, Nina rolled her eyes at her, then she too got up.

'Come on then, better do like the man says and get on with our day jobs. We can talk about all this later if you like.'

'Oh yes please,' said Beth. 'I'll give you a ring this afternoon, then, shall I? Before Harry gets home.'

Nina snorted. 'Yeah, hope I've got my phone by then. Anyway, the sooner you come out and make it official that you're a detective the better, love. Aren't you sick of pretending it's just a little whatchamacallit, a bobby?'

'Oh, a hobby,' said Beth, a little taken aback. 'Well, it's not really like that... I'm not pretending, not exactly...'

'Sure about that?' asked Nina, and for once there was no smile on her little face. 'Have it your way, babe.'

With that, she turned on her heel and walked out of the café.

SEVENTEEN

A little chastened, Beth decided there was nothing for it but to show up at work. It was certainly about time she got back to her paid employment. And besides, maybe someone at Wyatt's would be able to fill in some of the blanks that Harry had so conspicuously left her with.

Nina thought she should become a full-time detective, it seemed. But was Beth really ready to jack in her sinecure of a job, for an uncertain future as some kind of private eye? Could anyone support themselves doing that? She didn't want to spend her days tracking down lost dogs (who would all inevitably be found hiding from Katie's awful cockapoo Teddy in the furthest reaches of Dulwich Park).

But, as soon as she was settled behind her large desk, and contemplating the neat shelves of Wyatt's archives stretching back to the foundation of the school, she started to feel calmer and more comfortable. She'd be a fool to give up this post, she really would. Especially as she had almost finished the outline of her definitive biography of Sir Thomas Wyatt, the appalling old swashbuckler who'd set the school up, using the blood-drenched proceeds of his slave plantations in the West Indies.

This was an important job, and a story which needed to be told. If she could just find the clear space in her head to dedicate to it... She sifted through the documents on her desk, laying bare the purchases of land and souls that were the cornerstones of this institution. Just as she had opened up the right document on her laptop, and was carefully scrutinising the ancient, faded cursive handwriting in one of Wyatt's shameful ledgers, there was a knock at the door.

Despite herself, Beth looked up much too brightly at the interruption and sang out, 'Come in.'

It was Janice Grover, wife of the headmaster of Wyatt's, fount of all wisdom and mother of Beth's adorable goddaughter Libby. She was wearing a violet cashmere cardigan that looked as soft as a cloud, velvet jeans and little violet shoes that would surely have swallowed up Beth's entire clothes budget for a decade.

'Those are delectable,' said Beth enviously.

Janice preened a little. 'Tommy bought them for me, he said I deserved a treat.'

Beth smiled. Harry had bought her a coffee this morning – and he'd given her that special smile of his, too. Janice's shoes were nice – but after all, they wouldn't look quite right with Beth's ratty jumper.

'I'm so glad you've popped in. I was going to see if you were free for lunch, Janice. I wanted to pick your brains about something.'

'Let me take a wild guess. The SOCO tent in the village?'

'Am I that transparent?'

'Just a bit,' Janice said. 'Isn't it awful? Poor Bella Harrington.'

'Is that the name of the woman?'

'Yes. Isn't it ghastly about Len Broughton, too? The whole place is buzzing with it.'

'Are the two deaths connected, do you think? I mean, I

know this Bella worked for the council, but they must employ so many people...'

Janice was staring at Beth. 'Don't you know? Bella was Len Broughton's secretary.'

'No! Listen, can we go and get a sandwich right now?' said Beth, trying not to sound too keen. Yes, it was horrible having to discuss this poor woman's murder, but if she didn't pump Janice for all the details, she'd be kicking herself, as Harry certainly wasn't going to fill her in, whatever her mother might think. She needed to find out as much as she could, in order to make progress with the Len Broughton killing.

When Janice nodded, Beth slammed shut her laptop and locked the ledgers away. Sir Thomas Wyatt's awful crimes had to make way for much more recent evil deeds. But not forever. She'd be coming back to him, she swore to herself. At some point soon.

* * *

Beth and Janice took their places in the staff canteen queue, which was mercifully short this early on. They slid their trays onto an empty table and began to unwrap delicious sandwiches, freshly cut this morning by Wyatt's staff who were a little like house elves – super efficient and all but invisible. Beth sank her teeth into a sumptuous cheese and pickle doorstep and sighed a little. Then she dabbed her mouth with a napkin. She might as well just come out with it.

'The thing is, Wendy has asked me to look into the whole Len Broughton thing.'

'I heard your mum was... involved,' Janice admitted, showing the sort of tact that made her such a natural at her job, dealing with anxious, entitled parents on one side and the highly qualified, but sometimes touchy, Wyatt's staff on the other.

'But there are just so many other women out there who seem to have had flings with him too,' Beth said, a heavy frown gathering under her fringe. 'It's impossible to whittle down the numbers. I mean, I know the choir and the Bridge class group were both meeting until late that night, so any women who did those activities are out. But it still seems to leave hundreds roaming the streets of Dulwich who might have had a motive. And I have to find out who did it, or there'll always be a shadow of suspicion hanging over Mum. You know what it's like round here.'

'I certainly do,' said Janice ruefully. 'Well, I suppose we can definitely rule out Bella, now.'

Beth chewed slowly. 'I don't think so, Janice, not really. I mean, she could have killed Len, and then been killed by someone else who was upset at what she did. It doesn't mean she didn't murder him at all.'

'Oh goodness,' said Janice. Now there was a rare pleat appearing in her normally untroubled brow. 'I can see why it might seem a bit overwhelming.'

'A lot of the women gave Len money. Turns out he had a big gambling problem. I can't help thinking it's someone who did that, maybe handed over their life savings, then realised he was never going to pay them back. That might make someone angry enough to do him in.'

'Rather than hearing that he was actually married, or had multiple girlfriends? I suppose so... I think in a way your mum is the lucky one. She was the only fiancée – as far as I've heard to date.'

'That's something, I suppose,' said Beth, with a wince. 'But I really need a bit more than that.'

'Wait a minute,' said Janice, her eyes lighting up as she spied someone on the other side of the dining room. 'Yoo-hoo, Sal!'

She was beckoning to Sally Wainwright, the new art

assistant, who came meekly over, and then sat herself down at Janice's invitation. In her late twenties and with an endearingly open expression, Sally reminded Beth of a faun in the forest, fresh-faced and eager to please. When the introductions had been made, Janice plunged in.

'Sal, you used to work at the council, didn't you?'

'Just for a while,' said Sal in her breathy voice. 'I didn't love it.'

'Did you know Bella Harrington?'

Immediately the girl's face fell. Really, thought Beth, it was amazing how fast news got around. 'I was so shocked this morning when I heard... Yes, I temped in her office when she was away.'

'You mean... you worked for Len Broughton?' Beth said, trying to keep the growing excitement out of her voice. She didn't want to spook the girl.

Another expression, more complicated than the last, passed over the girl's open face. 'Yes. Just for a week or so. It was long enough, to be honest.'

'I've heard Len could be... difficult,' said Beth diplomatically. That was putting it mildly. The more she heard about him, the more he seemed like an octopus on turbocharge. A nice girl like Sal wouldn't have stood a chance with him and his overactive libido. And that was without even addressing the fact that he seemed equally grasping about money.

'Luckily he was away a lot on appointments,' Sal said. 'I was usually on my own in the office. Right up on the third floor, just near the lifts. It was pretty lonely. I was surprised, though – when he was in, although he was... demanding, he was very organised. He typed everything out himself on his computer, even though he had quite bad dyslexia and it took him ages. Then he printed the stuff, put it in folders and squirrelled it away. Everyone else did things digitally, but he always said he didn't trust technology. Not after something he called "the Y2K bug".'

'Y2K?' Beth was astonished. 'But it's over two decades since all that Year 2000 stuff. And it was just a big panic over nothing,' she said. She remembered her father poring over newspaper articles on the havoc that was about to ensue... then the clock ticked round to one minute past midnight on 1st January 2000 – and what happened? Absolutely nothing at all.

'Yes, Len said that was exactly why we should be on our guard. They'd cleverly not pulled the plug when everyone had been expecting it, so they'd do it at some other time instead.'

Beth tutted. There was little point in asking who 'they' were. People who believed in conspiracy theories like this had their firm beliefs – and it was nigh on impossible to shake them. At least Len and Wendy would have had a lot to talk about on that front. Wendy had been getting more and more of her 'news' from YouTube recently and had come up with a lot of very startling ideas that Beth had no truck with. Maybe she had found a kindred spirit.

But Len's habit of committing everything to paper could be extremely useful. Beth chewed away thoughtfully at her sandwich, while Janice and Sal chatted about this and that. It sounded as though Len's spreadsheets were almost as active as his bedsheets. What was the betting that he'd jotted down the names of all the women he'd fleeced? These could be Beth's prime suspects, and she would be able to cut out all the women he had not ripped off.

Just then, her phone started to ring. 'Oops, sorry, I thought I'd turned it off,' she apologised, then saw it was Nina trying to get through. 'Actually, I should probably take this. See you later, ladies,' she said, answering her phone with one hand and picking up her tray with the other.

'What's up, Nina? Apart from you finding your lost phone,' she asked, as she started walking back to her office.

Nina sounded uncharacteristically jumpy. 'Oh, erm, yeah. Told you I would. It's about the deaf in the village this morning?'

'Deaf? Oh, er, yes, I see. Yes, I've found out a bit more, her name was Bella Harrington, she worked for Len...'

'OK, didn't realise you'd be that far on already, that was quick work. Listen, since you know that much, I got to talk to you about it all. Friend of mine, wasn't she?'

'Was she? Why didn't you say this morning?' Beth asked.

There was a pause. 'Sorry, boss is shouting for something,' said Nina. 'Um, listen... when can we meet?'

Beth opened her office door and looked around. There was her abandoned work from this morning, the outline of her book that was now so tantalisingly close to being finished – and yet still so far away. 'Um, can I get back to you tomorrow? I've got so much on today...'

There was a pause. 'Yeah, yeah, sure,' Nina said, then the line went dead.

That was very odd. But Beth didn't have time to think about it now. She really did have a lot on her plate. She'd had a brainwave, and nothing was going to stop her getting on with this. She pushed her synopsis of the Wyatt book to one side and fired up her laptop, quickly opening the council website.

She had to find a way into the council buildings, she had to break into Len's office, and she had to lay her hands on the records of his disreputable behaviour – the files Sal had mentioned.

She felt a little frisson of fear at the thought of what she had to achieve. Goodness knew how many rules she'd be trampling on. She could easily get arrested, if not imprisoned, for such frankly illegal behaviour. But it would be worth it, wouldn't it, to get to the truth? She needed to get Wendy off the hook. And for once, Beth wasn't going to do it alone. She knew the perfect person to help her.

EIGHTEEN

Jake was a bit surprised when he saw Beth hanging around by the school gates when the final bell went at 3.30. As it was a Friday, he had no rugby practice that day, and Charlie was free too.

'I'm just going to walk along with you to your mum's,' Beth said to Charlie. 'And yes, Jake, we can stay for a bit. But only a little while, mind.'

Beth had rung up earlier to get a special dispensation from Katie to call in on their way home. Weekday meet-ups had been banned since Jake had fallen asleep in double Maths during the Gregory King debacle. Charlie at least managed to keep his eyes open but Katie had sniffed falling grades and both mothers had pulled back. It was hard enough to keep up with the punishing pace at Wyatt's if you were firing on all cylinders. If you were unconscious during lessons you were pretty much out of the game.

Katie, about to teach her next stretch class, had recognised her friend's determined tone and caved in. 'We do have an hour's window in the schedule. Whatever you've got to tell me that's so urgent won't take longer than that, will it?'

Beth, though pretty sure it would take longer than sixty minutes to persuade Katie that her idea was totally sensible, agreed airily. Now here they were on the doorstep. A couple of houses along, Beth could see Belinda McKenzie ushering her brood into her house. Belinda swept in without sparing Beth a glance. However her teenage daughter Allegra, now fully living up to her nickname 'Leggy' in a short, short skirt, smiled and raised a tentative hand in her direction. A little surprised, Beth waved back and then the girl disappeared into the big house and the door was slammed shut. Then Katie answered the door, and Beth put the incident out of her head. Jake and Charlie scampered off together, just as if they were still five and dying to play Lego, and Beth followed Katie into her huge, stunning kitchen.

Thanks to Katie's boiling water tap, seconds later they both had lovely cups of tea in front of them. Outside in the garden, the dreadful Teddy was throwing himself against the full-length Crittall glass doors, leaving horrible muddy smears that Beth could hardly see without wincing. If they'd been her windows, she'd have been spritzing them with Mr Muscle glass cleaner for all she was worth. But Katie just sat with her back to the situation. 'Don't worry, he can't possibly get through, the builders said you could drive a bulldozer at them and they wouldn't budge. So, what's so top secret that you can't tell me on the phone?' Her voice was full of amusement.

Beth looked into her mug for a moment to gather the courage necessary to suggest something that might well get them both locked up. 'It's like this...'

Five minutes later, she was amazed to see Katie's decisive nod. 'Yep. Sounds good. When are we going to do it?'

'Katie... are you sure?' Beth knew she shouldn't be trying to talk her friend out of this. It was her own pet scheme, after all, and pretty much essential if they wanted to make some progress. But on the other hand... neither of them was exactly suited to life in prison.

'I've said I need to throw myself into this investigation thing, haven't I? And you've done stuff like this before and it's gone OK.'

It was a statement, not a question, which was just as well, as otherwise Beth would probably have had to correct Katie's mistake. Yes, Beth had done equally reckless things before. But they had usually involved her getting clonked on the head in dark alleys and ending up in hospital. Still, she wasn't one to look a gift horse in the mouth.

'When shall we do it, then?' Beth faltered.

'No time like the present.' Katie drained her cup decisively.

'But the boys... their homework...' Beth was dumbfounded.

'I just meant let's do it tonight. Not this actual moment, Beth,' Katie said reassuringly.

Beth relaxed for a second. Then she realised that only gave them a very short time to prepare.

'I take it Michael will be home tonight?'

'Yes. I'll just say I'm taking Teddy to another obedience class.'

'But haven't you run out of options on that?' Katie and Teddy had either failed or been kicked out of all the courses in the area. Katie had even travelled as far as Peckham to get Teddy enrolled, but the outcome had been the same. He was dog non grata all over south-east London at this point.

'Don't rub it in! I'll just say another one's started up and they haven't heard about Teddy yet so they haven't banned him.'

'OK, great,' said Beth. Then with dawning horror, she realised something. 'But that means you'll have to take him with you when you come out!' She was pretty sure what they were contemplating was already madness. With Teddy in tow, it was positively certifiable.

'Oh, we'll just leave him in the car,' Katie said with a casual wave of her hand. 'He'll be fine.'

At that moment, there was an almighty crash as Teddy erupted into the kitchen, coated liberally in mud and panting with delight at having outwitted his foes, the evil windows, which now hung dejectedly open. That was going to be a very expensive problem for Katie to sort out in the morning. Tail wagging furiously, Teddy careered up to Katie and lavished big licky dog kisses on her.

'God, he's so strong!' said Beth, aghast, as Teddy celebrated his victory with a volley of barks.

'I know,' Katie said grimly. 'I'm going to sue those builders, they told me nothing could get through those doors.'

Nothing... apart from one very strong and determined cockapoo, apparently. 'Well, I'd better be going.' Beth leapt to her feet and called up the stairs to Jake, who trailed down obediently while Katie tried to shove Teddy back into the garden. As the sounds of a struggle intensified, she just called into the kitchen, 'Um, see you later, Katie, all right?'

'Yep, see you then,' called Katie. As Beth shut the front door, Teddy's barking and Katie's ineffectual shouts of 'Down, boy' were not giving her the best feeling in the world about their little mission later that night.

NINETEEN

Beth's misgivings had given birth to misgivings of their own by the time she parked the little Fiat outside Katie's place later that evening. Harry had got home at a reasonable time, for once, so she'd had to leave him and Jake in the cosy sitting room, peacefully watching a sci-fi thriller of no intellectual merit whatsoever, with Magpie and Colin fighting for sofa inches. It was a lovely domestic scene and the last thing Beth wanted to do was haul herself out onto the mean streets of Dulwich again and do something which she knew would have Harry telling her off big-time, if not actually arresting her, if he'd known what she had in mind. She'd had to say she was helping Katie with Teddy, which didn't sit well with her highly developed conscience, although it *was* sort-of true, as Teddy was having to come too. It was truer still, however, that Katie was helping her with a bit of breaking and entering. Anyway, it was too late for regrets. Luckily poor Harry seemed too tired to cross-question her.

She got out of the Fiat and rang the doorbell. She was amused to see that, a couple of doors down, every single light was blazing at Belinda's place. Now that everyone was watching their electricity bills like hawks, it was completely typical of the woman that she'd found a new way to flaunt her wealth via this ostentatious lightshow. Beth was still tutting as the door swung open.

'Katie!' she said in stunned surprise. She barely recognised her friend. Katie did happy colours, brights that suited her sunny nature and her status as the village's most bendy resident, thanks to all her yoga. But here she was, dressed from head to toe in black. Black sweater, black leggings, black boots... and swinging from her hand was what looked suspiciously like a black balaclava.

Meanwhile, Katie was goggling almost as much at Beth. 'You're not changed,' she said, giving Beth's usual jumper and jeans ensemble a once-over.

'Um, no. I didn't get the memo about the Special Ops team outfit. Can I just ask, how do you think we are going to get into the council offices? Because I'm not climbing up the outside of the building or anything,' Beth said firmly.

'Shh,' Katie said, looking over her shoulder and dragging Teddy out of the house on his lead. For once, he didn't seem hell-bent on escape. At least he was consistent in his contrariness, Beth supposed. 'I don't want Michael to hear.'

'But does he really think you're going to a dog obedience class, dressed like that? Tell me that isn't actually a knife strapped to your leg?'

'This? It's just an old toy one of Charlie's. But if you think it's a bit much...'

'Um, maybe just a tad,' said Beth, trying and failing to hold back a smile. Katie had the grace to blush and quickly unfastened it. 'Didn't Michael say anything about that, at least?'

'Honestly, at this point he wouldn't care if I was dressed up as Santa Claus. All he wants is for me to get Teddy out of the house. He's just eaten another batch of crucial paperwork.

Somehow, although it's Teddy who does it, Michael always makes me feel like it's my fault.'

Katie's voice had a dangerous wobble in it and Beth realised that her friend wasn't far from tears. She abandoned all thoughts of making her change into something more normal, and ushered her to the tiny Fiat. Teddy, shoved onto the back seat, immediately set about gnawing the floral seat cover, which Colin also hated with a passion. At least it would keep him busy on the journey, Beth hoped.

There was silence for a few minutes as they set off for the council offices, bouncing over the speed bumps that made Court Lane seem almost as hilly as the Lake District. At the junction at the top, Beth turned towards Forest Hill, trundling past the Horniman Museum's famous clock tower and the children's playground on the opposite side of the road where Jake and Charlie had loved to take turns on the helicopter-shaped climbing frame.

'So, what's the plan?' said Katie.

'You know Teddy's behaviour isn't your fault, don't you?' said Beth, at exactly the same time. They both laughed and the tension in the car dissipated. In her rear view mirror, Beth saw Teddy had laid his head down on the flowery oilskin cover and appeared to be falling into a blissful slumber. Long may that continue, she prayed.

'Yes, I know it's not because of me, really,' Katie said. 'And I don't take it to heart. Poor Michael, he's really stressed at the moment, lots of mergers.'

Beth nodded sagely. She knew nothing about publishing, except that it was a pond with five big fish, which was perhaps a few too many.

'On the plan front,' Beth said, after having pulled off a tricky right turn. 'Um, I was thinking...'

'Yes?' said Katie, all careful attention.

'Well, to be quite honest,' said Beth, sliding the car into the council car park opposite the big, undistinguished building that held its offices. 'I was really thinking of winging it.'

Katie sighed. 'I was hoping you wouldn't say that.'

But, as they sat and contemplated Beth's inability to show the Moriarty-like levels of planning ability they both knew the occasion demanded, Beth became aware of something else. The car park was suspiciously full, considering it was after-hours. And more cars kept arriving.

'Katie, I think we're in luck! Something's going on at the council tonight. Hopefully we can just blend seamlessly in.'

'Great,' said Katie, and they both got out. Though, when they were both standing in the car park, Beth realised Katie's outfit wasn't going to fit in anywhere – except at a cat burglar convention. And then there came a ghastly howl.

'You know, it would have been good if we could have left Teddy behind, really,' Beth said, as mildly as she could.

Katie looked back at the car. 'I know, I know. It's just that he's my alibi, isn't he? Like you said, I couldn't go to "dog training" and then not take him.'

They both looked rather desperately back at the car, where the volume of barks was increasing. Then the little Fiat started rocking back and forth, as Teddy bounced around inside. A couple of people walked past on their way into the council building and looked back quizzically at Beth and Katie.

Katie sighed. 'We can't leave him in there, you know, Beth. He'll just woof the place down.'

Beth did her best to suppress a selection of choice expletives. How on earth could they get anything done with that blinking mutt in tow? But she could see Katie had a point.

'Oh, all right then. But I bet they have a no-dogs policy inside.'

As they waltzed through the big double doors at the front of the building, Beth almost thought they'd got away with it for a moment. But just then, a security guard shouted out, 'Madam! Excuse me, madam with the dog there?'

Beth and Katie turned round resignedly. But the security guard just said, 'Ladies, you need to sign the book.' They looked at each other, did as they were asked, then they were on their way again. The stream of visitors was heading for what looked like a large public hall. There was a notice outside it, welcoming everyone to an open forum discussion on rubbish collection policy in the Dulwich area. No wonder there were so many people arriving – and with any luck the meeting would go on all night. It was a red-hot topic, with Dulwich now polarised between those who recycled everything, and kept their rubbish down to a weekly tiny bag, and those who firmly believed it was all pointless greenwashing, and cleaning out takeaway trays took more energy than could ever be justified. Beth and Katie followed along, until Beth spotted a bank of lifts and gestured to Katie to follow her. They peeled off, with Teddy's paws clicking gently on the polished tile floor.

Beth pushed the button for the lift, and they waited in silence, with Katie smiling and nodding at the odd person passing by.

'I can't believe they've let us take Teddy in,' Beth said under her breath.

'Maybe they think he's a guide dog and I'm blind, or something?' said Katie.

'Or could they think he's an emotional support dog?'

They both looked at Teddy, who was licking bits of himself with rather revolting enthusiasm. Beth shrugged. 'Well, it's worked so far, so let's not knock it.'

The lift pinged at that moment, and they whisked Teddy into it. Sal had told Beth that Len's offices were on the third floor, and she jabbed the button, just as they saw the security guard looking at them a bit more closely. Beth smiled reassuringly as the doors swished closed. They both collapsed against the mirrored walls of the lift and high-fived each other. 'What a team!' Beth said.

When the lift stopped on the third floor, they got out gingerly. There were no lights on, and Beth had only the vaguest idea of where Len's office might be located. The corridor stretched in both directions.

'Sal said it was near the lifts, but which door is it?' Beth said, stumped.

'Well, we'll try both ways. We seem to be on a lucky streak, so it shouldn't be too hard.'

As soon as they turned to the right, though, they spotted it straight away – due to the fact that the police incident tape was still stretched across the door. As the powers that be had decided Len's death wasn't suspicious, the office must have been searched after Bella's murder, as she had worked there, too. It took less than a second for Beth to pull that off and stuff it in her pocket. But there was still a slight problem. When Beth tried the handle to Len Broughton's office, it was very firmly locked.

TWENTY

Beth and Katie looked at each other, deflated. They'd got so far, against all the odds. It didn't seem right that anything should stop them now.

'Damn!' said Beth. 'I should have realised it would be locked, what with Len having died in there. Obviously they'd up the security.'

'What do we do now?' Katie said. 'You don't have a key, right?'

Beth shook her head sadly. 'I'll just have to go back to Sal and ask her who'd have a spare. You never know, she might have one herself that she forgot to give back...'

Both fell silent, recognising that they'd stretched their lucky streak a little too far. But, just as they were about to turn and retrace their steps, Teddy decided he had other ideas. His mistress was staring wistfully at the door. He knew just how that felt. He'd spent much of his young life being shut out of this or that, Michael's study, say, or Katie's walk-in wardrobe, both of which would be much improved, in his opinion, by a dash of cockapoo in their midst.

Katie was really looking unhappy. Hangdog, one might

almost say. Well, Teddy couldn't have that. Fresh from his triumph over the unbreakable metal kitchen garden doors back at home, he wagged his tail. Easy-peasy, he said to his mistress in a few loud barks. And, just as she was shushing him and dragging him away, he flung himself instead at the door with an almighty crash.

There was a brief, shocked pause as Teddy shook himself and the women looked from him to the door and back again, a faint glimmer of hope in their eyes. Then Teddy did it again. And again. And again. Just as he had before, at Katie's. Suddenly there was a splintering sound... It seemed the council had been scrimping on their office budget. The door, to Beth and Katie's astonishment, seemed to be made of not much more than plywood. Though it looked hardly damaged, that crack must mean something important had gone ping inside. Beth hoped against hope it was the lock.

Beth very gingerly pushed the handle for the second time that evening – and this time it gave. 'Oh my God! Well done, Teddy,' she said, bending to pat the excited dog, silently adding to herself, *words I thought I'd never say.*

Teddy, having been so clever and having been told he was a good boy, yes, a very good boy (which hadn't happened nearly enough in his short life, in his opinion) was quite excitable to start with, but as they cautiously advanced into the room, the melancholy feel of the place dampened even his high spirits.

All the evidence Beth had come across so far suggested Len hadn't been a nice person at all – he had misled her mother, broken her heart, and conned various women around Dulwich out of their money. He had been a liar and a cheat. But he was dead, and places belonging to the recently departed had their own solemn atmosphere. Added to that was the unmistakable aroma of stale pipe smoke. Beth couldn't fathom why her mother found it appealing. It hung heavy in the air, suggesting Len had been a very determined smoker, despite whatever rules might be in place. She looked at the ceiling and, sure enough, there was a disabled smoke alarm hanging down forlornly from its wire. Trust Len. Along with lots of dusty files, books, and what looked like an opened box of chocolates, she could also see several pipes on the shelves. Next to them was a mountain of pouches that she guessed contained the special tobacco her mother had loved the smell of.

It wasn't a large office, holding just a desk with a big chair, a couple of visitors' chairs in front of it, and a bank of filing cabinets. On the desk was a computer, and it was this Beth advanced towards.

Teddy lay down by the door, his vanquished enemy. He had clearly decided to keep an eye on it in case it decided to fight back. Katie turned on her phone torch and started going through the files on the desk.

'Um, what are we actually looking for, Beth?'

Beth, who was trying to gain entry to Len's computer, batted away the question impatiently. 'Oh, you know, lists... lists of women he was fleecing, if possible. He noted everything down meticulously... Sal said he did that on his computer, then printed it out for safekeeping... See if you can find anything stashed anywhere, files, folders, papers, something with concrete information we can use to start contacting people and ruling them out. Damn!'

'What's up?'

'Oh, I'm trying to work out his access code. I should have thought about this before, but I never use one myself. The office at Wyatt's is always locked and I don't need one at home. People usually use something familiar or significant, don't they? Trouble is, I don't even know his birthday. Blast it,' she said as the little line of dots did a sideways wiggle to indicate she'd guessed wrong again.

Katie was silent for a beat. 'You don't know his birthday... but you do know your mum's,' she said brightly.

Beth sighed. 'Yes, but Katie, he was lying to Mum. I mean, she wasn't really his fiancée, was she? As he already had a wife... not to mention about a billion girlfriends.'

'Still, you never know. Wendy obviously felt it was genuine at the time... maybe it was. Go on, Beth. Give it a go. What have we got to lose at this point?'

Beth stared at her friend across the shadowy office. Teddy, thank goodness, had subsided into a snoring heap over by the door, apparently exhausted by having finally done something useful at long last. Katie was absolutely right. She might as well give it a try.

She slowly keyed in the digits for her mother's birthday, deciding that she would concentrate on the day and the month, and make the assumption that Wendy would never divulge her year of birth to a man, belonging to that generation which considered it almost a duty to lie about your age. Then she pressed the enter key.

The computer did a merry little chime, and the screen started loading.

Beth and Katie stared at each other, open-mouthed. 'Well, what do you know? That's amazing, Katie. What a brilliant idea. Well done. Mum is going to be so thrilled when I tell her this.'

'When you tell her that you broke into Len's office? I'm not so sure about that.' Katie smiled as she came round to stand at Beth's shoulder. They both peered at Len's home screen. The wallpaper picture he'd chosen was intriguing in itself: it was Picasso's *Les Demoiselles d'Avignon*. Beth was just wondering why all those splintered aspects of femininity might appeal when she reminded herself that was hardly the reason they were there. What if that security guard downstairs finally wondered what on earth two women and a dog were doing, going up in the lift after-hours? They really had no time to waste.

Beth clicked on a few icons and a dispiritingly large number of files came up, all marked with dates. 'What is all this stuff?' She opened a couple up, and they were just minutes of meetings – stupendously boring meetings, by the looks of things. She sighed deeply. 'What would you do, Katie, if you were a philandering cheat who was trying to make money out of women who should have known better? Where would you put the evidence?'

'Well, I'm not sure why you think I'd be able to access Len's weird mind... it's hardly the way I live my own life. But I would say that, if ever there was something I wanted to hide from Michael – I mean obviously there isn't, but if there ever *was* – then I would put it in plain sight, with as boring a title as possible, so he'd be sure not to look. Something like, I don't know, "Maintenance work" or "Building repairs" or—'

But Beth interrupted her. 'Look! Here.'

They both stared at the screen. On the fractured background of the Picasso masterpiece, Beth had just laid bare a file. Its title was 'Maintenance and repairs'.

Beth's cursor hovered over the file. 'Shall I?'

'What are you waiting for?' Katie said.

Over by the door, Teddy roused himself and let out a piercing whine. Beth and Katie both looked up, but they could hear nothing. Beth shrugged and turned back to the computer screen.

Then Teddy whined again, more loudly. And, a few seconds later, both of them heard what had been evident to the dog. The sound of footsteps, pattering steadily on the lino floor outside, and coming inexorably nearer.

TWENTY-ONE

'So we just got terribly confused,' Katie was saying, her beautiful blue eyes opened to their saucer-like widest. 'I could have sworn the sign said this was the ladies.'

The security guard, though still looking sceptical, was softening by the second under the full glare of Katie's sudden ditzy blonde charm, which was apparently only enhanced by her clinging cat burglar outfit. Beth was doing her best to stay in the background, with the now softly growling Teddy. 'Shh!' Beth whispered into one of his silky black ears. 'Don't interrupt Mummy's performance.' She got an enthusiastic lick for her pains.

'Thank you so much, officer,' Katie now simpered, gazing admiringly at the thickset man. 'I don't know what we would have done if you hadn't come along. We were so, so lost.'

The guard puffed out his chest (quite difficult as the buttons were already straining to contain his sizeable paunch) and said gruffly, 'Well, you should really be more careful... I don't suppose you know but we recently had a, ahem, nasty incident on this floor. It really isn't a good idea for you to be up here after dark,' he admonished, as though they were naughty children.

Katie gazed at him admiringly. 'Thank goodness you're here, officer, keeping us safe.'

This seemed to mollify him. 'Well, in future, just remember, this floor is out of bounds. And no dogs upstairs.' He wagged his finger in Katie's face.

'Of course not, sir, quite right, yes, we'll be going now,' Katie babbled, ushering Beth and Teddy in front of her. As soon as they were clear of the office, they all scampered as quickly as they could to the lifts. Beth started pressing frantically at the 'down' button. As they waited, Beth sneaked a glance over her shoulder. Damn, the guard was still outside Len Broughton's office, and it looked as though he had noticed a tiny snippet of police tape that Beth must have left attached. All the doors were identical, and it seemed he hadn't realised, until now, that the office they had been inside was the one where both Bella and Len had worked. Now he was bending to examine the door. The damage Teddy had done really hardly showed, but...

'God, he's going to call us back to ask how we got in there,' said Beth, stabbing frantically at the lift button. 'Come on, come on...'

The guard stood stock-still for a moment longer, and then he fixed them with a beady eye. Beth could almost see the cogs start to turn in the man's mind. Now he was moving ponderously in their direction. He was getting closer... and closer... when thank goodness, there was a ding. Such a welcome sound! The lift doors swished magically open in front of them and they tumbled in. Beth hit the 'ground floor' symbol as though their lives depended on it. A few moments later, they were sidling out into the foyer.

They were in luck again. The recycling meeting had clearly just ended, and not in a good way, judging by the disgruntled faces they saw filing through the lobby and through the exit. There was a discontented murmur as people unlocked their cars, slammed doors, revved up the engines, and then found themselves queuing to leave.

'Quick, let's get in the thick of the line of cars. Then even if that guard raises the alarm, they won't be able to spot us,' Katie said.

The little trio ran the last few yards to the old Fiat and they all hopped in, Teddy curling up obediently on the back seat. Even he might have had enough excitement for one evening, Beth decided. She seriously needed to re-evaluate the dog after their exploits. He'd actually been incredibly useful for once.

'Maybe this is Teddy's metier. Maybe he's actually a bloodhound after all,' Beth said to Katie as she crashed the gears in her eagerness to join the cars nudging towards the exit. 'And what about you? That was an Oscar-winning performance of a dumb blonde femme fatale back there with the guard. Eat your heart out, Raymond Chandler.'

'Thanks.' Katie smiled. 'Honestly, how on earth could that guy think we were stupid enough to be looking for a loo in an office?'

'Men never seem to find it that hard to think women are idiots. But at least occasionally it's useful.'

'Anyway, I'm sorry we didn't get more out of it, after all the trouble we went to... we could have been arrested or anything, I suppose,' Katie said disconsolately.

'I don't think that guy had powers of arrest, much though he might want them. And anyway, who said it was a wasted trip? Look at this,' said Beth.

As best she could, with one hand still on the wheel and an eye on the queue of traffic edging towards the gates, Beth raised the hem of her jumper an inch. Under it, Katie could just see the corner of a file.

'Beth! How did you get that? I thought you were expecting the useful stuff to be on the computer?'

'I was, but then I remembered Len's Y2K fear. So about a

second before our friend burst in and broke up the party, I looked under Len's pouches of tobacco. He really loved that stuff – I thought he might hide anything important there. And bingo, I found this file. I shoved it up my jersey while you were schmoozing with the guy.'

'Well done, Beth! God, I hope it's got the key to all this in it...'

'Me too.'

'But I'm going to have to get Teddy home now. Michael will really be beginning to suspect something. It's ages since we were out so late at an obedience class. We usually only last a few minutes.'

'Well, Teddy's done good work this evening. Perhaps he doesn't need obedience classes after all. Perhaps he was just looking for the right job,' Beth said, though she hoped she wasn't speaking too soon. And, knowing Teddy's reputation as a more efficient destroyer of documents than the average office shredder, she wouldn't be letting him within a mile of this folder she'd just found.

'Tell you what,' she said, cruising down Court Lane now and preparing to let Katie and Teddy out. 'Shall we meet up tomorrow morning for a coffee and we can see what we've actually got here?'

'That would be perfect. Let's do that. And Beth...' Katie added.

'Yep?' Beth turned as her friend got out of the car and extracted Teddy.

'Thanks so much for this evening. It was great that we could help. Me and Teddy, I mean.'

Beth waved and smiled, but as she drove off down Court Lane to get back to Pickwick Road, she realised it had been ages since she'd seen Katie look so purposeful and energised. She'd been semi-joking when she'd said Teddy might be a natural detective, but it looked like Katie really wanted to take her at her word.

Had Beth just made a rod for her own back? Would all their investigations now be accompanied by a panting, drooling, overexcited cockapoo? She sincerely hoped not. Just then, her phone pinged. At the next traffic lights, she sneaked a glance at it where it lay on the passenger seat. A text from Nina. That reminded her – Nina had been desperate to get something off her chest. For a second, Beth wondered idly exactly what it might be. She decided to ring her first thing in the morning. And then put it right out of her head.

TWENTY-TWO

The next morning, Beth woke up late and had to all but run to her rendezvous with Katie at Mariella's. When she got there, it looked like her worst fears about Teddy were going to be realised. She heard the commotion long before she saw the cockapoo, who was busily tying his lead in knots, running round the outdoor table where Katie had obviously parked him, tied to a chair leg, in the hopes of having a quiet coffee inside.

What a shame. Teddy had been such a hero yesterday. But now he had reverted to type, and Beth was left wondering why Katie couldn't just have left him at home. She sidled past the yapping pooch, hoping he wouldn't show any signs of recognising her. It would be just dreadful if anyone thought she was his owner. She'd left poor old Colin shut up in her house. There was a time and a place for dogs, and at this important juncture in their investigation there simply wasn't room for a paw out of place.

She was slightly pink when she took her place inside the café, but not nearly as pink as poor Katie.

'Do you think I should go out and see what's up with him?' Katie said, trying to keep her head down. She was quite transparently also hoping no one would clock her as Teddy's mistress. But as she was already getting quite a few sidelong glances, and Teddy was pretty notorious, Beth definitely thought that ship had sailed.

'Let's try not to worry about Teddy for a second. What about this?' Beth said with a bit of a tah-dah, sliding the folder onto the table in front of them. Already, its edges were looking slightly bashed up, and there were a couple of damp stains. Beth brushed at them ineffectually with a tissue.

'What happened to it?' Katie said in consternation.

Now it was Beth's turn to look a little hunted. 'Colin. He's such a naughty boy sometimes,' she conceded. 'He's always had a thing about paper, ever since eating all those books of Harry's... It's possible I may even have encouraged him with that a little,' Beth said. Try as she might, she couldn't quite forget how she had smeared one of Harry's crates of whodunits with a tempting cocktail of crushed dog biscuits. That had not been her finest hour.

'Anyway, the contents are fine,' she added more brightly.

'Don't tell me you've had a look already,' said Katie, sounding a little disappointed.

'Not exactly, a tiny peek more than anything,' said Beth quickly. 'But I think you'll find this interesting...'

Just then, the waitress came over with a satisfactorily laden tray. Katie had ordered well: two very large cappuccinos, thoroughly dusted with chocolate powder, and a couple of chocolate and cinnamon buns so large that even Katie would have to do a significant amount of yoga to work one off.

'I thought we needed to keep our strength up,' she said a little defensively.

'It's all good with me, Katie. This is just what the doctor ordered. That's if the doctor's a massive chocoholic,' said Beth, immediately sinking her teeth into one of the still-warm pastries. Once she'd chewed for a satisfying minute or two, and brushed a few stray crumbs off the folder, she said, 'Well, let's get down to it, then.'

At first glance, once the contents of the folder were spread across the table, they were a bit of a disappointment. There were only two sheets of A4 fanned out, and there was precious little writing on them; just a few columns of what looked like figures, with headings above.

'Is that all there is?' said Katie, picking up the first piece of paper. 'And what does it even mean?'

'I know, I was pretty miffed at first, I kept looking inside the folder, as though something else was going to come out, something that was going to blow everything apart. But then I took a proper, hard look at this little lot.' Beth sat back and smiled, as though everything should now be clear.

Katie, distracted for a second by a particularly bloodcurdling yowl from Teddy outside, gave Beth a peevish look. 'It's all right for you, you love puzzles and crosswords and stuff. But it's not the same for me at all. I don't know what you're getting at. This means nothing to me.'

Beth sat forward immediately. She'd forgotten how thin-skinned Katie had been lately. Taking on Teddy had really overloaded her friend. Before the arrival of the cockapoo, Katie had been the acknowledged queen of yoga in Dulwich, and also a brilliant wife, mother, hostess – and friend. But the dog had been a stress too far. The way in which things had unravelled had shown Beth how hard her friend had been working before. Beth had always assumed Katie was naturally good at everything. Now she was beginning to see that Katie simply tried a lot harder than she did, and at things she didn't always consider important.

'I'm sorry, Katie. I get it, I really do. Yes, I do enjoy puzzles. I might as well come clean, I didn't just have a quick glance, like I said. I really had to study everything. Let me show you exactly what I found.'

Katie smiled at Beth, and Beth's shoulders went down in relief. She couldn't really have stood to have anything else come between them. Outside, Teddy was still yapping away, but Katie didn't seem as riled by it as she had been earlier. And, even as Beth listened, the noise died down. It sounded like Teddy was reluctantly settling at last. Good.

'Well, you see, it's like this...' Beth started, when a shadow fell over the papers they were examining. Beth looked up slowly, although from the outline on the table she was pretty sure who was suddenly looming over them. Who else in Dulwich Village was *that* tall, and *that* skinny? 'Belinda,' she said through gritted teeth, quickly covering the sheets of paper with the folder and making sure no writing was showing. Belinda McKenzie was the last person she wanted to be sharing this hard-won information with.

'Lovely to see you, Katie,' Belinda trilled, ignoring Beth as usual. 'I just saw your doggy outside, he seemed a bit neglected so I gave him one of my home-baked dog biscuits.'

'Oh! Did you?' Katie's eyes opened wide. Belinda's dog biscuits were infamous. She would never dream of cooking for her husband or children while there was an au pair around to exploit, but Belinda did enjoy whipping up batches of these treats, which were said to cause many of her own dogs' behavioural problems, not least appalling flatulence. Her children often threw them over her fence into Dulwich Park, where wise dog owners tried to get their charges to steer well clear.

'He wolfed it down,' said Belinda smugly. Outside, Teddy started up a keening wail.

'I'd better just, er—' said Katie, bolting for the door.

Belinda was silent for a beat, staring down at Beth as though she was something on the sole of one of her stratospherically expensive shoes. Today these looked very much like Christian Louboutin stilettos. Who on earth wore those on the school run? The woman was absurd. But Beth decided to remember her manners, and Wendy's many strictures that 'you catch more flies with honey than with vinegar,' and she tried a tentative smile. Immediately, Belinda rudely turned her back on Beth and sashayed down the corridor to 'her' table, from where she could keep tabs on her bunch of fawning admirers and see everyone else in the café. Beth breathed again as she left.

She couldn't have said exactly why Belinda always had this effect on her. It was probably a relic from school days, when a couple of the 'in' girls had always been ritually mean to the terminally uncool kids in the class. But Beth had a choice, now. She didn't need to hang out with the likes of Belinda, and try to gain her favour. And nothing Belinda did could really hurt her now. Could it?

She shook the thought off and was glad to see Katie reappearing, a rueful look on her face. 'I was too late to get the biscuit off him. I hope it doesn't affect him too badly,' she whispered, sliding back into her seat.

'Well, he's being nice and quiet,' Beth said.

'Mmm. It's a bit ominous,' said Katie.

'Well... let's take advantage of it,' said Beth bracingly. 'Look, I was just going to tell you what I'd found. Let's not allow Belinda to spoil things.' She nearly said 'Belinda and Teddy,' but stopped herself in time. Whatever the effect the dog had had on Katie's ordered life, she knew her friend loved him with the whole of her big heart. She was one in a million, that was for sure. Beth smiled, removed the folder from the table, and fanned the pages out in front of them again.

'OK, then. What's so obvious, that I just don't get?' said Katie in a small voice.

'It's not obvious at all, Katie,' said Beth reassuringly. 'But this column is figures, isn't it?' She pointed to a line of numbers dancing down the page. 'So I started from the premise that this had to be the money Len got out of various women. Quite a few of the figures are in the thousands range, and I think that's the kind of sum he was going for, judging from what Deirdre MacBride told me, anyway.'

'As much as that?' Katie goggled.

'Well, Deirdre didn't exactly say how much she'd stumped up, but I got the impression it was plenty. She's pretty well-heeled, you know, with that lovely house in the village. And all that weird tweed she wears is actually really expensive. I saw that jacket of hers in one of Mum's catalogues and it cost a fortune.'

'Look at these sums – two thousand, three thousand, even five thousand here. Do you really think this is all money he conned out of people? God, I just can't believe how many people shelled out,' Katie said, gawping at the list. 'Then what are these letters by the side of the numbers? Do you think they're...' Beth watched, as an idea dawned on Katie. 'Oh my God, they can't be, can they? Are they the initials of all the women he's taken money from?'

Beth nodded solemnly. 'That's what I'm assuming. If you have a look here, there's a D.M. with several figures next to it – I'm betting that's poor Deirdre MacBride herself.'

'I can't believe she was one of his women! She seems such a sensible person, I'm surprised she had any truck with him at all. She really doesn't seem the type,' Katie said.

'I think that was the key, he didn't have one. Unless it was simply a woman with money. Poor Deirdre, she's certainly seen through him now, though she's still pretty wistful. Anyway, all we have to do, I think, is work out who these initials fit. Then we'll have our suspects.'

'So this "W.H." here – do you think that's Wendy? How awful, Beth. But at least she doesn't seem to have parted with much.'

'No, thank goodness. Compared with some of the women, he hardly got anything out of her. Maybe that's why it lasted a good few weeks. He knew she had some savings stashed away.

Mum tells anyone who'll listen how great my dad was with all his life insurance policies. It must have been tempting enough for him to keep hanging on, trying to weasel it out of her.'

'That's so sad, isn't it? Anyone can see she really loved him.' Katie looked at Beth, her eyes troubled. 'I'm sorry, it must be so hard for you that she's been caught up in all this. But at least he didn't fleece her completely, not if this is accurate. Good for Wendy if she hung onto her money. And don't forget, he used her birthday as his password. That has to mean something. Look, there's someone here who seems to have given him, wow, a huge sum of money. Can that be right? It's over ten thousand pounds.'

'Yes, and have you seen the initials?'

'B.M. Now who could that be?' said Katie thoughtfully. 'I mean, those are quite common initials, aren't they?'

'They are. But there is someone I can think of...' Beth started to say. Just then, there was a huge peal of laughter from the table at the other end of the café, where Belinda and her coterie were laughing immoderately at something. From the way they were pretending to shush each other and looking around a little guiltily, it was clear that someone close by was the butt of their joke, and also that there was an element of meanness to it. Beth caught Belinda's imperious gaze and immediately looked away, but not before she'd seen the evil glint of triumph in the woman's cornflower blue eyes.

Beth turned to Katie, and raised her eyebrows.

Katie did a double-take that would have been funny under other circumstances. 'No! Not... No, surely not. I mean, there's the age gap, for one thing. And she's married...'

'Len was married, come to that.' Beth shrugged. 'Stranger things have happened. Although Belinda has denied even knowing him – but I wouldn't put it past her to lie.'

'Well, oh my gosh. Maybe... Wow. Belinda McKenzie and Len Broughton.' Now it was Katie and Beth's turn to snigger a little. Katie was usually very good about tolerating Belinda's outrageous behaviour, but her interference this morning with Teddy may have taken the biscuit, thought Beth. 'I don't know how we're going to prove it, though. Or any of these other names, come to that.'

'We don't really have to, not in a court of law. The police can do that, if it comes to it. At the moment, all we have to do is identify the most likely suspects. And a woman who lost a huge quantity of money to Len Broughton would certainly have a much better motive for bumping him off than my mother does. Let's not forget that's our aim. To clear Wendy's name, to find out who murdered Len's poor secretary Bella, and to get that killer off our streets, as soon as we can. In time for Mum's blessed Bridge tournament.'

'Yes...' said Katie. 'Yes, I know. It seems like rather a tall order...'

'You're not getting cold feet now, are you, Katie?' said Beth quickly.

'No, not at all. And I don't want to let you down. It's just that we do have other things we have to think about. Other things that are really important, too.'

Beth was at a loss. 'What on earth could be as important as getting my mother's name cleared and solving two murders?'

'Well.' Katie shrugged. 'How about the Year 8 disco?'

'Ah,' said Beth. And she had to admit that, even though she'd much rather pretend it wasn't happening at all, the disco was inexorably creeping up on them. Maybe Katie had a point.

TWENTY-THREE

The disco, and the decorations she hadn't yet made, now loomed large at Beth's little house in Pickwick Road. Normally, social events came and went and Jake's level of preparation for them was the same as it had been since he was a tiny child – a big round zero. He went to parties, sure, but they were at the houses of family friends of Beth's, and as Beth wasn't madly sociable at the best of times, they were usually at Katie's house. Jake didn't consider it necessary to wear special clothes, to look particularly clean, or to brush his hair to go to Katie's. And nor did Beth, come to that.

But the Year 8 disco marked a sea change. Charlie had asked for that specific pair of new jeans for the event, a seismic shock to his mother's system. Then, a couple of weeks ago, Jake had made his similar request to Beth.

She had got the sweatshirt he wanted, but the jeans had been sold out. She had immediately ordered them online, only to find they were unavailable in Jake's size. She had decided she'd try again in a couple of days... and then the Len Broughton situation had developed.

Now, when Jake loped into the kitchen on Saturday afternoon, and said in a carefully offhand manner, 'Those jeans come yet, Mum?' she answered him in the same faux-casual way.

'Not yet, hon. I'll have a look and see what's holding things up.' She sat at the table, idly playing with her mug of tea, until he sauntered out. Then she ran to get her laptop. Once she'd got on the website again, she saw her worst fears had come true. The jeans were still out of stock in Jake's size, and the rest had vanished too. Why hadn't she snapped up the bigger ones when she'd had the chance? He'd probably have grown into them by the time the disco came around. Or he could have shuffled around in the smaller size. But now there was nothing for it.

'Um, Jake?' she called up the stairs.

There was a pause. Then a slightly suspicious voice replied, 'Mmm?'

'Those jeans...' Beth began.

Immediately, Jake was thundering down the stairs, his bottom lip protruding, as it always had, on the rare occasions he was in a mood, from toddlerdom upwards. 'I knew you hadn't bought them. Are they too expensive or something?' He stared at her.

'No, Jake, no, that's not it. Money isn't a problem, I've told you that,' she said, crossing her fingers behind her back. Sometimes it wasn't so much a problem as a crisis, but there was no need for him to know that. 'It's just that they're out of stock. Are there any other ones you like?'

'*Those* are the ones I wanted,' he said. 'I don't like any others.'

'OK, well, as I said, they aren't available. What is it you like about them?' She was genuinely curious. To her, they looked indistinguishable from the jeans he had on now, and the other pairs no doubt strewn around his room.

'Oh, you wouldn't get it. They're just... cooler,' Jake said, then started to go very slowly back up the stairs, head hanging.

'Jake, wait, listen. I'll get any other jeans you like. Just let me know, send me a link.'

'It's fine. I wanted those. Don't worry. I'll just go in... whatever,' he said. The words were brave enough, but the mood conjured up was of Cinderella, dressed in rags and destined for a life of miserable drudgery.

Beth went back into the kitchen and sighed. She knew how important it was to have the right labels when you were Jake's age. But she also knew how much it really didn't matter, in the grand scheme of things. The girls surely wouldn't notice what make his jeans were, and she hoped that those worth their salt wouldn't care anyway.

Yet Dulwich was the sort of place where appearances did count. The grown-ups were much more bothered than they should be about the right kind of car, house or spouse, let alone the teenagers. Look at Belinda McKenzie, for goodness' sake. She was obsessed with status, measured by having the right accessories. Beth was really sorry that Jake wouldn't be able to swagger into the disco in the 'right' jeans. But he might as well get used to it. And the sooner he realised a person's heart was more important than the label on their clothes, the better.

That didn't mean, however, that Beth was immune from awful pangs of guilt, as her constant refreshing of the jeans website proved. Unfortunately, Jake's size was staying stubbornly out of stock. She'd even discussed the jeans debacle with Katie, but Katie had got in early with her order and Charlie's had arrived weeks ago. Katie, bless her, wasn't smug about this, but there was nothing she could do to sort the situation out.

Beth went to bed feeling she was getting RSI in her forefinger from her constant refreshing of the jeans website. But by the next morning she was resigning herself to Jake toughing it out as the only boy in horrible jeans at the disco (which she hoped his rational mind would tell him was not going to be the case), and beginning to turn her mind to the decorations issue, when she got a call from her brother Josh.

'Where are you, Joshy? When are you coming over?' she was asking him, when her doorbell rang. 'Hang on a sec, just need to get this,' she said into the phone, as she opened the front door.

There was Josh, large as life, standing on her threshold with a very young, very pretty girl just behind him. He had a huge smile on his face, from successfully carrying off a prank. Typical, thought Beth, but she couldn't begrudge him, it was so lovely to see him after all this time. 'Josh! How are you?' she said, ushering him in with a kiss and giving the girl a hug too. She knew how hard it was to be one of Josh's many girlfriends.

'Julie-Ann, meet my sister,' said Josh, waving at the girl in an offhand way. 'Now, where's that little nephew of mine?'

'Not so little,' Beth was just saying, as Jake crashed down the stairs two at a time.

'Uncle J!' he said, while Josh stood back and marvelled.

'Well, a lot can change in a couple of years,' Josh said, clapping Jake heartily on the back. 'Glad to see you're not a titch like your mum,' he added, smartly moving out of Beth's range. 'Here,' he said, flinging a package at the boy. 'Got you these during our layover in New York. Someone told me they're all the rage.'

Jake took a pair of jeans out of the bag. The expression on his face suggested he had just been handed the Holy Grail. 'Wow! Thanks, Uncle J,' he breathed, and bombed back up the stairs again.

'I think you've just made your nephew very happy. If those are the brand I think they are, I've been trying to get them online for weeks. How on earth did you know?'

'Come on, sis, everyone knows they're in,' Josh said lightly.

Beth raised her eyebrows to the heavens above, then remembered her manners. 'Come in and sit down. Cup of tea?' she said, shepherding them both into the kitchen. Josh planted himself by the window, admiring the changes in the garden.

'Can't believe you've finally got this place into some sort of order at last,' he said, not noticing Beth's hackles rising. 'You wouldn't believe what it's been like, Julie-Ann. The table was so big you could hardly get round it, and the garden was about ninety-five per cent weeds. Though where on earth are our goalposts?'

'You may have noticed, Jake's got a bit big for those now. You might get a bit more than you bargained for, playing him at football these days,' Beth said. 'Anyway, what's up with you?'

'Came back to see Mum, like we discussed. So how much did you know about what was going on?' Josh asked rather sharply, which was out of character. He was usually so laid-back he was almost comatose.

'I told you, I had no idea. Even when she got me to go with her to the funeral, I had absolutely no clue she thought she was engaged to the guy. Engaged! Honestly, it was unbelievable. Women fighting each other, calling each other names. I bet that poor little vicar hasn't recovered yet.'

'Mum tells me you're sorting everything out for her. About the murder and that. And it's going to be done and dusted by the time the Bridge tournament comes around.'

Beth rolled her eyes. 'She's got a lot of faith in my abilities, all of a sudden. I'm doing my best. But there are a ton of suspects. And as far as I know the police still don't think Len was murdered anyway, though his secretary certainly was.'

'Won't Harry let you have the inside track on it all? That's how you get most things done, isn't it?' Josh said, ducking quickly as Beth chucked a tea towel at him.

'Did you get that from Mum? That's what she thinks. I've hardly seen him since all this kicked off, and he's on overtime today. I wish he would tell me stuff, but he doesn't. Sorry, Julie-

Ann,' Beth said. 'My brother never thinks before he speaks. You get used to it eventually.'

Julie-Ann just smiled brightly, and Beth suddenly wondered whether she actually understood English. She had yet to say a word, or do anything except smirk prettily.

'As you're here, Josh, you can give me a hand, can't you?'

'What with?' said Josh, staring around the kitchen. 'You've already done the washing-up.'

Beth tutted. 'A hand with *all these problems* would be nice. With Mum, with these murders... And with Jake and the disco.'

'Jake and the disco? That sounds more like it,' said Josh, smiling at Julie-Ann, whose face suddenly lit up. God, yet another girl who'd got it badly, thought Beth. It wouldn't be long before her brother tired of the poor thing. Beth hoped she wouldn't want to cry on her shoulder.

Then the doorbell rang again.

Who on earth could this be, Beth wondered, as she pattered off to answer it. Harry would be back late, he'd already sent her an apologetic text with several kisses, and he had a key anyway. Wendy would inevitably be playing Bridge round about now, however sad she still was about Len. She hadn't been expecting Josh, but he always loved surprising her. Beth definitely didn't have any more visitors scheduled.

TWENTY-FOUR

Beth swung open the door, to find Katie and Charlie on the doorstep. Charlie smiled at her and ducked past, thundering up the stairs. Katie looked on indulgently. 'He got the message from Jake about the jeans! I thought it would be OK as it's a Sunday. And I decided I'd stop by too, so we could finish off that chat we were having in the café yesterday.'

'About the disco?' Beth asked, ushering Katie in.

'No, about all those initials. I thought if we had a proper brainstorm we might get a bit further... I mean, Belinda McKenzie can't really be... Oh, hello, I didn't realise you already had company,' Katie said, having reached the kitchen where Josh and Julie-Ann had obviously been enjoying a covert smooch.

Josh leapt up, all boyish grin and floppy fringe, while Julie-Ann hid her pink cheeks by bending over her cup of tea.

'No need for an introduction to this reprobate,' said Beth, prodding Josh with her elbow. 'And this is Julie-Ann. Julie-Ann, this is Katie, if you're looking for yoga classes while you're here, she is simply the best.'

Julie-Ann looked up immediately, but instead of discussing

it with Katie, she searched out Josh's eyes instead and seemed to be checking if doing a class would be OK with him. Beth sighed inwardly. There was really no hope for the girl if she was going to try and get Josh to take her decisions for her. He had enough trouble forging his own path, flitting restlessly from danger zone to hot spot, never staying in one place long enough to put down any roots. True to form, he swivelled away from Julie-Ann's gaze and instead pulled out a chair for Katie and made a big fuss of her.

'You're looking as gorgeous as ever, Katie. How's that boy of yours? Is he as tall as Jake? I barely recognised my own nephew,' he said.

As Charlie had been taller than Jake for almost all of his life, and was still two inches in the lead, Katie only smiled. 'Great to see you, Josh. How long are you around for? Your poor mum has had quite a time of it.'

Immediately Josh was vague and distant. 'Oh, you know. I've got to do what the news desk tells me,' he said, fooling no one. Josh wasn't tied to one paper – of course not. He was a freelance, and he turned up at the world's worst flashpoints as and when it suited him.

'Has Charlie done his weekend homework?' Beth said, keen to steer the conversation away from potential bumps in the road. 'I'm not sure Jake has got down to all his.'

'Oh, he told Charlie he had on WhatsApp,' said Katie.

'Well, that's great then,' said Beth, who knew when she was beaten. 'And I suppose the jeans are big news.'

'When is this disco exactly?' asked Josh. 'Julie-Ann and I might be able to lend a hand, you never know...'

'It's been looming so long, it's one of those things that I thought was never going to come round. But it's on Monday. If you're serious about going, Josh, that would be brilliant,' said Beth, sniffing a way to get out of the ordeal. If Jake's cool uncle could go instead, and keep a beady eye on his nephew... but

Beth realised that was going to be the trouble. Would Josh be vigilant enough? Was he going to think it was funny, when he heard what Jake and Charlie had been pressured into doing? She hoped not, it would be totally the wrong message to give the boys. Obviously they had never been going to go through with it, but Beth and Katie had promised the school they'd be keeping an eye on their lads. Much as she might want to delegate the onerous duty, Beth realised she couldn't.

'Yeah, we could pop in. Quite a blast from the past, the Wyatt's Year 8 disco,' said Josh with a reminiscent smile.

'Of course, I forgot you were at the school too,' said Katie. 'I wonder if things have changed much.'

'Some things never change,' said Josh with a searing sideways glance at Julie-Ann. The girl blushed painfully. Oh spare us, thought Beth.

'So you'll be going round to Mum's? Are you staying with her?' Beth knew her brother wouldn't be trying to cram himself and his girlfriend into his mother's cluttered little house, but she just wanted to stop the flirting. It did the trick.

'No,' said Josh, in an uncharacteristically firm tone. 'We've got my flat, remember?'

Josh had always kept a pied-à-terre in an area referred to by those who lived there as 'East Dulwich' but which Beth, as a village girl, knew was actually Peckham.

'You've still got that place? Really?'

Josh shrugged in an offhand manner but it was proof of how well he was doing. To keep a London flat empty and visit it only every couple of years was a luxury very few could afford.

'It'll probably need a bit of a clean,' he acknowledged. Beth shivered inwardly at the amount of hoovering it would need to get up to her standards after all this time. But that was very much Josh's problem.

'OK, well, that's great that you'll be nearby, anyway. Any idea how long you're staying?' As soon as the words slipped out,

Beth realised how futile they were. The moment Josh lost interest in anything, he was off. It was usually a matter of days, as far as visits home went. Now he just shrugged. 'Well, while you're here,' said Beth quickly, realising she'd have to act fast to capitalise on his presence. 'Like I was saying earlier, you can maybe help out a bit. And not just with the disco.'

'Help out? What with? Looks like you've got this place sorted,' Josh said, staring round the room.

'I'm not asking you to tidy my house. I wondered if you could give me and Katie a hand, looking into all these women. I mean, who better?' Beth said this with a sideways smile. She didn't want to hurt poor Julie-Ann, but surely the girl knew by now that Josh was an incorrigible flirt, at the very least?

'These women?' repeated Josh. 'Don't know what you're on about.'

'Let me explain a bit,' said Katie.

Beth blessed her friend for intervening. She could already tell that Josh had gone slightly into shutdown mode, a method he had deployed in the past to shrug off all his mother's attempts to get him to lend a hand with tasks that she deemed too 'masculine' for her, like taking the bins out and so on. But he would be on much better behaviour with Katie, because he knew her less well – and because she was a very attractive woman. Beth watched as Josh leant forward and listened intently to Katie, who was telling him all about the lists of initials she and Beth had found. Julie-Ann, meanwhile, was watching with a slightly frozen look on her pretty face. Poor love. She might as well get used to it, though, Beth thought. Looking on while Josh flirted was going to be a big part of her life for the next couple of years.

For the umpteenth time, Beth wondered where Josh had got this side of his nature from. She was absolutely useless with the opposite sex herself, and still considered it a bit of a miracle that she'd ever got together with Harry. Her mother, until this Len business, had seemed oblivious to men, and her late father had been the very model of devotion, though no one could say Wendy was easy to live with. Yet this family had produced the uber-flirt that was Josh, a man whose interest in his girlfriends had only once looked as though it was going to outlast the best-before date on the milk carton in Beth's fridge. She sighed.

'What's up, Beth? Don't you agree with me that we should all try and nail down these initials? One of these people might be our killer,' said Katie.

'Oh, yes. Yes, absolutely. Sorry, I was miles away there for a minute. But you're right. Maybe while we're all here we might be able to work out a few more of the people. We think we know a couple, but there are others here...'

'Yes, what about A.D., for example? Does that ring any bells?'

'I've been thinking about that one. What if it's Angela Douglas, the head of the College School?'

'Miss Douglas? Really? But she's so frosty. And she's about a hundred years old,' said Josh.

'I wasn't suggesting she'd appeal to you,' said Beth sharply. 'Anyway, she's only in her fifties. And Len was sixty if he was a day.'

'There's still the frostiness thing,' said Josh, unrepentant.

'OK, well, anyway. I think Angie Douglas is in the choir. And the choir members were all together afterwards at the crucial time, so I think that lets her out. There's an F.H. here. Mean anything to anyone?' There were blank stares all round. Beth carried on looking down the list. 'What about C.B.?... Oh, I think that might be Cheryl Brandreth.'

'Cheryl Brandreth... that name rings a bell,' said Katie with a frown.

'She's in charge at the library, at the end of Eynella Road,' said Beth.

'Oh yes, I know her! But isn't she one of the Bridge gang?

They were all otherwise engaged, weren't they, that night?' said Katie.

'Damn, yes. They were all downstairs in the Rosendale pub after their meeting,' Beth remembered.

Katie squinted at the writing. 'There's a B.T. here?'

'That's got to be Bernie Troughton, hasn't it?' Miss Troughton was Angela Douglas's devoted deputy at the College School. 'But I can't believe she would have fallen victim to Len's charms.' Beth shook her head.

'It's just about possible, I suppose. But wouldn't she be in the choir with Angela, then? I thought they did everything together. And until this Len business, I really did think that meant everything,' said Katie.

'You live and learn.' Beth shrugged. 'But yes, if she's in the choir, then that lets her out too. It means we've crossed a few off the list.'

'Who's this B.M., then?' said Josh, reading upside down.

Beth and Katie looked at each other. 'Well, we think that could be...'

'None other than...'

'Belinda McKenzie,' they said together, collapsing in giggles.

'No! You've got to be kidding me. That blonde bird with the legs up to her eyebrows who's always treating you like a squashed bug, Beth?'

'Thanks. Yeah, that one,' said Beth.

'Right. Well, we'll just have to see about that, won't we?' Josh sat back, a lazy smile unfurling across his handsome face.

'What do you mean, Josh?' Beth said, instantly on edge. 'What on earth are you thinking you might do?'

'Relax, sis, isn't this what you got me on board for? To sort things out for you, the way I always do?'

Beth spluttered. That very much wasn't the way she saw

things. But across the table, she caught sight of Katie who was looking at her meaningfully.

'I think what Beth meant to say is, we're very grateful for the help,' Katie butted in with a big smile.

'Er, yes. That would be super helpful,' said Beth, inwardly cringing at the thought of all the havoc Josh might unleash. He didn't really know Belinda well, but had long been aware she was a fellow mum at the Dulwich schools – and a massive thorn in Beth's side. Heaven alone knew what Josh might say to the woman, if he had an attack of big brother protectiveness. If it all went awry, then Beth would be left to pick up the pieces, while Josh departed on a plane to the next festering hellhole before you could say reckless idiot.

On the other hand, Beth very much didn't want to tackle Belinda herself, and she knew that Katie, although proving very useful already this time around, was just too polite to ask the straight questions that needed to be put. Perhaps getting Josh involved was a necessary evil. She sat across the table from him and smiled as enthusiastically as she could – but in her lap, she crossed the fingers on both hands.

TWENTY-FIVE

Beth washed up the last glass and straightened out the tea towel so it would have a chance to dry overnight. Colin was snuffling in his basket, harking back in his dreams to a time when he'd been able to chase rabbits with ease. Magpie was licking one paw while eyeing him contemptuously.

It was time Beth went up to bed, but her mind was still buzzing with all they'd discussed over dinner. Katie and Charlie had stayed, as had Josh and Julie-Ann, and it had been a fun evening, although Beth had been sad that Harry was working yet another weekend and stuck at his desk until late. Her spaghetti carbonara – the only thing she had the ingredients for at such short notice – had gone down a treat for a change, and no one had minded finishing off the few old tubs of ice cream that had been languishing at the back of the freezer for pudding. Each flavour had glinted with ice crystals from the many times it had partially thawed and been refrozen, but it tasted none the worse for that. There had been no vegetables in sight, but Katie hadn't said a word of disapproval and in fact had hoovered up her own portion of pasta with flattering haste. Beth was sure she and Charlie would be on double rations of spinach tomorrow, though.

In amongst all the jokes and the chit-chat, they had discussed the Len situation very thoroughly. Josh, who'd initially seemed to be in denial about the seriousness of the matter, had volunteered to question Wendy more carefully on any sums she might have given the man, plus he was absolutely determined to sort out Belinda McKenzie as well. Goodness knew what Julie-Ann would be doing while all this was going on – Beth hoped she wouldn't be relegated to cleaning Josh's flat for him.

While Josh seemed up for being a lot more helpful than she had initially thought, it was as tricky as ever to pin him down to a timetable. This would have been particularly useful with Belinda. Beth certainly didn't want to encounter the woman moments after Josh had done his worst. But Josh wasn't quite sure when he'd get round to anything, he had various people he wanted to visit, and of course he'd be spending quite a bit of time with Wendy, and then there was showing Julie-Ann the sights...

Well, the sights weren't going to take long, Beth thought mulishly. Then she realised that was unfair – they had the amazing Wyatt's Museum of Art on their doorstep, as well as the almshouses and chapel also built by Wyatt, not to mention the park and the village... But still. Trying to organise Josh was like nailing jelly to a wall. Just the thought of his evasions made Beth feel tired enough to go to bed at last. It was lovely to snuggle in with Harry, who was just home and exhausted, and to feel her troubles falling away as he rolled over sleepily to give her a hug. They settled down like happy spoons in a cutlery drawer – well, a teaspoon and a serving spoon, at any rate – and Beth felt sleep claiming her. Once again, she realised she hadn't had a moment to call Nina and arrange the promised meet-up.

Never mind. Time enough tomorrow to sort everything out, was her last waking thought.

* * *

Once Harry had given her a long, lingering kiss or two the following morning, and departed reluctantly for work, Beth reached for her phone. She was going to get Josh to confirm his appointment with Belinda McKenzie, if it was the last thing he did. But when she dialled, the phone rang with that far-off foreign-sounding ring tone again. And there was no answer. What? No! Surely he couldn't have skipped the country already.

He'd been there, large as life, in her kitchen only yesterday, with what sounded like a week's worth of plans to get through – not least offering their dear mother Wendy the type of solace she would only accept from her wonderful son. Beth snorted. And now this. He must have rushed to the airport the moment he'd left her house. And now he wasn't even picking up. She sent him a terse text and got reluctantly out of bed.

Jake was just shambling out of his room, in his uniform already but looking very much as though he'd slept in it. She wrapped her scuzzy old dressing gown a little more tightly round herself and realised the apple hadn't fallen far from the tree on the sartorial front.

'You need to brush your hair,' she said, moving past Jake a couple of minutes later as he hunched over a bowl of cereal in the kitchen, and ruffling the top of his head.

'Hey, mind out! It took me ages to get it looking like that,' said Jake, carefully re-tufting his locks. Beth did a secret grimace behind his back while she was waiting for the kettle to boil, but she muttered a sorry.

'Wasn't it great that Uncle Josh brought those jeans for you?'

A beaming smile lit up Jake's face and at once she could see the happy-go-lucky toddler he'd once been, beneath the gangling almost-teen she was now housing. 'Yeah. Uncle J is brill.'

'Certainly is,' said Beth somewhat heavily as she poured boiling water on her tea. She sloshed in some milk, put the cup down and took a quick peek at her phone. Nope, nothing yet in response to her call and text. She wondered if she should try him again. Where on earth could he have flown to in the middle of the night? But the thing with Josh was that there was always going to be some god-forsaken country that needed him a lot more, in his judgement, than his much-neglected homeland.

Jake's head was now bobbing up and down in time to his phantom music, and she was just wondering if she ought to insist he took his earbuds out when her phone finally rang. She scrabbled to pick up the call before it went to voicemail.

'Hello?'

There was a hollow sound, and then Josh spoke, as though from the bottom of a distant well. 'Hey, sis. Sorry, had to cut and run. It's all kicked off over here.'

For once, Beth didn't even bother asking where he'd got to. He must have left more or less the moment he'd taken his leave of her yesterday. 'You could have WhatsApped. What's happened to all our plans? I thought you were going to take care of Belinda McKenzie for me. Not to mention Mum.'

'Spoken to Belinda already. Quick chat on her doorstep last night, en route for Heathrow. It's no go on that one.'

'What do you mean, "no go"?'

'She says she never had any sort of relationship with Len Broughton. Didn't know the guy at all.'

'And you believed her? Oh come on, Josh. Of course she would say that, wouldn't she? She's not just going to come out and admit it. Especially not to my brother.'

'If you felt like that, why did you get me to do it?'

Josh now sounded miffed, and Beth was about to insist that he'd taken it upon himself to do the honours with Belinda. But the reception wasn't great, and if experience had taught her anything, it was that she wasn't going to win an argument with her brother. If all else failed, he'd simply pretend the line had gone funny, put the phone down, and she wouldn't hear another word from him for months.

'Anyway, Beth, I've got some experience dealing with liars, with these guys in this part of the world, not to mention anywhere else, and I'd just say one thing...'

There was a long silence and Beth started worrying the connection had gone. 'Yes? Josh, can you hear me?'

Another pause, and finally Josh spoke again, his voice sounding even tinnier now. 'She was telling the truth. I'm sure of it. And there's another thing, don't know whether you've thought of it...'

'What? What?' said Beth impatiently. Across the table, Jake finished his cereal at top speed. It seemed this yelled conversation was putting a serious crimp in his breakfast, despite the earpods. He slung his bowl in the sink, bobbed his head in Beth's general direction (this now took the place of a goodbye kiss) and wandered out into the hall. The next thing she heard was the front door slamming. Damn it all. She was sure there were a million things she ought to be saying to him. But she had to concentrate on Josh, while she had him on the line. 'What is it, Josh?'

'...jumbling up the words. You know, like I always do.'

'What? I missed the first bit of that,' she yelled.

'Oh, OK. I was just saying, don't forget, Len was supposed to be dyslexic, wasn't he?'

'According to Sally at the school, yes he was. As I told you last night. So what?'

'So... have you considered that all those initials might be wrong?'

'But they do fit people we know had a connection to him. Like A.D., Angela Douglas...'

'Well yes, OK for her. But dyslexics often reverse letters, don't they? I should know. So what if B.M. doesn't stand for Belinda at all? What if it ought to be M.B.? Is there an M.B. who ought to be in the frame?'

Beth thought hard for a moment. 'Oh my God, Josh, that's so cunning. You could just be right.'

But *M.B.* Why did those initials ring such a strong bell? She racked her brain. If Belinda really wasn't a contender, there *was* an M.B. that they ought to be considering, she was sure of it. She just needed to dredge that little bit of information up to the surface of her mind again. 'That's so clever. I'll get right on it, Josh. Josh? *Josh?*'

But all Beth could hear now was a whistling, echoing sound. It looked as though Josh had finally reached whichever warzone needed his attention so badly and cut the line. She was just about to hit the off button herself when she heard a faint sound. 'Oh, is that you, Josh?'

Suddenly Josh's voice was loud and clear again. 'Yep. Nearly forgot to say, keep an eye on Julie-Ann for me, will you?' he said. Then the phone really did go dead.

'Julie-Ann?' Beth squeaked indignantly, even though she knew Josh was no longer listening. So he'd skipped off, shirking his duty to their mother... and had now even added to Beth's burdens, by giving her his current girlfriend to babysit. Well, that was just great. All right, he'd provided a steer on the next step in the investigation – but at what cost? Beth took a sip of her tea, then almost spat it out. It was pretty much stone cold.

Oh, never mind. She chucked it down the sink, then picked up her handbag, jacket and scarf. She needed to get going today. If Josh was right – and she had to admit that, however annoying he was, he sometimes did hit the nail on the head – then she had a new suspect to check out. Urgently. She needed to get to work, have a proper look at Len Broughton's notes again, and wait for that name to float up from her subconscious. It couldn't take that long, could it?

TWENTY-SIX

But in the end, Beth had one of those mornings. Well, perhaps she should say, yet another of those mornings. Because, every time she tried to get down to studying her sheets of A4 from the raid on Len Broughton's office, someone else would interrupt her.

First of all, it was lovely Janice, with some charming pictures of Beth's goddaughter Libby. Libby was utterly gorgeous, and Beth usually thoroughly enjoyed browsing through snaps of her looking impossibly cute with Janice's fluffy new tortoiseshell kitten (who was very aptly called Cashmere). Today, she was itching to get on.

Then, just as she had finally finished her last bit of filing and was pulling the Len folder towards her at last, there was a sharp rap at the door. It was quite peremptory. For a second, her blood ran cold, thinking it might be Janice's husband, Dr Grover, the head of the school and the man to whom Beth owed the outline of the book she had been not quite writing for a regrettable number of years now. But when she'd said, 'Come in,' the face that peered round the door belonged to Sal instead. A palpably nervous and rather upset Sal, at that.

'Do sit down, Sal, what can I do for you?' asked Beth. The other woman's eyes looked suspiciously glassy; Beth hoped she wasn't going to burst into tears. But Sal took a seat, sniffed determinedly and spoke up.

'I just wondered... I heard your other half is in the police. Do you know what's going on with Bella Harrington?'

'I wish I did,' said Beth honestly. If only Harry told her as much as people thought. If only he was around to tell her anything *at all*. But he was working twenty-four/seven on the Bella murder at the moment, and even if he hadn't been, he was a stickler for confidentiality. It was inconvenient for Beth's investigations, but she still respected and loved him for it. If she had the misfortune to be involved in some ghastly crime – as a victim, rather than an investigator – she prayed she'd get someone as upstanding as Harry on her case. 'He gives me no information at all. And I haven't heard a whole lot on the grapevine, either,' Beth added, thinking suddenly of Nina. She must get back to her, there was something her little friend wanted to tell her, and it might be about Bella Harrington. 'Is there something that's worrying you particularly?'

'Apart from the fact that someone whose job I did has been murdered? And it's not at all clear why?' Sal raised her eyebrows at Beth. 'Of course, I'm really sad about Bella, it's an absolute tragedy. I mean, I never really met her, but no one had a bad word to say about her, and Len was certainly not easy... but I have to say I'm actually scared. What if whoever killed her thinks I know more than I ought to, as well?'

'Do you think that's why she was killed?'

Sal blinked. 'Well, don't you? If the rumours are true, and Len was murdered because of something he was up to in the council, then it makes sense that Bella was killed too because she knew too much.'

'But what would she know about, exactly?'

Sal seemed to be losing patience a bit. She shifted in her

chair, and almost glared at Beth. But, Beth was glad to note, that meant she was a lot further away from tears than she had been.

'I wasn't in that role for very long, and I didn't like working for the council for many reasons. But even in the short time I was there, I could see there were plenty of opportunities for greasing palms, here and there, to get the decisions people wanted. You know the Wyatt Estate has a stranglehold on things like who can build where?'

It was a rhetorical question; in common with everyone who lived in the centre of Dulwich, Beth's own property was subject to the whims of the Estate. She nodded.

'Well, the Estate can put pressure on the council, to get building work vetoed. Not in the centre of the village, because it controls everything there already. But on the outskirts. And likewise, people are willing to pay the council... to put their views forward to the Estate.'

'You're saying there's corruption going on? And you think Len Broughton knew about it?'

'With his job, he must have known. And it makes sense that Bella did too. But I'm going round telling everyone I know nothing. And please say the same if anyone asks.'

'Of course I will,' said Beth. 'But I have to say, I've been working on an entirely different assumption, that Len was killed through jealousy or revenge, something to do with all his affairs. And maybe Bella just knew too much about that side of his life, and perhaps worked out the identity of the killer. I don't think anyone would assume you'd be up on the ins and outs, if I can put it like that, of all his flings. Not after a week. I mean, surely it would take months?'

Sal looked a little calmer at this thought. 'Well, I just hope you're right, Beth. Because otherwise, I have a horrible feeling that my days are numbered. I've moved out of my flat temporarily and I'm staying with friends, and I'm changing my phone number too, just in case. And I've applied for a few jobs, out of the area. The faster I can move on from all this, the better.'

'Well, don't rush too much. It would be such a shame if you left Wyatt's. It's almost certainly nothing to do with you, all of this. And the police are looking into everything, and so am I. So you've got plenty of people working to sort things out.'

'It can't happen fast enough for me. I tell you, I'm not getting a wink of sleep,' said Sal, getting up and making for the door. On an impulse, Beth shot up and gave her a quick hug before she left. The poor woman, she must be going out of her mind with worry.

No sooner had Beth sat back down at her desk and started to puzzle over Len's A4 pages again – there was an F.H., for instance. Could that be Harriet French, just the wrong way round? – than her phone went off. She looked at the screen, about to ignore whoever was calling, then saw with a sigh that it was her mother.

'How are you doing today?' Beth said, as gently as she could, still studying the lines of figures and initials. There was total silence from the other end of the phone, and then a stifled sob. Oh no.

'Mum? Mum, what's up? I thought you were feeling a little bit better?'

'Josh... Josh has gone!'

Beth sighed. 'I know, Mum. It was an emergency,' she said, trying to sound calm, while she inwardly felt like shouting at both her brother and her mother. But doing either wouldn't help one jot. Josh was way out of yelling range, and raising her voice at Wendy only caused more of the type of sniffling she was currently being treated to anyway. 'Would you like me to come over?'

'That would be wonderful, dear,' said Wendy, already sounding a lot more dry-eyed, and ringing off abruptly.

TWENTY-SEVEN

Feeling she'd been played, Beth had no choice but to scoop up the A4 sheets again, put them back in her shoulder bag, and scoot out of the door. She had her hand on the doorknob when her phone shrilled for the second time. 'I'm just coming, Mum,' she said quickly.

'It's me, babe. Forgotten about us meeting up, have you?'

'Oh, Nina! No, I haven't forgotten. It's just been a manic couple of days. I've been meaning to ring you at least twenty times, but things keep getting in the way... Anyway, I've got to rush round and see Mum now, but how about meeting up after that?'

'OK. All right. Yeah, why not,' Nina said, but she was uncharacteristically downbeat.

'Is everything all right, Nina?'

Her friend sighed gustily down the phone. 'S'pose. Anyway, I'll tell you in a bit, yeah? Quite a story. It's going to knock your rocks off.'

'Is it? OK then, sounds good. See you at Mariella's later.'

Beth puzzled over the chat as she made her way to Wendy's. There was something up with Nina. Something she couldn't quite put her finger on. But as soon as she was through her mother's front door, all thoughts of anything else vanished from her mind. Wendy was sitting, sobbing, in her kitchen, drooping over a brimming glass of something that looked suspiciously like sherry.

'Mum! It's not even midday yet, and you're drinking.'

'What does it matter, Beth? What does anything matter, without Len. And now Josh has gone, too.'

'But you've still got me, Mum.'

'Exactly,' said Wendy darkly. 'It's the Bridge tournament in a matter of days and you're no further on, despite all your promises. What am I going to do?'

Beth clenched her jaw in frustration. Then she silently counted to ten, and tried a different approach. 'Come on, now, Mum, get your coat on. We're going for a walk.'

Wendy tried every delaying tactic in the book, just as Jake had done as a small child, but once she was out of the door, safely bundled up in a warm coat and her innumerable scarves, she perked up hugely.

'Look, look at the acers! Aren't they beautiful, Beth? You didn't tell me the colours had turned already,' Wendy said.

Beth tutted inwardly. Now she was responsible for describing autumn to her mother in blow-by-blow detail, as well as everything else? But she decided not to rise to the bait.

'Gorgeous, isn't it? Let's have a quick turn round the park and you'll be right as rain. It's a shame Colin isn't with us, he'd be loving this.'

'Who? Oh, that old fleabag mutt of yours. Such a silly name. Now Katie has a lovely dog, doesn't she?'

Beth swallowed. There seemed to be scarcely a single safe topic left to discuss with her mother that didn't immediately make her want to throttle her – or, on the other side, didn't irritate Wendy beyond belief. As they were already getting on so badly, she might as well just come out with it and ask her about the money she'd given to Len Broughton. But, just as she was struggling to frame the question, someone hailed her from the other side of the way. Beth squinted across, the October sun getting in her eyes.

'Who's that handsome man? He seems to know you, Beth,' said her mother, plunging off their footpath with a surprising turn of speed and bustling over to get a closer look.

'Mum!' said Beth in alarm, following slowly and reluctantly. She still had no idea who the guy was, but he had now stopped and was apparently chatting with Wendy. Tall, with an aquiline profile, hair with a hint of red gold, a very angular face... the penny dropped.

'Oh, er, Chris! How are you?' said Beth, flustered as she caught up with Wendy. 'I didn't recognise you with your clothes on.' She gestured at his jeans, tweedy jacket and tightly wrapped scarf, then realised what she'd said and blushed furiously. 'Oops... I just meant, um, out of your SOCO stuff, oh Lord.' She turned to Wendy, trying to get things under control. 'Chris is one of Harry's team at the Met—'

'Chris Campbell. Forensic pathologist,' Campbell said, taking Wendy's hand and bowing deeply over it. Beth had forgotten those strange bows. But the sensation of being slightly wrong-footed was quite familiar. Now he was giving her one of those searing glances again. 'How have you been, Beth? Been missing the team?'

Beth started to shake her head vigorously, then stopped herself. 'Oh, you're joking. Yes, I see. Things are going fine, thanks. How about you?' she finished primly.

'Mustn't grumble,' said Campbell with a slightly fixed set to his face. 'Well, I shan't keep you ladies from your stroll.' He bowed again, and was soon striding out of sight.

'What a marvellous man, so masterful, so tall and rangy,' sighed Wendy.

Beth turned to her, astonished. 'You seem very interested in men, all of a sudden.' She couldn't keep the accusatory tone out of her voice.

'Well, I may be old, Beth, but I'm not dead yet,' Wendy admonished her daughter.

'You're not old,' said Beth automatically. She'd been saying it for years, every time Wendy prompted her to. But it was also true. Her mother had decades ahead of her. The business with Len had been a shock – and a disaster – but there was no reason why Wendy shouldn't hook up with a man who was less unsuitable, and enjoy another happy relationship, like the one she'd had with Beth's father. 'I can give you Chris's number if you like,' she said with a mischievous glint in her eye.

'Oh, don't be silly dear, there'd be no point, would there?' Wendy said, but just then she got distracted again and was suddenly dodging behind one of the big oak trees close to the path.

'What on earth are you up to, Mum?' Beth asked, mimicking her mother and pressing her back against the comforting trunk of the huge old tree. 'Jake used to love hiding behind these oaks.'

'Well, exactly, dear. Didn't you see who that was coming through the park gates?'

'What? No, I didn't see anyone, still can't for that matter,' said Beth, craning out from behind the tree. Her mother hooked her arm and pulled her back.

'For goodness' sake, don't let her see you.'

'Who, Mum?' Beth was mystified, and getting not a little fed up with this one-sided game of hide and seek.

'Margery Brinkwell,' Wendy hissed out of the corner of her mouth. 'Honestly, Beth, I really think you need to get your eyes tested. First you didn't recognise that handsome man, and now you seem to have missed that dreadful woman, I can't think how.'

'I've only ever seen her a couple of times, and one of those was when you were braining each other with hymn books in the church,' said Beth, glossing over the fact that she'd interviewed Margery Brinkwell in the Dirty Dog and was pretty convinced her hands were clean of whatever happened on Len's last night in his office. 'And as for Chris, well, the sun was in my eyes.'

'Be like that. But the longer you leave it, the worse your sight will get,' said Wendy.

Beth was about to remonstrate, even though it had all the hallmarks of one of those endless bickering sessions with her mother that never really got resolved, when her phone rang. She looked at the screen. It was Nina.

'Mum, I've really got to take this. Are you OK getting home from here?'

Wendy popped her head out for a second, and checked the coast was clear. 'Of course, of course. Margery's gone now so I'll just tootle back. And Julie-Ann's coming over to stay for a few nights. So you go on ahead,' she said with a shooing motion.

If Beth hadn't been conscious that she'd been putting Nina off for days, she'd have been a bit more circumspect about leaving her mother. But as it was, she turned round, accepted the call, and told Nina breathlessly she was on her way.

''Bout time too, babe. Got lots to tell. But I'm not sure you're going to like what you hear. Just remember, whatever I tell you, don't... don't hate me, will ya?'

'I certainly won't,' Beth assured her, but her brow was furrowed when she ended the call. What on earth had her friend had been up to now? Nina was a law unto herself, that was for sure. She felt the first prickling of alarm. For once, she had sounded deadly serious. And that, in itself, was no joke.

TWENTY-EIGHT

By the time she reached Mariella's café, Beth was agog with curiosity. But she had to stifle it as there was a queue, and Nina was standing cheek by jowl with one of the biggest gossips in Dulwich – Belinda McKenzie.

For a second, Beth fulminated. Was there a minute in the day when blinking Belinda wasn't in a café? Then she realised that the only reason she knew her nemesis spent half her life sipping cappuccinos was because she did the exact same thing, too. Luckily, Belinda was in front of Nina and Beth sidled in behind, hoping she'd be unobserved. Belinda was so tall in her skyscraper heels – stacked cork numbers that were as silly as they were expensive – that she surely wouldn't be able to pick out Beth's features even if she did turn round, she was so far off the ground.

Belinda kept her eyes straight ahead, probably appalled at having to line up like a mere mortal. Normally one of her coterie of mum pals popped in early to hold 'their' table against all comers. But today, someone had clearly slipped up. Heads would roll, Beth was sure of it. It would be quite fun watching, she thought – then she wondered what on earth she had become. Seeing Belinda bullying one of her pathetic followers should definitely not be a highlight of her afternoon. She, after all, knew only too well what it was like being on the receiving end of the punishment the woman was no doubt gearing up to dish out.

The queue was moving quite swiftly now and it wasn't long before Belinda was teetering away to her seat. Beth was relieved when she and Nina were pointed to a table at the other end of the café. Beth slung her bag on the table and shrugged off her jacket. 'So. What's on your mind, Nina?'

Nina, who was faffing with the zip on her white puffa coat, mumbled something with her head down.

'What was that? I can't hear a word,' said Beth.

Nina, exasperated, looked up and almost shouted, 'I know what you're going to say!'

'About what?' Beth was baffled.

'Oh, I should have just told you right out. But I was... I dunno. Ashamed, or something.'

Beth patted her friend's arm awkwardly. This didn't sound like the Nina she knew and loved. 'Look, tell me now. I'm sure you'll feel better once you've got it out – whatever it is.'

Just then, the waitress came over for their order. Beth sighed at the timing, but maybe this would be easier if they had some fuel to see them through. She ordered eggs on toast, thinking this was the closest she was going to get to lunch today. As usual, Nina confounded her expectations by ordering only a cup of tea.

'Aren't you going to be hungry?' Beth said as the waitress departed.

'Couldn't choke down a snorkel, the way I feel,' Nina said sadly.

Beth goggled a little then said gently, 'What on earth is it, Nina? Do tell me.'

'Bella Harrington, innit?' Nina said succinctly.

'Is it? I mean, what is it about poor Bella Harrington? Walking past those planters is just awful, I quite see if you're spooked...'

'Nah. I knew her, didn't I?'

'Oh yes, you did say. Where from?'

'Council. Temping.'

'Riiight.' Now it all made sense. Nina had a long and varied career as a freelance secretarial troubleshooter, cutting effortlessly through filing snarl-ups that had lesser administrators tearing out their hair. 'I see,' said Beth. 'Oh, I'm really sorry, Nina. You must be so sad about, um, what happened to her.'

'No. I mean yes, I am sad, course I am. But that's not the thing.' Nina turned her head away. The food arrived, and Beth did a little faffing with cutlery and a napkin, while Nina chewed her nails.

Once Beth had cut off a lovely chunk of eggy bread and swallowed it, she gave her full attention back to her friend. 'Look, Nina, if that's not it, or not entirely it, then what is the problem, exactly? What do you have to feel guilty about? You worked with Bella, and it's really sad she died. But it's not like, I don't know, you stole her last biro or deliberately trashed her filing system or something, is it?'

Beth turned back to her plate, and sawed away again at her toast. It was just that little bit overdone. Meanwhile, there was total silence from Nina. And it wasn't the kind that comes from someone peacefully enjoying their cup of tea. It was the kind of thick, troubling lull that is brewing with undercurrents. Beth looked up sharply, to find Nina's little face working.

'Nina! I wish you'd say it, whatever it is. We're friends, aren't we?'

'We are now. But will we be after I've spilt these here bees? That's what I don't know.' Nina took a crumpled tissue out of her coat pocket and blew her nose thoroughly.

'There are no, erm, bees you could spill that would make me

look on you differently,' Beth said, reaching out and patting Nina's arm again. 'Honestly.'

On the other side of the table, Nina took a deep breath. 'All right. Don't braise me though, if you don't like what you hear. So... Bella and I had a big blow-out a couple of months ago. We were properly on no-speakies for ages, before she died. Well, I was doing the no-speaky bit. She kept wanting to "talk",' Nina said, making quote marks with her fingers.

'I can see why you feel bad about falling out with Bella,' said Beth. 'But...'

'Nah, that's not all, though. We fell out... because we both discovered we'd been seeing the same bloke. In my case, a long time ago, but still. When it came out, she was proper blobs-macked. And she kept on and on wanting to rabbit on about it. In fact, a call to me was probably one of the last ones she ever made.'

Beth fell silent for a moment. 'Really? But... I don't understand. I thought your phone was lost? And anyway, wasn't Bella seeing... Len Broughton?'

'Yep. You've got it.'

Beth stared at Nina, her chin almost hitting the table, as her friend went on. 'I didn't make that last call to Bella, but there were lots of others on my phone. And yes, she was seeing Len. So, Bob's your lobster. *Now* do you see what I mean?'

TWENTY-NINE

All Beth could do was goggle at her friend. 'That means... you and Len? No! No? Surely, Nina. I mean, he was how old exactly? And what about Wendy...'

'Nothing wrong with an older man. And it wasn't just me and Wendy, mate. Me and half of Dulwich Village. Course, you got to believe me, I had no idea. None at all. About Wendy, the wife, none of that. And it was all over with me and Len, oooh, years and years ago.'

'But you knew about Bella,' Beth blurted and, despite herself, it had come out in an accusatory tone.

'See? This is what I was afraid of,' said Nina, stirring her tea dejectedly. Then her shoulders started to shake. She was crying.

Beth was horrified, and writhed in her seat. 'I'm so sorry, Nina. Please don't cry. I didn't mean that the way I said it... I suppose I was just a bit, well, shocked.'

'Not as shocked as I was, when I discovered what he was up to. Believe you me,' said Nina. With that, she pushed herself up from the table and, before Beth could stop her, she was threading her way through the crowded tables and out onto the street. Beth abandoned her eggs and scooped up her bag to follow, dropping a couple of notes on the table to pay for everything, but her path was blocked by an au pair failing to get her twin charges into their huge stroller. By the time she got outside, Nina was long gone. She rang her straight away, but the call went to voicemail.

Damn. What was she going to do now? She couldn't deny that she was taken aback. Her mother, and Nina, sharing a lover? Even at a distance of some years, it still didn't bear thinking about. What on earth had Len Broughton been up to? Had he been on a mission to seduce every woman in the village? If so, Beth supposed she could count herself lucky. She'd never even clapped eyes on him before his disastrous funeral. And she rather wished she hadn't been to that.

Beth turned round one last time, hoping to spot a flash of white coat or a jaunty gingery curl. But Nina must be miles away by now. Maybe it was just as well. It would give Beth time to assimilate this bombshell, and work out how on earth it played into the whole Len/Bella/murder thing.

Just then, a heavy hand came down on her shoulder. 'Oh, for heaven's sake, what is it?' Beth said shrilly, before she turned and saw Belinda McKenzie staring down at her with a most unfriendly look on her face. It was all she needed right now.

'Where is that brother of yours?' Belinda said, with no preamble at all.

'Fine thank you, how are you, Belinda?' Beth said, trying to make the woman feel bad – though she knew that was a lost cause. She was also playing for time. Josh had only just confronted Belinda about Len Broughton. If Josh was right, and the initial letters in Len's spreadsheet had been transposed, then Belinda probably had every justification for feeling quite hacked off about his impertinent questions. But Beth certainly didn't want to have to apologise to her. She smiled up at Belinda, yards above her, with as sunny and innocent an expression as she could muster at this short notice.

'We were supposed to be discussing a meeting today. I need to get in touch with him,' Belinda said tersely, flicking a sheaf of her golden hair over her shoulder and almost blinding a woman behind her. She turned, but when she saw it was just a nanny she wheeled back to Beth without a word of apology.

'Sorry!' Beth exchanged a grimace with the poor woman, who was rubbing her smarting eye with one hand while trying to push a buggy with the other. 'Josh? Um, now where has he got to?' Beth feigned an expression of deep concentration while Belinda tapped her foot in its fancy shoe. 'But didn't you have a chat with him already?'

Belinda looked at her as though it was none of her business. Then she unbent a little. 'Yes, if you must know, we did have a quick rendezvous. But he promised he'd call to arrange a proper dinner meeting soon.'

Aha, thought Beth. That's the way it goes, is it? Josh had successfully confronted Belinda about Len Broughton, been convinced that she hadn't, in fact, been involved with him, and had then done what he usually did with any half-presentable woman. He'd started flirting and made a commitment that he had absolutely no intention of keeping.

Well, Beth wasn't going to pretend that she liked the way Josh went about things. But it was a lot less irksome when it was Belinda who was left in the lurch.

'You know, he never tells me anything. Do you have his phone number?'

'No, I don't, actually,' said Belinda slowly.

'Would you like it?' said Beth, trying to keep a wicked gleam out of her eye. She'd always wondered if Belinda had a little crush on her big brother. It looked as though she'd been right. And it would totally serve Josh right if she passed his details on.

'Oh, yes please,' said Belinda quickly.

Beth was a little surprised at her keenness. She was married, after all. But perhaps Belinda was trying to even the score, since the whole village knew about her husband and his ooh-la-la with the French au pair. And Beth did know how appealing Josh could be when he put his mind to it. Well, good luck with pinning him down, thought Beth, as she obligingly texted over Josh's number. She then made herself scarce, before Belinda could place a call and realise her brother had scarpered to a country far, far away, rather than have a tête-à-tête dinner with Dulwich's uber-mummy.

There wasn't any point in heading back to work to finish the day, thought Beth. And anyway, she now had so much to chew over, she wouldn't be able to concentrate at all. So she toddled back to Pickwick Road instead. She got a very ill-deserved hero's welcome from Colin, and took him quickly round the block to stretch his elderly legs. There was so much guilt involved in being the custodian of a sweet soul like the Labrador. She wished she could take him everywhere with her, but it really wasn't possible. And these days he was so tired, half the time he only pretended to want to go for walkies.

Back in the kitchen she made herself a cup of tea and sat down at the table. She sighed, thinking over everything she'd heard at Mariella's. It was so hard to believe that Nina, her irrepressible friend, could have felt a connection, even for a moment, with a man like Len Broughton. There was at least a thirty-year age gap, and Len had been a serial philanderer and a chancer as well. Beth had always thought Nina had such good antennae about people, instinctively knowing who was on the 'straight and barrow', as she'd probably put it.

Yet maybe this was why Nina was now so wise – because she had once been badly burnt by the awful guy. You would think, then, that she would go out of her way to warn other women not to make the same mistake. Suddenly she remembered Deirdre saying that someone who didn't look like a 'Dulwich type' had spoken to her about Len. It had to have been Nina. But Wendy, certainly, would have taken no notice of any voices of doom about 'her Len'. She had been in the grip of an obsession, and nothing and nobody could have put a damper on that – apart from the grim reaper and a churchful of evidence of his sneaky ways.

Women could certainly be wilfully blind when they wanted to be. Men were probably the same, but somehow the example of Belinda, this afternoon, floated to the forefront of Beth's mind. There she was, a woman who no doubt considered herself at the apex of Dulwich society. Yet she had had no qualms about lowering herself to ask the person she despised most in the world to help her find a totally worthless man. Not that Josh was really that bad, Beth corrected herself quickly. He wasn't taking money from women. He dated them one at a time. He was a good uncle. And he was still her dear brother.

Her phone, lying on the table in front of her, suddenly burst into life. It was a call from an unknown number. Beth hesitated for a moment, then pressed reply.

'Beth? Beth, is that you?' It was the voice of a hesitant, even scared young woman. Could it be someone with information on Len Broughton?

Beth sat up a little straighter. 'Yes? Who is that? How can I help?'

'Oh, it is you, great.' The girl now sounded relieved. 'It's Julie-Ann.'

Beth's mind went blank for a second. Then she remembered. Josh's girlfriend. Left behind in the UK, for Beth to keep an eye on. Just what she needed. Her prayers for more information on Len Broughton had not been answered.

'How are you getting on, Julie-Ann?' Beth asked, hoping she sounded more enthusiastic than she felt.

'Oh, you know... staying with your mum at the moment. And I'm at a bit of a loose end, now Joshy's gone.'

'Yes, I bet,' Beth murmured sympathetically. For a second, she considered asking the girl where Josh had flown off to so hurriedly, and why. But that wasn't really fair. Even if Julie-Ann knew, she'd probably feel bad about telling Beth. Josh was sure to have made it plain one way or another that he wasn't interested in sticking around to look after his weepy heart-broken mother. Nor would he want Wendy or his sister ringing him every five minutes, nagging him to come back.

But wait a minute. Just because Josh had left Julie-Ann in the lurch, that didn't mean Beth had to as well. Perhaps she could press her into service on the mystery? Julie-Ann had the advantage that no one knew her in Dulwich, so nobody would associate her with Beth and her investigations. 'Well, if you're not busy with Mum... maybe you could help me out a bit with a couple of things?' Then a thought struck her. Had Josh actually dumped Julie-Ann? Was that why she'd been left behind, like a lost sock in the washing machine drum? 'Um... I don't quite know how to put this, but Josh is coming back for you at some point, isn't he?'

Julie-Ann laughed. 'You betcha. Did you think we'd split up? No, he's not getting away that easily.'

Beth laughed along, but decided to enlist the girl's services quickly, just in case. Julie-Ann almost bit her hand off, so keen was she to do something more taxing than mop up Wendy's tears and wait for her boyfriend to return. They agreed to meet right away in the village.

Beth was surreptitiously pulling on her pixie boots when she heard a snuffling sound behind her in the hall. It was Colin, with a hopeful look on his face.

'Oh, Col. Well, I suppose you can come too,' she said. Fate seemed to be telling her she was in charge of all the lame dogs today. Not that Colin was lame, exactly. Just that little bit stiff. She clipped on his lead and they pattered off together, Colin's tail now finding a rhythm of happy wagging that seemed to propel them both along.

In a matter of minutes, they'd got to the meeting place, just round the corner from the planters where poor Bella Harrington had met her doom. Colin settled down on the cold pavement, never averse to grabbing a nap whenever the opportunity presented itself. Beth moved from foot to foot, trying to keep warm. There was more of a nip in the air now as the year unspooled.

Across the way she could see the Village Primary, where they would be furiously practising the school nativity play already, in the desperate hope that it would have achieved some sort of coherence by Christmas time. She missed those days. Things were a lot slicker at Wyatt's. No sheep fell off the stage in terror when the Angel of the Lord appeared, and Joseph was absolutely never heard to remark that the baby Jesus was ugly. Somehow the show was the worse for it. But obviously she was very proud of Jake for being part of such a wonderful institution.

'Beth? Hi, sorry, it took me a bit longer than I...'

Beth gathered her thoughts and gave Julie-Ann a quick kiss on the cheek. The girl looked a little wan today, maybe as a result of Josh's hurried departure.

'Don't worry. Great that you're here. Now, did Josh explain to you all about Len and what we're trying to find out?'

'Yes. Yes of course, I was sitting in the kitchen with you all, don't you remember?'

Beth instantly felt bad. The girl had been there the whole time, how awful.

'Well, now's your time to shine,' Beth said brightly, to make up for overlooking poor Julie-Ann. 'I'd love it if you could do a bit of digging for me. If I ask those SOCO officers over there,' she said, pointing to the white tent. 'They'll tell me nothing. They know about me and Harry, and they won't want to get into his bad books by passing on any information they shouldn't. But they don't know that I know you, you see, so they'll tell you what's going on and then you can tell me.'

'Um, OK,' said Julie-Ann, looking baffled. 'But why on earth would they tell me anything?'

'Because you're a very pretty, persuasive girl,' said Beth, who felt a bit like shaking Julie-Ann at this point. 'And because you're going to take them a coffee and get chatting and then you're going to press, very gently, very sweetly, for some information. Do you think you can do that?'

'Erm...' Julie-Ann looked a little doubtful about this gambit.

'Great! It'll be easy, honestly. They'll be so bored and cold, poking away in that tent all day. They'll be thrilled at having an interruption. Believe me.'

Julie-Ann still wasn't looking convinced. 'All right... but what on earth should I ask them?'

'Well, how about cause of death, time of death, any leads on the killer, things like that?'

'Right. Um, Beth, I'm really not sure...'

'Nonsense, you'll be brilliant,' said Beth heartily. 'Now, let's just pop and get some lovely cappuccinos for them. Honestly, they can't resist a hot drink, police workers. It's like they've never seen tea or coffee before.'

Beth steered the reluctant girl into Mariella's, after tying Colin to an outside table, and soon they had four coffees balanced in a cardboard tray. Beth propelled Julie-Ann outside again and pointed her in the direction of the white SOCO tent. She just about managed to restrain herself from giving the girl a hefty push between the shoulder blades. She shook her head. Some people were natural sleuths... and some weren't.

Just then, out of her peripheral vision, she saw a flash of white. She'd know that coat anywhere. It was Nina, streaking past her as fast as she could. Of course. She'd be heading to the Village Primary for pick-up time, to get little Wilf. Honestly, Beth thought. Call herself a detective. She should have worked that out and been standing waiting for Nina. This was her chance to make things up to her. Without thinking, she dashed over the road, deaf to Colin's whines. He'd thought he was about to be liberated from his table, but he'd just have to wait a few minutes more.

Outside the Village Primary, Nina was hunched into her coat, turned away from the road, and standing a little apart from the gaggle of mums who were usually her pals. Beth rushed up to her and put a hand on her shoulder. When Nina turned, all she said was, 'Huh. It's you.'

'Yes, it's me, and I'm so sorry. I was wrong to be so judgemental about all that... Len business. Look, it's nothing to do with me who you see. It was just a shock that you and my mum—'

'Yeah, yeah, you've made your point. No need to rub it out,' said Nina, turning away.

'Nina, come on, you must know I didn't mean anything by it. All this has been hard. I mean, my mother hasn't looked at another man since my dad died. And then finding out about all the others... it's thrown me off balance a bit. But I know you were seeing Len quite a while ago. Maybe he wasn't as, erm, active then.'

Nina turned round at last, and Beth was mortified to see a tear trembling from her lashes. 'Nah. He was always Jack the bad, he was. But you know how it is. You work with a guy... you get close...'

Beth realised this was the way that she and Harry had got together, though he would no doubt be furious at any suggestion they were on the same team, even now. Despite his addiction to Golden Age whodunits celebrating the talented amateur, Harry was firmly of the belief that modern policing was the domain of professionals only. But Beth brushed over all that to reassure Nina. 'I know, I mean, look at me. Loads of people meet their partner at work.'

'Yeah. But loads of people don't meet their *married* partner who's also screwing everyone else at work, do they?' said Nina dolefully.

'Well, you didn't know that when you first met him, did you? You were temping, he was the boss, his word went. I mean, it's a classic. And then, when you found out the truth about Len afterwards, I'm sure you were every bit as upset as my mum.'

'Yeah, and with probably more reason, too,' Nina added cryptically. 'Soon as I found out what he was like, I knocked it on the bed.'

For a second, Beth's mind led her places she didn't want to go, then she realised what Nina meant. 'Of course. I'm just so sorry you had to go through all that, Nina. It must have been awful. So he really didn't tell you he was married?'

'Course not. What do you take me for? He was a real "liar, liar, pants on the fryer", that geezer. But somehow, he had a lot of charm,' Nina reminisced with a faint smile. 'I couldn't hate him, even after—' she stopped abruptly.

'Even after what?' Beth said, intrigued.

'Oh, nothing. Just everything that happened, I s'pose,' said Nina. 'Look, here's Wilfy-boy.'

Nina's little son ran up to them and locked his arms around Nina's legs in an exuberant greeting that risked knocking his mum flat, something Jake hadn't done for years. It was a sad day for a mother when her son decided he was too old for hugs, Beth thought.

'I'll let you two get on,' said Beth, a touch wistfully, though she was glad they had gone some way to sorting things out. She retraced her steps to Mariella's and untied Colin from the table. Then she looked over at the SOCO tent, and saw Julie-Ann was doing sterling work, chatting away with a couple of the team, who seemed a lot more appreciative of her charms than Josh. Beth waved at her, and mimed a telephone, mouthing *call me*, and was stumping back to Pickwick Road when her phone shrilled in her pocket.

But to her surprise, it wasn't Julie-Ann but Katie. 'What time do you want to meet tonight?'

'Tonight?' Beth echoed blankly, searching her dusty memory banks for an outing that had slipped her mind.

'Yes! Don't tell me you've forgotten about the Year 8 disco? *Again?*'

THIRTY

Beth mentally crossed her fingers as she trudged home, her phone to her ear. 'Of course I haven't forgotten about the disco,' she said, wincing at the thumping lie. 'Um, great. What time do you think we should get there?'

'Well, the official kick-off is at seven, so how about we get there at six fifteen?'

'That seems... early,' said Beth. There were a thousand things she'd rather do with her evening, thank you. Even putting out the bins was suddenly looking compelling, and as for taking Colin round the block for the umpteenth time, well that would be Nirvana by comparison.

'We've got to get into position, help with the set-up... put up our decorations... and you know we promised Mrs Montgomery we'd be on hand,' said Katie, gently insistent.

'Oh, damn. I mean, fine, OK then,' said Beth. She couldn't go back on her word to the frankly terrifying head of Year 8, any more than she could leave Katie in the lurch. And blast it, she'd completely forgotten about the decorations. 'So I'll meet you with Jake at, what, just before six fifteen?'

'No, no, the boys will be making their own way. Honestly, it'd be social death if they rocked up with us.'

'Oh? Great, that makes me feel even more like going,' said Beth. 'I suppose we don't have to eat beforehand, though,' she said, cheering up slightly. 'We can just graze on sausage rolls.'

Beth could almost feel Katie's shudder down the phone. 'If you must,' she said. 'See you later, then.'

When she turned her key in the front door, the first surprise was the sound of the shower running upstairs. Jake normally showered right before bed, so for a second Beth wondered whether Harry had got home early for once. But the sight of Jake's schoolbag, overflowing on the stairs, and his enormous trainers in the hall, were both incontrovertible clues. It was her son up there. Jake was voluntarily subjecting himself to extra hygiene measures.

Beth couldn't help grinning. This was the most obvious sign yet that things were changing with her lad, apart from the trendy jeans. He'd obviously worked out that cleanliness was appealing to the opposite sex. Beth felt quite proud. When he thundered down the stairs a few minutes later, she nobly forbore to mention his dripping hair or the cloud of something that smelt suspiciously like Harry's rarely deployed aftershave that trailed after him. She hoped it would wear off a bit by the time he went out, otherwise he might have the girls fainting for all the wrong reasons.

As Jake stood there, in his new jeans and very clean sweatshirt, Beth realised he was becoming a handsome young man; the spitting image of his dad, in fact. Not for the first time, she turned away from him to hide a tear at the fact that poor James was missing all this, and she had to clear her throat before saying, 'So I'll be off to meet Katie at the school for six fifteen. And you just come along when you're ready. Are you meeting Charlie?'

'Yeah. OK, whatever,' said Jake, grabbing a bag of crisps from the cupboard. 'Laters.'

* * *

Beth was in a thoughtful mood as she walked through the chilly streets that evening. She'd considered changing, then dismissed the idea. She didn't want to upstage Jake's special new jeans, courtesy of Josh, did she? And also, she couldn't be bothered. She was exhausted, having had to venture into the loft to see if, by any strange chance, there were any disco-suitable decorations lurking up there. Of course there hadn't been, but she'd hastily grabbed some Christmas tinsel and baubles, and that would just have to do.

The evening wasn't about her, after all, she thought, as she scuffed along in her old boots, swinging her bag of ancient festive tat. This was Jake's chance to shine – although she hoped he wouldn't take that too literally. The idea of him prancing around the dance floor like John Travolta was enough to make her toes curl.

It wasn't difficult to turn her mind to other matters. She was still reeling at the news that Nina and Wendy, of all people, had both been involved with Len. She couldn't imagine two women more different from each other. Len had definitely had eclectic tastes – or totally indiscriminate ones.

She'd had a quick call with Harry earlier, before leaving the house, explaining she'd be out at the dreaded disco. He'd obviously felt a little sorry for her, as he'd let slip the results of the post-mortem on Len Broughton. They were still going with natural causes, despite Wendy's certainty that it was murder, but Harry admitted there had been an unusually high concentration of nicotine in his bloodstream. Though, as the man had been such a dedicated pipe smoker, that was perhaps not much of a surprise. Beth had tucked the information away, to mull over later. There must be some reason why that particular word, nicotine, struck a bit of a chord with her. Where had she heard it recently? Or something similar? She shook her head. For now, she had to focus on Jake, and make sure he sailed through this disco without blotting his copybook any further with the school.

Of course, the whole thing was ridiculous – even without Beth and Katie hovering all night, she was certain that neither Jake nor Charlie would put a foot wrong in their interactions with the girls from the College School. Both were kind and polite, and as thoughtful as boys their age could be. Maybe that wasn't saying an awful lot. But neither had those laddish tendencies that led to the sort of toxic showing off that might include picking on girls in order to win points with their peer group.

If it hadn't been for that frightful Gregory King, there was no way they would ever have put a toe out of line.

These thoughts took her right up to the gates of Wyatt's, where Katie was waiting nervously. She was wrapped in a long black velvet duster coat, and her hair gleamed like spun gold under the streetlights, helped out by glittery combs at the sides. Beth glanced down at her own pixie boots and surreptitiously tried to buff them up a bit on the back of her jeans. They exchanged the regulation Dulwich double-kiss and linked arms as they strolled up the path to the Great Hall, a bit hampered by Beth's bag trailing bits of tinsel and Katie's much larger carrier of snazzy-looking handmade decorations. The Hall was quite a sight, every light shining out into the night, while a big sign was strung up over the entrance, bidding everyone welcome to the Year 8 disco.

'Wow, it's so splendid,' said Katie, marvelling as they entered the hall. Beth realised Katie had hardly been inside the school, thanks to its sensible policy of keeping parents firmly outside at pick-up time. For Beth, the heady cocktail of furniture polish and hymn books, with a faint note of adolescent boy, was the familiar backdrop to her working life. But, she admitted, the place did scrub up nicely. As well as a huge and beautiful arrangement of rust- and rose-coloured chrysanthemums, there was another banner inside, advertising the disco, and there were beaming members of staff on hand to direct the parent helpers to their stations.

First stop was the cloakroom, where Katie shrugged off her lovely coat – and revealed an even lovelier black velvet cocktail wrap dress, which she wore with sheer tights and velvet Mary Janes with a stacked heel, almost giving Belinda McKenzie's shoes some competition.

'Oh my God, Katie, you didn't tell me you were going to dress up,' said Beth, mortified. Admittedly, the thought had flitted into her own brain for a second – but even then she'd only really contemplated swapping her current jeans for a slightly cleaner pair.

'It is a bit of a special night,' said Katie mildly. 'But don't worry, Beth, you look great,' she said, putting so much jolly conviction into her words that Beth instantly felt even worse.

Beth shook her head sadly. 'Oh well. Jake wouldn't recognise me if I wore anything different. Mind you, that might be a good thing. Why didn't I think of it?'

But in truth, she had nothing in her wardrobe that would have fitted the occasion like Katie's simply perfect dress.

Just then, things got even worse as Belinda McKenzie strolled by in a plunging red dress slit to the thigh. Her stilettos were so high she had to grab the wall for support. Then she stopped, and swung round carefully.

'Oh hi, Katie. You look nice,' she said, bending for a kiss on both cheeks. 'Glad someone's made the effort,' she added, with a sniff in Beth's direction, then she lurched off again, the shoes giving her the slightly off-balance motion of a camel swaying through the desert.

'What on earth is she even doing here?' hissed Beth, as she and Katie made their way towards the main hall.

'Well, her boy Billy is in Charlie and Jake's year,' said Katie in a low voice. 'And isn't her daughter a prefect at the College School? She might be here too.'

'Oh Christ! How can I have forgotten that she'd be around? I don't know how I let you persuade me into this,' Beth said peevishly, pulling at her tatty old jumper, as though that would suddenly magic it into the slinky evening number that was obviously required.

'Oh, come on, now, Beth, it's going to be fun,' said Katie. 'And besides, I didn't persuade you. It's a three-line whip, remember? Neither of us had a lot of choice.'

Beth pursed her lips, but she supposed Katie was right. As they entered the hall, however, one of the dads on the door pressed a plastic goblet into her hand. She took a sip and instantly things started to look up.

'What the hell is in this? I hope we're not giving this to the kids,' she said to the father, who on closer inspection turned out to be the parent of a boy in Jake and Charlie's class.

'Don't worry,' he said with a wink. 'It's only the mummies and daddies who'll be getting the good stuff.'

'Come on,' said Katie. 'That looks like the refreshment table over there, that's our station.'

'Great, I'm starving,' said Beth.

'We're supposed to be serving the children – but whatever,' said Katie, catching sight of Beth's cross expression. 'You might feel a bit better after a sausage roll... or two.'

THIRTY-ONE

In fact, it took at least three sausage rolls before Beth regained her equilibrium. They weren't even that nice, but she chomped them down while Katie flitted about, making their stand look wonderful with her handcrafted, carefully constructed decorations – and Beth's tired old baubles.

Beth coughed, almost choking on the greasy pastry. She hadn't had anything to eat before leaving home, and seeing Belinda on her work territory had given her quite a shock. She much preferred it when the woman only cropped up in the usual Dulwich cafés. But Katie was right, Belinda had a child in Year 8 at Wyatt's so of course she had every right to be here.

From her vantage point behind the refreshment table, Beth could now see Belinda's daughter, Allegra, amidst a gaggle of other girls who must be College School prefects. While Wyatt's closed the disco to all but Year 8 pupils, College School prefects were trusted to help run things.

Again, the girl was living up to the nickname 'Leggy'. Tonight she was wearing a micro mini, revealing legs even more spectacular than her mother's. She also had the family trademark sheaf of long blonde hair – but unlike her parent, she had a sweet and guileless look in her large blue eyes. She was clearly the leader of the little pack of girls, but she seemed to be wielding her power for good, and not evil – the girls were all laughing and joking and seemed very happy together, something that was not at all the case with Belinda and her band of admirers.

Suddenly, Katie nudged Beth and Beth almost choked on her fourth sausage roll. 'What's up?'

'Don't look now, but it's Charlie and Jake.'

Sure enough, Beth watched as her son and his best friend sidled into the vast room, transparently self-conscious and staying well away from the knots of girls that were forming around the sides of the room.

The lights, which had been beaming out, were suddenly dimmed and the disco ball in the centre of the room started spinning, sending splinters of silvery light around the room. At the same time, Dr Grover, the head, stepped forward. 'Welcome, boys, girls and parents, to the Wyatt's School Year 8 disco. I won't try and say anything cool, but I would just like to thank all those who have worked so hard to make this evening happen. And I wish you all a wonderful night. And now, as they say on *Strictly*, keep dancing.'

There was a round of applause, almost entirely from the parents, and then the music started up in earnest. The first track to blast out was 'Celebration' by Kool and the Gang, a song which Beth estimated had been released in 1980, so it seemed a fair bet that the evening's playlist had been put together by someone's dad, rather than any of the kids themselves. Katie raised her eyebrows at Beth, but was soon bopping along to the song as best she could in the cramped space between their trestle table and the wall.

Meanwhile, the students were now almost squirming with

embarrassment. It seemed no one was bold enough to put a foot onto the dance floor. Instead the sexes divided like the Red Sea, boys on one side and girls on the other.

'Oh my Lord,' said Katie. 'Do you remember your first disco?'

'Mmm,' mumbled Beth through another mouthful of sausage roll. She really must stop or there'd be none left for the kids. 'It was just like this. My mother wanted me to wear a "nice dress", a frilly number with a sash and little bows and everything. So I refused and wore Josh's jeans. All the other girls were in these super-cool outfits... I spent the whole evening eating the snacks,' she added. Then she looked down at her old sweater, and then at the sausage roll in her hand, and put the last bit down carefully.

'I loved my first school dance,' said Katie, still bouncing along to the beat, closing her eyes. She was clearly being transported back to a carefree teenage time when, no doubt, the boys had vied to dance with her and all the girls wanted to be her friend.

'Two plates of sausage rolls, please,' came a small, squeaky voice. A boy, almost on a level with the table, eyed Beth hopefully.

'Of course, of course,' she said, loading up the paper plates. He'd need all those if he wanted to grow a bit. Though, as she knew to her cost, sometimes there wasn't quite the correlation between calories and height that one might wish. She brushed a lion's mane of crumbs off her jumper and kicked the resulting pile under the table.

As the boy tottered away with his groaning plates, Beth turned her attention to the dance floor again. Some of the bolder girls were now standing under the disco ball. In the middle of the huddle was one girl who was taller, blonder, more beautiful than the rest... of course it had to be Allegra McKenzie. Beth swivelled to look round the hall and, sure enough, there was Belinda, gazing on proudly as her daughter dominated proceedings. But though Allegra was definitely no shrinking violet, Beth watched as she encouraged all the girls in her group to take a turn in the centre, twirling and dancing and drawing admiring stares from the boys.

A small queue of hungry lads and lassies had formed, so Beth turned back to her duties. When she next looked up, she caught sight of Jake and Charlie. Charlie was tapping his foot, lounging against a pillar, effortlessly cool. Jake, however, had his eyes fixed on one thing and one thing only. Beth moved her head to see what had got his attention. But it was more a question of who. Jake was staring right at Allegra McKenzie, and the expression on his face was not unlike his mother's when she spotted a particularly fine chocolate cake. It was a mixture of yearning and ravening hunger – but it also contained that backwash of regret, that suggested he already knew his heart's desire could really be quite bad for him.

Beth must have made some sort of strangled sound, because Katie turned to her in alarm. 'Are you OK?'

'Yes. Yeah, I suppose so, anyway. Listen, shall we get a drink? Another proper one,' she said, pushing Katie's fruit juice away.

Katie gestured to the queue, which was now stretching a fair distance. 'Maybe when we've dealt with this lot. Why, is there something up?'

'Oh, I just saw something I didn't much like the look of,' Beth said, smiling automatically at the boy in front of her and helping him to sandwiches and crisps. 'Here, what on earth is Belinda up to now?'

Belinda McKenzie had pushed herself into the middle of the dance floor, where a few clumps of girls – and one or two brave boys – were gyrating to Boney M's 'Rasputin'. Beth was beginning to wonder if there were going to be any tunes from this century. But, more pressingly, could it be possible that Belinda was deluded enough to give them some sort of exhibition of dancing? She always had an unstoppable urge to be centre stage at every carol concert and parents' evening Beth had attended over the years. But what on earth was she thinking of, disrupting the disco? Both her son and her daughter were surely going to be crucified by her attention-seeking. Although, Beth supposed, they might actually be used to it. Poor things.

Belinda stood in the middle of the room, and gradually the dancing around her stopped. By the time the song came to an end, she was alone on the dance floor. She swished back her hair, and spoke up. She had no need of a microphone, her ringing tones easily reaching every corner of the large hall.

'Forgive me for this tiny interruption,' she said with a self-deprecating laugh. 'I just wanted to announce, on behalf of the PTA, that there will be a prize tonight for the best dancer. So, children, get your grooviest moves on!'

At that, Belinda twirled on the spot, executed a flawless curtsey, exposing lots of leg thanks to her red dress's side slit, and swept away, leaving silence in her wake. Beth looked over at Jake and Charlie, who had that wooden look on their faces that meant a grown-up had done something cringeworthy. Then the next song started up. It was 'Killer Queen'. Beth was beginning to suspect whoever had put together tonight's playlist had a sense of humour, if not very current musical taste.

'Did you know Belinda was head of the PTA?' Beth hissed to Katie.

Katie nodded. 'Well, come on Beth, of course she is. Who else?'

Beth sighed. It did make perfect sense. But really, was there a single aspect of Dulwich life that woman didn't want to dominate? Beth didn't bother to answer that one. It had even looked for a second as though she was in the centre of the Len

Broughton business too, though Beth was now willing to accept Josh's theory that those initials might be down to dyslexia. It made sense. Beth really didn't think Belinda would ever willingly give her husband Barty grounds to winkle her out of her enormous mansion and part her from her splendid lifestyle.

But thinking about Len Broughton made her realise that Katie was right, this evening was a valuable opportunity. There were bound to be women here who had, at the very least, a glancing knowledge of Len, even if they weren't notches on his bedpost – a bedpost that must be so whittled down by now that it could only resemble a particularly fragile matchstick.

'Hey, do you remember any of those initials on the Len spreadsheet that match the mums or teachers here tonight?' Beth nudged Katie.

Katie, who was just nibbling her first crisp – the plain variety, of course, to avoid additives – nearly choked at this. 'You're not serious? We can't go around asking people questions tonight.'

'Why on earth not?' Beth's eyes were wide. 'You did say you thought there'd be some of his exes here.'

'Well, I did, but that was to make sure you came,' said Katie with a sideways smile. 'I'm definitely not asking any questions. What if the boys see what we're up to?'

'So? They'll just think we're being sociable.'

'Beth, have you forgotten we're supposed to be here watching them?'

'I haven't, but it doesn't take two of us, does it? Not really,' said Beth with a shrug. She peered over to Jake and Charlie. They were still lounging in a would-be casual manner on the fringes of the dance floor. Beth was sure they weren't fooling anyone, as Jake kept stealing glances at the biggest and giggliest group of girls, where the happy shrieks of Allegra McKenzie occasionally pierced the air. She certainly was having a fine old time, Beth thought grumpily. Then she realised it was hardly fair to dislike the girl, just because her mother was the literal worst person in the area. She dragged her eyes away and scanned the rest of the room.

'Look over there, Katie. I can see Angela Douglas. Now she was definitely on the list, and she was at the funeral, too.'

'Tell me you're not going to accost her,' Katie said, scandalised. 'She's like, well, Dulwich royalty or something.'

Angela Douglas, head of the College School, did indeed have a regal air, and tonight her long black crepe dress with its silk organza panels, and her double string of pale, glowing pearls made her look more queenly than ever. She was talking to Dr Grover, and at her elbow was her deputy, Bernie Troughton. Here was Beth's opportunity. Bernie oversaw the archives at the College School – she was Beth's opposite number, to all intents and purposes.

'Well, all right, Angela Douglas is pretty intimidating. But don't forget, it looks like she's on Len Broughton's list. We have to catch the killer, or my mother is in the frame. And I don't want anyone accusing Wendy of murder. Harry told me tonight the post-mortem turned up a lot of nicotine in Len's bloodstream – I'm pretty sure that's not good for you. What if someone, knowing he was a smoker – and that seems to be everyone – gave him extra nicotine somehow? If Angela was mixed up with Broughton, then she'd know about his pipe and that makes her a suspect just like anyone else.'

Just saying the word nicotine had made Beth think, though. She had that strange déjà vu feeling again – what was that word she'd heard that rang all these bells? But Katie was speaking.

'God, I don't know how you do it, Beth. But if you really want to go ahead and grill her, then I can't stop you,' said Katie. 'Don't worry, I'll keep an eye on the boys.'

Now that Beth had scored her point, she felt very reluctant to slip out from behind the buffet table and sidle up to Angela Douglas. She'd talked big to Katie, and it was all true, but the woman was also seriously scary. Beth had heard tales, from mothers with girls at the school, about just how firm the head could be when she chose – and how small she made people feel. Beth was already small. And she didn't really want to feel any smaller. But it was now or never...

THIRTY-TWO

Beth did her best to glide through the knots of pupils, the boys busily stuffing their faces with crisps and snacks, the girls trying not to look quite so much like animals at feeding time but still managing to snaffle their fair share of the food on offer. The large group of girls containing Allegra McKenzie was the hardest to edge around, it was constantly moving, and at its centre 'Leggy' was holding forth, while the crowd screamed with laughter at her every word. Beth dodged them, and almost came up against Belinda McKenzie herself, but she pretended she couldn't see Beth and simply lurched past her on her high heels.

Finally, Beth reached the little group around Dr Grover. Angela Douglas, with her serene yet austere beauty, was surveying the crowd, while Bernie Troughton was telling Tom Grover a long story and he was trying to look interested. Beth nudged her way in, helped by Grover who hailed her like a long-lost friend.

'Beth, wonderful to see you. Doing sterling work with the refreshments over there, with Charlie's mum, isn't it? Has Jake had a dance yet?'

As usual, Beth was impressed by the head's effortless memory for names. 'I'm not sure if Jake is going to make it onto the dance floor tonight, he'll be pretty much doing a solo if he does,' she said, smiling as she looked at the acres of empty space. It was still a ratio of one boy to ten girls out there.

'Oh, you'd be surprised,' said Dr Grover with a wink. 'By the end of the night, they'll have lost those nerves. I don't know if you've met Angela Douglas? And this is Bernie Troughton.'

'Bernie and I have our archives in common,' Beth said, although she knew full well that the College School's records were crammed into one broom cupboard and Bernie was much too busy with her duties as deputy to look at them from one term to the next. 'But I think you and my mother might have a mutual acquaintance, Miss Douglas.'

'Oh, who might that be?' said Angela Douglas, looking down at Beth as though she was an interesting specimen she might just consider collecting.

'Erm, Len Broughton,' said Beth, with only the faintest suggestion of a quaver in her voice, though she did clutch her plastic goblet of punch a little more tightly.

Immediately, Angela Douglas's face changed colour, her pallor going from aristocratic to corpselike at a stroke. Meanwhile, Bernie Troughton's cheeks went the other way, becoming so suffused with blood that she resembled a plum tomato.

'That man! The hurt he caused...' Bernie Troughton thundered. Angela put a long-fingered hand on her friend's arm, and she immediately shut up.

'I was acquainted with Mr Broughton, yes,' Angela Douglas said with steely composure. 'But I think perhaps not in quite the way your mother was. Our paths crossed over plans to enlarge the school. The planning department at the council became involved, and was quite obstructive. Len took it upon himself to try and smooth the way... he was very kind. And I was able to help him in his efforts...'

Beth suddenly realised this might be tantamount to a confession, to having bribed the man. She listened even more intently.

'...But all that was over and done a year ago, I do assure you. I got the shock of my life at the funeral. There was so much... upheaval... from some of the ladies attending. None of that seems to fit with the Len I knew. But then, how well do we ever really know people?'

Angela Douglas delivered this last line in a particularly piercing voice, staring directly at Beth. And, if Beth had felt like a specimen before, she now felt like one that was undergoing a particularly unpleasant dissection.

'Bernie, you were as surprised as I was, weren't you?' Angela turned to her friend.

A complicated expression flitted over Bernie Troughton's doughy features. She was still flushed after her burst of protective anger earlier. But now she looked as though she was hiding some thoughts which didn't entirely accord with Angela Douglas's.

That was interesting, thought Beth. If only she could get Bernie alone, perhaps she could drill down a little into what Angela's relationship with Len Broughton had really been like. Because, from the looks of things, someone was hiding something.

Just then, there was a whoop from the dance floor, and Beth whipped round to see what was going on. Thank goodness, it wasn't Jake, but some of the other boys did, indeed, appear to have lost their inhibitions at last, and were trying to breakdance on the parquet floor of the Great Hall, with little success. They were drawing a lot of attention to themselves, though, and the knot of girls including Allegra and her friends drifted over, like iron filings attracted to a magnet.

Now Beth could almost see the idea catching on in other

groups of boys, and suddenly quite a few launched themselves forward and started throwing very odd shapes, like embryonic dad dancing. Why were boys at posh schools so hopeless at this, Beth wondered. She'd loved her late husband James madly, but gosh, he was awful on a dance floor. If the success of their marriage had rested on that first bop together, then they would have been divorced within a year. Luckily he had a lot of other very good qualities up his sleeve, not least giving her Jake.

She looked towards her son, wondering if he would feel the pull to strut his stuff, as the other boys were doing. She was confident he would hold out, stick to the wallflower role that Beth had made her own during similar discos when she'd been young. But no. To her growing amusement – and slight horror – he and Charlie were now leaving their safe corner, rather tentatively admittedly, and shuffling onto the dance floor. To Beth, it now seemed as exposed a spot as the high diving board in an Olympic final. But then, thank goodness, the music changed to Lady Gaga's 'Poker Face' and Beth relaxed a bit. Surely anyone in the world could dance to this.

She excused herself to Dr Grover and his guests, getting a sharp glance from the head for her pains. She was pretty sure that tomorrow, her friend Janice would be asked by her husband to get a good explanation out of her. But for now, her priority had to be getting back to Katie's side, so they could clamp their hands over their eyes – and peer at their sons' antics through the slits in their fingers.

'Have you seen?' Beth asked, a little breathless, as she wiggled behind the refreshments table. She was sure it hadn't been quite this snug at the beginning of the evening. Maybe she'd had one too many sausage rolls.

'God, yes, I can't look,' said Katie, staring straight at the boys.

'Nor can I.' Beth was equally mesmerised. 'I really didn't

think Jake was the type to get out there and, you know, *do his thing*,' she hissed. 'He certainly doesn't get that gene from me.'

'Well don't look at me,' said Katie. 'Charlie said on the way out that nothing on earth would get him dancing tonight. And now look at him!'

Beth squinted over at him. It really wasn't a pretty sight. His arms and legs were flailing this way and that. She thought irresistibly of a cricket jumping from bush to bush, and nearly laughed. But then she looked across at Jake and it really wasn't funny any more.

'Do you think they took some kind of bet to see which of them could look more, I don't know how to put this kindly, idiotic?' said Beth, mortified. Jake was now trying out a step that looked like some sort of adaptation of a Highland fling. 'He's going to fall over if he's not careful.'

Katie shook her head sorrowfully. Then she perked up and nudged Beth. 'Do you know, I think it's working. Maybe there's method in their madness.'

'I hope so, or I'm having my son committed,' said Beth glumly. 'What do you mean?'

'Look at the girls.'

Beth swivelled her head. There were groups of girls all round the room, dancing quite enthusiastically now, and clearly enjoying themselves. 'I don't get it.'

'Not those girls. That lot.' Katie pointed, as subtly as she could, at the largest group which, as usual, had Allegra at its centre. They had stopped their own dancing and were apparently drinking in the sight of Jake and Charlie's contortions. Allegra had her hand over her mouth, but her sparkling blue eyes were alight with something that wasn't the casual contempt that Beth might have expected from a McKenzie. Was it... no, surely it couldn't be? Not admiration?

At that moment, a large, shiny and very expensive handbag

thudded down on the trestle table in front of Beth. All the plastic cups jumped and juddered, and even the leaden sausage rolls quivered. 'Any chance of getting a drink round here?' said a very loud, very posh voice.

THIRTY-THREE

'What would you like, Belinda?' Katie asked politely as Beth's nemesis flicked back her silky blonde tresses. Compared with her daughter's flaxen hair, Belinda's mane looked that little bit brassy under the lights. For the first time, it occurred to Beth that she must dye it. Poor Belinda. It really was hard work being her. A second later, all her sympathy had dried up as quickly as a grape in the desert.

'Champagne, please. I don't mind if it's not vintage,' Belinda said impatiently. 'Failing that, I'll take a prosecco, if it's properly chilled.'

'Um, we're only doing snacks, as you can see,' said Beth, waving a hand at the sad remains of the sausage rolls. 'But I think there's white or red screwtop over there, Belinda. Take your pick.'

Belinda shuddered. 'God, the very idea! Anyway, what on earth does your son think he's doing, Beth? And what are all these Christmas baubles doing on the table? Did you get the date wrong or something? Maybe you can't afford a calendar?'

Beth took a breath. The last thing she wanted was a public

row with Belinda. But the woman had just insulted her decorating skills, her timekeeping – and her boy. She'd gone too far. Before she could wade in, though, Katie had interrupted.

'They're supposed to be mini disco balls,' Katie fibbed loyally. 'And whatever he and Charlie are doing, it looks like your daughter is quite intrigued.' She raised her eyebrows at Belinda, who wheeled round to glare at the little tableau. Sure enough, there was Leggy McKenzie, giggling prettily, while watching Jake and Charlie. Then she actually blew them a kiss.

Belinda was just about to stride off, when Beth detained her. 'Just wondering... I know my brother had a chat with you about Len Broughton—'

'Dear Joshy. Trying to protect his mother after she made quite an error of judgement,' said Belinda, making Beth fume. 'But he was on the wrong track with all that. Of course, I could have said more...'

'Could you, though, Belinda? I bet you don't know a thing about what really happened.' Beth crossed her arms firmly over her ratty jumper, and stared straight at Belinda. Yes, she'd been right, there was the faintest sign of dark roots in that expensive head of hair. Then Belinda gave a cruel smile.

'You should be asking that friend you hang around with, the chubby girl with the terrible jobs. She knows where the bodies are buried, that's for sure. Quite literally, in this case.'

For a second Beth couldn't even think who Belinda meant. Then when she realised, she leant forward over the remnants of the sandwiches, squaring up to the woman sneering down at her.

But Katie put a restraining hand on her arm and broke in. 'Thanks very much for the tip, Belinda. You're so well connected, I bet you know exactly which other people we should be talking to. I mean, you did know Bella Harrington, didn't you?'

Belinda looked at Katie in surprise. 'Don't tell me she's got you running around doing this stupid detective act as well? All right, I knew Bella. Not very well, but yes, in my position, you do come across all types,' she acknowledged with a graceful shrug.

'What position is that, exactly? I thought you were a stay-at-home mum?' said Katie.

'Silly, I meant my position in the community,' said Belinda, as though it went without saying. 'But yes, I'm a full-time mum as well. If you do it my way, it's all-consuming. I'm there for them twenty-four/seven, you know,' she said earnestly. 'As for Bella, she once worked for me as a nanny,' she went on, blithely unaware of any contradiction. 'Only for a couple of weeks, mind. She kept asking for time off at weekends, which was ridiculous. With gifted children like mine, you really need to stay on top of their needs all the time. Be really vigilant,' Belinda finished.

To one side, peering around Belinda's svelte form, Beth could see Allegra was now approaching Jake and Charlie. She seemed to be offering to tip some of her drink into their cups. While the two of them hesitated, a teacher swooped in and intercepted. It was Sam Radley, the bony Maths head. With pursed lips, he took Allegra's cup, sniffed the contents and carried it away, pausing only to have a brief word with Angela Douglas, who immediately looked over at the refreshment table. Beth almost ducked, a reflex when dealing with cross teachers. But Belinda was still talking.

'Did Bella know much about what went on in Len Broughton's office, do you think?' Katie asked.

'Well I would imagine she did, she was his secretary after all. That man, who would get involved with him, honestly? Hey, Beth? If anyone had skeletons in his closet, it was Len.' Then she laughed uproariously at what she'd said. 'Oh, that's too funny...' Belinda started, but then she got a tap on the shoulder. She turned round, to face none other than the College School head, Angela Douglas. And it looked as though she was not happy. Not happy at all.

THIRTY-FOUR

Beth and Katie were sitting at the kitchen table later that same evening, both nursing large glasses of Tesco special offer Chardonnay. Although it was only just 10 p.m., it felt as though the disco had lasted forever. So much had gone on.

Belinda had just been telling them how dreadful Len Broughton was (something Beth thought she already knew pretty well) when Angela Douglas strode over and let the cat out of the bag. Allegra McKenzie had been necking her mother's ninety per cent proof vodka all evening, and had been pretty generous in doling it out to her friends, too.

'Thank goodness Jake and Charlie had the sense to say no to that booze,' said Katie, lifting her glass to her lips once again.

'Hmm,' said Beth, who privately thought the odd shot of vodka might have explained a lot about the boys' dancing.

Katie took another hefty slug of her drink before speaking again. 'I wonder if it was because of all that stuff with that awful boy, whassisname, Geoffrey Tring.'

'Do you mean Gregory King?' asked Beth with a smile. 'At least we've got a bit of a surer grasp of what happened to Bella now,' she said more sombrely. 'Whoever killed Len must have thought Bella was on to them.'

Katie raised her glass to her mouth again – and missed it by miles. 'How much wine is there in this alcohol?' she said, overcome by giggles.

'Well, it's a lot less than in Allegra's cup... but maybe more than, um, we're used to,' said Beth, realising her friend was quite tipsy.

She was relieved when she heard the rattle of Harry's key in the door. Normally, she'd worry he might wake Jake, but tonight, after all the excitement of the evening, including Allegra and her mother being led away for a 'quick chat' by Angela Douglas and never coming back, she was pretty sure he'd sleep soundly.

'Hello, hello, hello, what's all this then,' said Harry as he stood in the kitchen doorway.

'You sound like something from a 1950s cop show,' said Katie, getting the giggles again.

'I see, it's like that, is it?' He glanced swiftly at the all-but-empty bottle on the table and seemed to draw his own conclusions. 'Can I have a drink with you, or is this a private party?'

Beth shot up to give Harry a kiss, get him a glass and fish another bottle out of the fridge. Soon they were all nibbling on crisps and laughing as Katie recounted the story of Allegra and the bootleg hooch. When she got to the bit about Belinda knowing Bella Harrington, though, Harry seemed to prick up his ears. Gone was the relaxed posture and the arm draped round Beth's shoulders. He listened intently, and when Katie had finished he seemed to speak reluctantly.

'I know I'm always the killjoy telling Beth not to meddle in this stuff. But Katie, I never thought I'd have to say the same to you.'

'Well, don't then,' said Katie, on another gale of laughter. But Harry didn't join in.

'A woman is dead. Not to mention Len Broughton himself.'

'Are you any nearer to finding out exactly what happened to Bella?' said Beth.

Harry gave her an old-fashioned look. 'Maybe it's time I walked Katie home,' he said.

'Oh no, don't be silly, it's no distance, I'll be absolutely fine,' said Katie, standing up – then immediately collapsing back down again on rubber legs. 'Oopsie.'

'Exactly,' said Harry. 'It won't take me five minutes. And maybe you should drink some water when you get in,' he suggested for good measure.

'Yes, ossifer,' Katie joked. Well, at least Beth thought she was joking. She bid them both goodbye at the door and then trailed back to rinse their glasses and put the kitchen to rights.

But something she'd heard that evening was still playing on her mind. Now what was it exactly? It eluded her as she immersed her hands in the soapy water. It remained just out of reach as she dried up and put the glasses away. But, just as she switched out the kitchen light, it came to her. 'Ah!' she said, as darkness fell.

THIRTY-FIVE

Beth bounded out of bed the next morning, ready to take on the world – and then stopped abruptly as a headache ripped across her cranium. She hadn't drunk that much last night, had she? Not nearly as much as Katie... or Allegra McKenzie. But every fibre of her body was telling her that she'd had more than enough, thanks.

Harry was still tucked up, sleeping the sleep of the just – he had arrived back late after seeing Katie home, but not too late to be thanked enthusiastically by a still-tipsy Beth.

Now she was reaping the full harvest of a night of unaccustomed drinking. She tiptoed downstairs, hoping Katie felt a bit better than she did, as she stood shivering in the kitchen waiting for the kettle to boil. She gulped down two paracetamol tablets with some water from the tap, then turned and tried to look breezy as Jake clattered down the stairs. He stopped dead when he saw her.

'All right, Mum?' he said doubtfully.

'Yes, yes, all good,' Beth lied through gritted teeth. She felt like clutching her head and howling, but giving her son a merry smile would have to suffice. 'Cereal?'

'I'll get it. You sit down and, um, take it easy,' Jake said, uncharacteristically chivalrous.

'Did you enjoy the disco?' Beth asked him.

'Um. Yeah. It was... different,' said Jake with a secret smile.

Beth wondered what he was remembering. She had a strong suspicion it was something to do with Allegra McKenzie.

'Allegra's going to be in terrible trouble at school, I would imagine,' she said in a faux-casual manner.

Jake blushed painfully. 'Yeah?' he said. 'Um, where's the milk?'

'In the fridge,' she said, forbearing to add, *where it always is*. He obviously wanted to get off the topic of Allegra McKenzie as quickly as possible, by any means necessary. It looked like her fears were justified. Jake was in the grip of a crush. On Belinda McKenzie's daughter, of all people. How on earth had this happened? Admittedly Allegra was beautiful and, on the evidence of last night, quite a live wire. Ordinarily, Beth wouldn't want to visit the sins of the mother on the daughter... but just look who that mother was.

She knew she should give the girl a chance. Yet at the same time, Beth was instantly convinced of the urgent need to make sure that this romance, if such it was, was nipped in the bud with the sort of ruthlessly aggressive pruning that even leading lights of the Dulwich Open Gardens set would wince at. What on earth could she do to make sure it didn't last?

But, as Beth trudged off to work a few minutes later, she realised that trying to stop teenagers having crushes on unsuitable people was a mug's game, from the Montagues and Capulets onwards. The Wendy Cope approach, allowing the star-crossed lovers to get to know each other better and hoping that familiarity would wreak its usual havoc on the mysteries of attraction, was by far the best way forward. Beth didn't know Allegra at all, but with Belinda as her mother, she was willing to bet the girl had to have some faults. She must surely be arrogant. And, at worst, she could be a chip off the old block, and just managing to conceal it well.

Beth realised she hardly knew Belinda's husband Barty at all. In the far-off days when she'd been on the guest list for McKenzie parties, she'd done little more than say hello and goodbye to him, finding him a daunting figure. Tall, and always wearing clothes that looked as formal as a three-piece suit, even when he was relaxing at the weekend, Barty had not exactly sought her out either. He was the type that, while he was talking to her, would keep scanning the room over the top of her head for more important people to mingle with.

A lavish host, Barty always plied his guests with plentiful top-notch booze, but she couldn't really have said anything about his likes or dislikes, and as for the secret yearnings of his heart, these were locked safely away behind his tweed waist-coats. He was 'in finance', a mysterious place to be as far as Beth was concerned. She had spent quite a lot of her adult life 'in penury', and the twain never really did meet. The McKenzie lifestyle, involving private school fees for three from birth to eighteen, with all the ponies, piano lessons and private tutoring that Belinda could throw at the situation in between, was a long way from Beth's frantic back-of-the-envelope calculations. That was before her job, and the arrival of Harry, had made Jake's school fees possible. What on earth would she and Barty have to talk about?

But it was likely that Allegra took after both parents, and Beth now felt she had missed a trick in not getting to know the guy. For all she knew, Leggy was a daddy's girl. She could even be really nice. Beth sincerely hoped so.

As she unlocked the door of the archive office, Beth realised she was going to have to put all that aside. There were more important things to be getting on with today. Not, of course, her filing, which was now cascading out of its in-box and onto her desk. No, it was the Len situation that had to be top priority.

No sooner had she had that thought, than her phone shrilled in her pocket. She fished it out, and her heart sank a little. It was Wendy.

'Hi, Mum,' Beth said as chirpily as the paracetamol would allow. 'How's it going? How's Julie-Ann settling in?'

To her great surprise and tremendous relief, Wendy actually sounded quite bushy-tailed this morning.

'She's such a joy, Beth. You know, it's absolutely wonderful to have somebody around who understands exactly how I like my tea.'

Immediately, Beth was smarting. She had taken infinite pains to learn this art, mastering the slightly off-the-boil water, the hasty dunking of the teabag, and the overuse of milk which produced the distressingly pale grey cup that Wendy preferred. And then added tons of sugar to. But, on the verge of saying something sharp, she stopped herself. It was to her own great advantage if Wendy loved Julie-Ann. So what, if Wendy never acknowledged her own efforts to get things right? Her mother wasn't going to change now. She was incapable of giving Beth the approval that – despite herself – she still yearned for.

'I'm so glad it's going well,' Beth said gently. 'She seems like a very nice girl.'

'Oh, she's lovely. So pleasant to have around the house. And such a good listener. *She* doesn't mind me telling her all about Len.'

Again, Beth bit her lip. She had listened to what felt like hours and hours of wailing on that very subject. And in fact, now she wouldn't have minded if her mother had droned on about Len some more. At this stage, it might have been useful for her investigation, and she could have found out whether Wendy knew about the man's gambling habit. But as Wendy only wanted to sit and cry (Beth's least favourite thing) she hadn't really encouraged it.

'I hope you're getting on with things. Not long till the tournament now, Beth.'

'Right. Is Julie-Ann there? Maybe I could have a quick word,' Beth said. It was true, she did need to talk to the girl, but it also served to distract her mother from her daughter's many shortcomings. A few seconds later, Julie-Ann came on the phone.

'How's everything?' Beth said, instinctively lowering her voice, though if her mother was doing any eavesdropping, it would be at the other end of the line, not here in the office.

'Yeah, all good,' said Julie-Ann, sounding more cheerful than anyone at Wendy's house had a right to be. Beth marvelled, yet again, at how well things had worked out. But she really needed to have a debriefing session with the girl. With any luck, she'd picked up at least a nugget or two of useful information by now.

'Shall we get together for a coffee? Today, in the village?'

'Lovely, I'll just ask Wendy when she's fr—'

'Without her,' Beth said urgently.

'Oh. Oh yes, I see. Well, she's off to Bridge in about half an hour, how about then?'

Beth agreed that would be perfect. Then, once she'd finished the call, she wondered whether it was even worth starting on her paid work for such a short time. The answer, as ever, was a resounding no. So she took a sheet of A4 and wrote her own version of Len's list.

Margery Brinkwell – as Len's wife, the prime suspect. But it sounded like the truth when she said she'd been nowhere near his office that night.

Harriet French – claimed to have had a tryst with Len on the evening of his death, but Margery said she was a habitual liar. No motive, if true that she didn't mind his other women.

Here, Beth had a tiny epiphany. Harriet French must be that F.H. on Len's list! He must have been doing that letter switcheroo thing he'd done with B.M./M.B. Cheered by this, she went on.

Bella Harrington – out of the running. But why was she killed? What had she seen, what did she know?

Angela Douglas – or perhaps Bernie Troughton? Hard to imagine Angela getting her hands dirty with a murder, but Bernie? A different prospect. She would definitely kill to protect her BFF.

Choir members – Beth reluctantly had to acquit all of them, as they'd been boozing away at the time of Len's death.

Bridge classes group – ditto

And here, reluctantly, Beth put her pen down. Because the next name she had to write was that of a dear friend.

THIRTY-SIX

On one hand, Beth couldn't believe that Nina, little Nina, her brilliant bubbly friend, had an evil bone in her body. But she also knew that, behind that chirpy exterior, she was ruthlessly efficient. As a single working mum for many years, she was an expert in getting things done without apparent effort. In between sorting out messy offices, feeding, clothing and loving little Wilf, and having plentiful cups of coffee with Beth, had she also bumped off her ex-boyfriend – and Wendy's great love?

It was just impossible to believe. Apart from anything else, it also then tied Nina into the killing of Bella Harrington. And, though Beth thought she might be just about capable of removing Len if he did something that really annoyed her, she had liked Bella.

Yet the evidence against Nina was compelling. Bella had had a phone call from Nina shortly before her death. Had Nina lured Bella to the LTN planters, just so she could plant her in them? It was an assumption Beth didn't want to make – but what on earth could there be, by way of an innocent explanation?

Beth furrowed her brow. In a way, she was surprised Harry

hadn't swooped in and arrested Nina already. Maybe (a tiny disloyal voice said) he just hadn't quite got there yet? Well, it left time for Beth to sort things out.

Because, no matter how black things looked, she refused to believe Nina had done it. And that meant that someone else was out there, walking the streets of Dulwich, with the blood of two murders on their hands. Beth couldn't let that state of affairs continue. She had to catch them, and as quickly as she could.

* * *

Getting a murderer bang to rights was easy enough in theory, Beth thought twenty minutes later as she puffed up to Jane's café, where she was meeting Julie-Ann for the promised coffee. But it was not easy in practice. For a start, you had to contend with all the people milling around Dulwich Village at this time of day. As well as the mummies ferrying their little ones to super-important baby gym classes at St Barnabas village hall, there were also the first Christmas shoppers out on the prowl, hunting down gifts from Romeo Jones, the dinky deli specialising in beautifully wrapped panettone at £39 a go, or Townsends, the candle and mug emporium that proved an irresistible magnet to all females in the area between the ages of twelve and ninety-two.

She was just swerving an au pair who was driving her charge's pushchair like Boudicca in a hurry, when she caught sight of a familiar face. Mrs Hill, her mother's next-door neighbour – and gardener par excellence. Normally, she would have held the party line and shunned her, as Wendy was still in a fury about the Japanese knotweed palaver. But seeing the woman out of the blue jogged something in her memory. Len and his pipe. Len and nicotine. And something that someone had mentioned, that wasn't quite tobacco... It was the last golden bell falling into place on a slot machine. Ker-ching!

'Oh, hi, Mrs H, how are you?' said Beth, rushing to her side before the woman had time to register how odd it was that Wendy's daughter was treating her like a long-lost friend. 'Just wondering... Mum was thinking of planting something in her garden, something that sounds a bit like, erm, nicotine?' She could just see Margery Brinkwell saying it so casually in the Dirty Dog. Harriet French, and the beautiful displays she created on her allotment. 'What could it be, erm, smoking, vaping, something like that? You're so brilliant at all the gardening stuff, I just know you'll think of the name.'

'Nicotiana, you mean?' said Mrs Hill, her eyebrows perfect arches. 'It does smell gorgeous. But it's really not a particularly exotic plant, you know, Beth.'

'Oh yes, that's it! So it's easy to grow?'

'Well, I suppose so. But it's quite poisonous. You probably wouldn't want any in your garden, no matter how annoying your mother gets,' Mrs Hill said with a slightly twisted smile.

'What? Oh, no, it's for a... friend.'

'Well, tell your... friend, she's missed her moment. Nicotiana flowers in summer. There hasn't been any around for ages.'

Beth's face fell and Mrs Hill chuckled. 'Well, must get on.'

Mrs Hill walked quickly away, leaving Beth's bright idea in tatters. Harriet French, allotment owner, part-time lover of Len and potential poisoner with nicotiana, was now off the hook – like all the rest of them.

By the time she had got herself together and made it to Jane's, Julie-Ann was already sitting in the café with two cappuccinos and two huge cupcakes, which did a lot to cheer Beth up. She slid a plate and mug across to Beth. The girl really was very pretty, Beth thought. Josh might be a scamp, but he had good taste.

Julie-Ann raised her limpid eyes to Beth's. 'So, it's great to get together. Your mum is such a hoot.'

'Isn't she just?' said Beth, while inwardly reeling at the word. With her daughter, Wendy was less of a hoot, more of a boot. And her neighbour apparently thought Beth ought to poison her. But she wasn't going to get into all that. 'Any news?'

'On what?' said Julie-Ann. 'On Joshy? No, he's so busy with work, he scarcely has time to ring,' she said, a shadow of sadness dimming her loveliness for a moment. 'But he's texting lots.'

'Not Josh,' said Beth quickly. Too-busy-to-ring didn't sound like a good sign, if she knew anything about her brother and his affairs. But the last thing she needed was for the girl to start getting morose. 'I was thinking more about anything the SOCO team might have told you? Or possible suspects... you know, Mum's theory about Len having been murdered.' She hissed the last few words, leaning across the table, though by now there could hardly be a soul in Dulwich who wasn't privy to Wendy's darkest suspicions.

'Well, your mum is quite down on Margery Brinkwell, but I suppose that's only to be expected,' Julie-Ann said, stirring her cup thoughtfully. 'I mean, she's the wife.'

'Yes,' said Beth with a shrug. 'Unfortunately. Or maybe I mean fortunately. If it wasn't for her, maybe Mum would actually have married the guy herself. And then she'd be in the frame.'

'Hmm,' said Julie-Ann, her eyes round and slightly unfocused.

'Anything else Mum is banging on about... er, I mean, that she particularly has on her mind?'

'Well, she's been getting together a bit with a few of the others, you know, the Len's Ladies group...'

'Hang on, what?'

'Oh, that's what they've named themselves. They're sort of

like a club. I mean, not the hoity-toity ones, like Margery Brinkwell or even that headmistress lady...'

'Angela Douglas?'

'Mmm, not her. But some of the others, like Harriet French. She grows flowers to die for, your mum says. But she always tells the most amazing stories. Like that she saw a UFO land in the village one time, and there are zombies in the little graveyard in the high street.'

OK, thought Beth. It looked like Margery Brinkwell hadn't been far off the mark about Harriet French, though she sounded less like a habitual liar and more like a sad case who was a bulb or two short of the full display. 'Who are the rest?' Beth asked.

'Oh, the ones who were at the Bridge classes or the choir that night.'

'I see. All the ones with alibis, then. The ones we don't really need to worry about.' Beth couldn't keep the disappointment from her voice. She'd thought for a second that this unholy alliance of exes might have been a way of getting a little further with the investigation. But, like everything else at the moment, it seemed to be a dead-end. Though it sounded as though she could now rule Harriet French out, at least. She only hoped the woman's tales of polyamory were as far-fetched as the talk of zombies.

'Yeah, they're very chatty, the ladies. They were round last night. Funny how they all get on so well.'

'Well, I suppose they do all have that special something in common.'

Julie-Ann looked blank.

'*Len*,' Beth clarified, mentally slapping her forehead.

'Oh yeah. And of course they're all pretty stunned about Len's baby.'

Beth, who'd been about to take a sip of her coffee, nearly choked. 'His what?'

THIRTY-SEVEN

Beth sat across the table from Julie-Ann, her eyes streaming as she tried to swallow. Julie-Ann just looked on in mild surprise. Finally, Beth choked the words out. 'What... what did you just say?'

'Yeah, Len Broughton's love-child or whatever. I suppose he's not a baby any more. Didn't Wendy mention it?'

Beth was silent for a beat. Wendy had not mentioned it, for the very good reason that, over the last few days, Beth had been allowing Julie-Ann to absorb her mother's demands, so she'd slackened off on the phone calls. Now she felt remiss. Very, very remiss.

'She didn't say a word to me,' said Beth, not clarifying that was because they had hardly spoken – although Julie-Ann probably knew that as they were in the same house. 'Tell me about it.'

'Well, it started off just as a bit of a rumour, but then a couple of the ladies did spot Len, ages ago you know, with a pram or whatever. And it turns out he did say something to Wendy about it. Just really vague, you know.'

'What on earth did he say?'

'Oh, something like he had a kid but the mother didn't want him to acknowledge it...'

'Typical! Absentee father, not contributing to the child's life.'

'Oh, but it wasn't like that. Not according to what he said to Wendy. She was telling me about it last night. The mum didn't want him around, refused to let him have anything to do with it.'

'Really?' said Beth, wondering why on earth her mother hadn't told her any of this. But Wendy already thought Beth disapproved of Len. She must have decided news of this child would just have made things worse.

'Wendy reckoned he was a real gent, not forcing her to have an abortion in the first place,' Julie-Ann went on.

'What a prince,' said Beth.

Julie-Ann nodded, the irony apparently flying right over her head. 'Your mum said it must have been hell for him, having to watch his kid grow up, with no involvement at all.'

This time, Beth just tutted. It looked as though Julie-Ann, living with Wendy for all of a couple of days, had definitely drunk the Kool-Aid and now Len was a paragon of virtue. 'Any idea who this woman was?'

'The mother? No. I mean, Wendy was keen to piece it together... but one of the others in the group was really trying to make everyone drop it. She kept on saying something really odd.'

'Odd? What do you mean?' Beth leant forward again. This was getting interesting. But just then, she heard a dry cough behind her shoulder. She wheeled round, only to see Belinda McKenzie standing right behind her. How much had the woman heard, she wondered.

'Beth. Your brother in town again yet? I've left messages on the number you gave me but he's not got back to me.' Belinda's tone was clipped. Given that Beth had last seen her and her daughter getting a thorough dressing-down at the disco, it must have taken a bit of courage for Belinda to approach them. Either that, or she wanted to get in touch with Josh at any price.

'Er, no, he's still, erm, on an assignment. Julie-Ann, you might know when he'll be back, though?'

'Oh, he's moving around so much, Afghanistan, you know, Ukraine I think.' Once again, the girl's eyes went cloudy with the strain of remembering. 'But we've got a definite date to talk tonight. Can't wait to chat to my hon. Anything you want me to pass on to Joshy?' Julie-Ann was radiant at the very thought, and apparently oblivious to any threat that the beautiful and predatory Belinda might pose.

'Oh no,' said Belinda, with a terrifyingly wide smile. 'Just give him my love. Well, I gave him quite a lot of it myself last time we, er, met... but there's always plenty more, just for him,' she said, her voice dripping with unmistakable meaning.

It seemed totally wasted on Julie-Ann. 'Lovely. I'll certainly let him know. It's so nice when really, really old friends keep in touch, isn't it? I bet you know him from school. Wait a minute, he said he had a really lovely kind Religious Education teacher, I bet that's you, isn't it?'

Belinda goggled in silence at Julie-Ann for a second, colour sweeping her face, then with a sort of infuriated squawk she turned on her heel and pranced out of the café. Beth swung back to look at Julie-Ann, who was taking the daintiest sip from her cup. 'She's in a bit of a hurry. Takes all sorts, doesn't it?' The girl shrugged. And then, as Beth watched, one of those large limpid eyes closed in just the suggestion of a wink.

'Julie-Ann! You're full of surprises,' said Beth with dawning respect. It took a lot to get the better of Belinda McKenzie. As Beth knew only too well. She'd been trying for years and never managed it. Julie-Ann was clearly a ninja-level practitioner of dark arts Beth could only dream of.

'Never mind all that,' Julie-Ann said modestly. 'What were we talking about before we were so rudely interrupted?'

'Oh yes,' said Beth. 'It was about Len's love-child... What on earth was it...? Ah, that's right. It was about one of the women in the group. You said she kept saying something odd?'

'That's right. Yep, it was really strange. The others were asking who the mother could be, was it right to keep the child from his father, didn't he have a right to know, and all that. And also shouldn't Len stump up something for the upkeep, even if the mother had said not to. Then this lady just came right out and said it and we all just looked at each other.'

Beth wrinkled her forehead under her plentiful fringe. 'Well? What did she say?'

'She said... "Let sleeping lions lie."'

THIRTY-EIGHT

Beth wandered out of the café, and spent a good ten minutes deep in thought outside Tomlinson's. Anyone passing might have thought she was gawping at the gorgeous display; little glass bud vases in jewel colours, an artful throw that Magpie would have loved kneading into shape with her sharp claws, a row of sachets of pot pourri, labelled *Jardins Francais*, tied with gorgeous velvet ribbons... it was all seriously tempting. But it was going in one eye and out the other. Beth was in a daze.

And she spent the rest of the day in the same trance, after Julie-Ann's curveball in the café. Any nuggets the SOCO team might have confided were completely forgotten, while Beth mulled over the phrase 'let sleeping lions lie' obsessively.

On the plus side, it meant all the filing got done in the archive office, while she was on autopilot. She even attempted to work on her much-delayed definitive biography of disgraced swashbuckler Sir Thomas Wyatt. But this was a bit too ambitious, in the circumstances, and it wasn't until she heard the school bell ring for the end of the day that Beth realised she'd been sitting, near-paralysed, for several hours, with the ledgers from the blood-soaked Wyatt plantations open in front of her.

Normally they were shocking enough to give her nightmares, but today she couldn't recall a single word she'd read.

It felt disrespectful to the people who had lived such awful, brutal lives because of Wyatt, not to give their stories her full attention. She slammed the ledgers shut, grabbed her bag, locked the door, and then stopped dead again.

What on earth was she going to do?

That phrase, 'Let sleeping lions lie,' echoed round her head continuously. There was only one person she knew, in the whole world, who would ever have uttered those words. And linking her to the matter of Len Broughton's secret love-child had thrown up some ideas that Beth just frankly could not get her head around.

Or was it that she didn't want to? She'd had enough trouble picturing a relationship between Len and this person in the first place. And now, it was even more disturbing to think that there was a permanent reminder of the affair walking the earth. Even if that reminder was in the shape of one of the sweetest children Beth knew.

Beth forced her feet to move, she said a mechanical goodbye to the porter, she walked out of the imposing Wyatt's gates, and she was just about to trudge home, when someone hailed her. Someone with a voice as loud as a foghorn, and an uncanny ability to cut through all the turmoil in Beth's head.

'What... what are you doing here?' Beth mumbled.

'Waiting for you, innit? Got time for a quick one?' said Nina.

Normally these words were music to Beth's ears. Not today. 'Erm, well, Jake will be home, I should really... I mean, maybe tomorrow? Or the next day?'

'So you've heard, then,' said Nina flatly. Even her curls seemed to have lost their bounce today, and her eyes were downcast.

'What's up, Nina?' Beth said.

'Come off it, babes. Who do you think you're pooling? This is me, innit. I know you know.'

'What do you know I know?' said Beth, playing for time.

'I know you... Oh, let's not do this. Fine, if you don't want to talk about it. But don't pretend you haven't heard. I bet it's all over town, even though I told those biddies to drop it.' Nina turned to go, and instantly Beth was full of remorse. She put out a hand and grabbed Nina's soft coat.

'No, come on, I'm sorry. I'm just having trouble thinking it all through. Wilf... and Len Broughton. I found it hard enough to believe that you were one of Len's Ladies in the first place. And now this. You never breathed a word to me about having Len's *baby*. I feel a bit – well, taken aback. And also, have you thought, if things were different, if my mother had had a child too...'

Here, Nina snorted, sounding much more like her usual self.

'OK, but you know what I mean. Wilf and I could have been related...'

'Nah, mate. You're definitely overthinking it all there. I've said to you before. It was a mistake, that whole thing with Len. But Wilf's the best thing that's ever happened to me, you know that. He's the bees' squeeze, as far as I'm concerned. But Len, nah. I didn't want him in my life. It was a one-off. Well, a few one-offs... and then Wilf came along. I wanted to keep it on the download, because I knew everyone would be judging me.'

'I'm not judging...' Beth started, but Nina gave her an old-fashioned look. 'All right. Maybe a bit. But you've got to admit, it's a bit close for comfort. With Mum and all.'

Nina shuddered. 'That was Len all over. Honestly, he was like one of them hamsters on heat.'

'Dogs,' Beth corrected absently.

'Whatevs!' said Nina, flicking the thought away. 'Wendy was welcome to him. And the rest of 'em, too.'

'No wonder someone bumped him off,' said Beth. 'God. You realise...'

'That this puts me right in the frame? Yeah. I got it. That was another reason why I was staying silent as the gravy.'

Almost without being aware of it, their feet had automatically led them to Mariella's. 'How about it, then?' Nina cocked her head.

'Yes. Of course,' said Beth. 'You grab a table, I'll get the coffees.'

As Beth queued, she looked over at her friend. Nina was sitting, hunched, still in her coat, even though the café was warm. She looked like a dejected little bird, perching on a telegraph wire on a very cold day. Poor Nina. What she must have gone through.

When she turned back, she saw that behind her in the queue was Bernie Troughton, who must have sneaked out of the College School for a quick snack. Sure enough, her plate was loaded with carbs. It was now or never, Beth decided.

'Erm, Bernie...'

'Christ, Beth! You do get around, don't you? First the disco, now this café,' said the woman, her brick-red face taking on an even ruddier hue.

'Sorry. It's just about, well, to put it bluntly, the night Len Broughton died.'

'That dratted man!' Bernie Troughton said, shaking her head.

'My thoughts exactly,' said Beth. 'I'm asking everyone... as you know, my mother—'

'Ah yes. She was one of the throng, wasn't she? Well, Angela is out of the frame. No doubts about that,' said the woman heavily. 'She was home the whole time.'

'How do you know? Um, if I could just ask?' Beth said timidly.

'I was there too, obviously.' Miss Troughton suddenly put her plate down with a bang.

'Oh, are you not going to...?' Beth asked.

'Suddenly lost my appetite,' she replied tersely, stomping off.

Beth barely had time to feel guilty before she got served and then made her way to where Nina was sitting. As she passed her friend's coffee over, Beth had a thought. 'You know, you could probably contest Len's will. Get something for Wilf.'

To her surprise, Nina guffawed. 'You gotta be kidding, babes. There won't be a scrap left for us. Not when Margery Brinkwell's had her way. And if your mother's got any hopes in that department, you'd better tell her to think again. No, my main worry at the moment is whether or not your boyfriend's going to arrest me.'

'Harry? Why would he do that?' Beth's eyebrows shot up.

'He's had me down at the station twice. Hasn't he said?'

Beth sat back in shock. 'Not a word! If he had, I would have rung you, I promise. And you didn't say anything to me, either. What's he been asking you?'

Nina grimaced. 'Turns out, the final call Bella Harrington got that night was from me... you know, when she got bummed off like that.'

Beth blinked. Nina's colourful way with words still had the power to surprise her on occasion, though usually she was able to translate everything fairly well these days. 'Oh, killed, yes. I see.' Then the rest of Nina's sentence struck her. 'Wait a minute, you rang Bella? What about?'

'That's the thing. I lost my phone that night. The call wasn't from me. Then whoever pinched it left it on my doorstep. It was there when Wilf and I went out the next morning.'

'Someone stole it? But don't you have a passcode on it?'

'Nah, mate. Wilf kept getting it wrong when he was gaming

on it, getting me locked out. He's not having his own phone till he's at secondary. So a code's more treble than it was worth.'

'Do you have any idea who took it?'

'Nope. Not a glue,' Nina said with a frown. 'I was at a meeting of Len's Ladies that night, though. Any one of 'em could have grabbed it. But because of that, and because I've only got Wilf as an alibi for when Len died – we were alone in the flat and Wilfy was tucked up in bed – Harry seems to reckon I did it.'

'I'm sure he doesn't,' said Beth bracingly, her mind teeming with schemes to get Harry to talk to her about all this – and to make him see sense. Nina couldn't possibly have done it. Could she? 'I can see why loads of people wanted to kill Len, but why would you have wanted to get rid of Bella?'

'Harry thinks it's because she was about to let the bat out of the bag about Wilfy. And he says maybe she was trying to blackmail me, getting me to pay her to keep it shut.'

THIRTY-NINE

Oh dear, thought Beth. That was actually a really good motive. But of course she couldn't come out and say that. 'Blackmail! He's always telling me off for suggesting that,' she said robustly. Then she realised that wasn't the main point here. 'I mean, you didn't want anyone to know about Wilf, that much is true.'

'Whose side are you on, babe? Would you want people to know Len was your Jake's dad?'

'Definitely not. I mean, he isn't... but I see what you mean. Blackmail, though... Are there any sums that have gone out of your account that would match up with that? I know the police look through bank statements for things like that.'

Nina suddenly looked close to tears. 'Why don't you just come out and say it? It's obvious you think Harry's got me bang to bikes.'

Beth shook her head. 'I really don't think that... at all. I know you're innocent. You wouldn't harm a fly, let alone kill two people. It's ridiculous, and I'll tell Harry that. But if there's any suspicious activity in your bank account, you should tell me so I can explain it to him.'

Nina looked at the table, and started drawing little circles with her spoon in a pool of spilt coffee. 'Thing is, now you mention it...'

Beth had a sinking feeling at the pit of her stomach. What on earth was going to come out now? What had Nina been up to?

'Well, last couple of jobs I've been doing. I've got them to pay me cash in hand, off the books, you know. That way there's a bit less to bother the Revenue. Everybody does it.'

'Do they?' Beth said. She certainly didn't. But there wasn't much opportunity for such jiggery-pokery, working for an old-established institution like Wyatt's School.

'It's coming up to Christmas pretty soon, and I could do with the extra,' Nina said, eyes wide.

Beth sighed. It wasn't a terrible crime. It wasn't double murder, for instance. But it was illegal. No wonder Nina hadn't wanted to bother Harry with the information. 'But you being paid in cash wouldn't show on your bank account, would it? They'll be looking for large sums leaving the account, as though you were paying Bella off.'

Now Nina blushed a fiery red – the first time Beth had seen this phenomenon. Her face clashed badly with her curls and she looked incredibly uncomfortable. 'Thing is, I did make a couple of big cash withdrawals as well. My cousin Katrina – you've met her – is, um, planning a bit of an escape fund. Got a violent ex. Or someone who ought to be an ex, if you know what I mean. I was passing it to her, but she's not going to stand up in court and say that, she can't let him find out.'

'That's really kind of you, Nina. But it couldn't have been worse timing. You will have to say something to Harry. Or maybe I can explain? He just needs to clear the point up, there's no question of court or anything.'

'Yeah,' said Nina, head down. 'Well, at least it gets me off the book.'

It certainly explained the money aspect, Beth thought. But

privately, she wondered. There was still the issue of the call to Bella on the night she died, and Nina's story about mislaying her phone and then finding it outside her front door sounded thin. Then there was her lack of an alibi, apart from Wilf, on the night Len had died. It would have been easy for her to slip out of her Herne Hill flat and hop on a night bus up to the council offices. Len would have let her in, as there was unfinished business between them. And then who knows what might have happened?

Beth stopped herself there. Nothing had happened, and that was what she was going to tell Harry. The whole thing was preposterous. Nina, adorable little Nina, was not a murderer, and that was all there was to it.

'Look, don't worry. I'll get Harry to see reason. In the meantime, just keep your mind off it all as best you can. If you hear anything else about Len from those, um, biddies, that you think would be useful, pass it on to me, but otherwise just concentrate on other things. How's the nativity play going, for instance?' Beth asked gently.

It was the right change of topic. The Christmas show at the Village Primary was always a hot ticket, though the performances were lukewarm at best. Jake had spent his career at the school being an also-ran ruminant right at the back of the stage, before a surprising promotion to a reindeer at the end of his stint there. Even then, he hadn't been Rudolph, of course, though his nose had been daubed with lipstick by a yummy mummy helping out backstage and he'd had to glow his way through all Wendy's festive photos as a result of the fact that peach shimmer proved completely indelible.

A smile spread across Nina's face at last. 'Wilf's being a Wise Nan, I'm really pleased, though I was secretly holding out for him to be the Angel of the Law. But maybe next year.'

'Oh I'm sure he'll get it then. That's if he doesn't get Joseph.'

'Oh no, that's going to girls now. It's Elsie Becksmith this year. Mary is being played by Wilf's mate Rex. And they've stopped having a doll as the baby Jesus. This year it's a pillow, as that's gender neutral, and depending on how that goes down, it might be a fruit or a vegetable next time.'

Beth couldn't help giggling. Although if it somehow made children keener to eat their five a day, maybe it was a good thing. At Wyatt's, the school favoured a simple no-frills carol concert, with all the old favourites. The candlelit procession into the Great Hall last year, with a Year 7 boy (obviously not Jake) doing a solo of 'Away in a Manger', had been spine-tinglingly beautiful. And the grand finale had been a rendition of 'Hark the Herald Angels Sing' that had raised the rafters of the ancient building.

'I wonder what kind of fruit or veg they might go for?' said Beth, keen to keep this line of distraction going. Nina was cheering up by the second.

'I'm thinking a giant mango might be good.'

'Or maybe a marrow? They could at least draw a face on it...'

Such musings occupied them happily until every speck of cappuccino was gone, and Beth reluctantly shouldered her bag. 'Listen, I'd better be off. But tell me if, um, you hear anything, won't you?'

'Yeah. And I'll be on the blower if your geezer arrests me,' said Nina succinctly.

They parted with a hug, and Beth started wandering back to Pickwick Road. She'd only got as far as the SOCO tent by the LTN flowerbeds when she saw a familiar figure. For a second, she wondered if she could just saunter past and pretend she hadn't recognised him, but then she realised that would be too rude. Especially as he'd seen her and was smiling widely at her.

'Chris! I'm surprised you're still here,' she said.

Chris Campbell performed his usual strange bow, his blue eyes raking her slight figure. 'Beth, how goes it?'

'Ugh. You don't want to know. Any progress?' she asked, gesturing at the tent.

'Just finishing up. Interesting case.'

'Oh really?' she said, perking up. 'Do you know anything about nicotine poisoning, by any chance?'

'Nicotine poisoning? Any particular reason why you would ask that?' His eyes were now blue slits, boring into her.

Beth tried to be offhand. 'Oh, just someone said something about a plant, nicotiana...'

'Ah yes. But of course it's much easier to kill someone with a cigarette than with a plant.'

'What, by waiting for them to die of cancer?' Beth attempted a joke.

'A bit hit and miss. But take fifty to sixty milligrams of nicotine and it's job done, depending on the weight of the individual,' he said. The dry delivery reminded Beth of his years of clinical training.

'Is that the sort of thing they teach you at medical school? Or did you pick it up later, when you were working in hospitals?'

'Well, they teach you how to recognise the symptoms, rather than how to create the poison, when you're a junior doctor. But making a simple nicotine reduction at home would do the job pretty well.'

'Oh, I'm such a bad cook, I wouldn't have a clue what to do,' Beth said quickly.

'Nonsense, your coffee is delicious,' said Campbell with fervour. 'And anyone could do this. Packet of twenty, dash of water. Boil it down nicely. That's all you'd need. And if you ate just one Benson & Hedges raw, as it were, that would kill someone as, ahem, petite as you, too.'

Campbell now had the pleased smile of a conjuror whose trick has come off well, but Beth's face betrayed only shock. She mumbled a farewell to the pathologist. If she'd turned round, she would have seen him standing staring after her, looking bereft. But she was just focused on getting home and working out how on earth this information fitted into what she already knew. She passed Tomlinson's on her way, and turned, despite herself. There was something about the place that was calling to her... unusual, as she normally had a fairly powerful allergy to unnecessary spending. She shook her head, but remained deep in thought all the way to Pickwick Road. In fact, she didn't even realise she had a visitor until she was almost at her front door.

'Katie! How lovely. Are you going to come in for a cuppa?' she said, almost automatically, while wondering how long her friend might stay and when she could get on with wrestling with these elusive ideas flitting through her brain.

Then Katie turned to face Beth – and Beth was horrified to see her face was blotched with tears. She ran forward the last few steps and for the second time that day was hugging a friend in need.

'I'm probably just being ridiculous...' Katie said, as Beth fumbled with her keys and got the door open, ushering her friend in and hoping against hope that the kitchen was reasonably tidy. Despite her OCD tendencies Beth was constantly in fear of being caught out in some sort of mess, perhaps a hangover from the days in her childhood home when she'd done Wendy's cleaning for pocket money, and then had to face a critique every time on her multiple failures, most notably not cleaning above the door lintels and on top of the light fittings (hard when you are a not-very-tall child destined to grow into a short adult, or 'petite' as Chris had just coyly put it). She had dreaded Wendy's finger coming away from some surface or other with dust still on it.

She pattered into the kitchen first, saw that the place was gleaming, and relaxed. 'Let me take your coat. Sit down, and I'll pop the kettle on. Tell me all about it, Katie.'

'Oh, it's so silly really,' Katie said, sniffing into a tissue. 'I'm overthinking things. Michael says I do that a lot.'

'I've never known you to overthink,' Beth said stoutly. 'Or underthink, either. I'd say you do just the right amount of thinking.' The kettle clicked off and she sloshed the water into two mugs, and passed one to Katie, then got out a packet of chocolate digestives which had miraculously survived Jake and Harry. 'Start from the beginning.'

'Oh, I suppose it was discussing the disco that started it. In a way, I was disappointed that Michael didn't make time to come too.'

'It wasn't a parents' event, though, Katie. I mean, we went because we had to, didn't we? The others there were all part of the PTA or whatever. And Charlie probably wouldn't have wanted his dad watching him all night too.'

Katie sighed. 'I mean, you're probably right, Beth. But I just thought it would be nice... we're not doing much as a family at the moment.'

Beth thought for a minute. She was the world's worst outing planner, and she, Jake and Harry really didn't do a lot as a unit – except co-exist in reasonable peace and harmony, which she supposed was a big thing. But Katie was great at this 'making memories' stuff. 'What about when you go down to Cornwall?' Katie had a stunning and very bijou cottage tucked away in a particularly scenic part of the county. It was tiny, so surely they got plenty of quality time squashed together there?

'We've hardly used it recently. In fact, Michael has even started saying we should get rid of it... you know, cost of living stuff and whatever.'

Beth's eyebrows rose. This would be a blow for Katie, who had spent endless hours sourcing exactly the right shade of seagrass stair carpeting to set off the original bare stone floors of the fisherman's cottage. And also, if the mega-wealthy Michael was having to retrench, what hope was there for the rest of Dulwich?

'Well, you do have a say, Katie. If you don't want to get rid of it, put your foot down.'

Katie chomped thoughtfully on a digestive. In itself, this was surprising as she usually shunned everything except brownies as toxins. Brownies were, apparently, the exception that proved the rule. She nodded slowly, as though the idea had never occurred to her. Then she shrugged. 'I just need to think about other things. Anything new on our investigation?'

Now Beth felt awkward. She didn't want to reveal too much about Nina's shocking position as prime suspect. Katie wasn't a gossip, but she was on great terms with everyone in Dulwich and it wouldn't be long before one of her many friends mentioned something in passing... Beth would explain things then, but she wanted to try to talk to Harry about the whole thing first.

'I'm not sure I've really got a lot further on...'

'I did have a bit of a breakthrough,' Katie said, butting in and cheering up a bit. 'I saw that woman from the building firm – you know, oh gosh, I can't remember her name now... the matriarch with the high heels...'

Beth thought for a moment, then she had a eureka moment.

FORTY

'You must mean Aggie Price?' said Beth. Aggie was the head of one of the two rival clans of builders, the Rutlands and the Prices, that had accidentally fitted the good folk of Dulwich with wonky conservatories for decades, while they fought amongst themselves. 'That's brilliant, Katie. Where on earth did you spot her?'

'Don't tell anyone, but I think she came to give Belinda a quote on fixing her shoffice. She was right outside her place in a van as I was walking past with Teddy. She said what a handsome dog he is,' Katie added proudly.

It was true, thought Beth darkly. He was handsome and, like many attractive males, he knew it and milked it endlessly to his advantage. 'So did you ask Aggie about Len? How on earth did you get the conversation round to that?'

'I just came right out and said it must be a big loss to the building industry round here, having a council leader like Len out of the picture. She said yes, and what a shock they'd got when they'd heard – both the families had been at a builders' convention north of the river that day and got into a fight at closing time at a pub near Kentish Town.'

'Sounds absolutely typical of that lot – and of course it does give all of them a perfect alibi. Were there any arrests?'

'I decided not to get into it too much, I just nodded as though that was always happening to me as well on nights out.'

'Well done, anyway, Katie, that's amazing – we can cross both those tribes off our list, then. That's definitely progress.'

'I wish we could eliminate all the cheated-on husbands and boyfriends that must have had an axe to grind with Len as well.'

'I do, too. Some of them are already out of the frame – the ones accompanying the women at the Bridge sessions and the men in the choir, for instance. As for the rest of them, the more I think about it, the more these don't seem like crimes by angry men. I mean, if a bloke was angry with Len, wouldn't he go and punch him on the nose? And why kill Bella Harrington?'

'I see what you mean. Yes, it doesn't sound very masculine, I suppose. What does Harry think? How's he getting on? Do you have any sense of where he's got to?'

'No. It's the same old story, really, Katie. I know he has an obligation to keep things confidential... but it would definitely help if he didn't,' said Beth, knowing that she was going to have to raise the issue of Nina with Harry at her first opportunity and feeling a bit queasy about it. Not only was she keeping it from Katie, her partner in the investigation, but also she wasn't sure how far she could reasonably get with Harry. And Nina was putting so much faith in her. *No pressure, then, Beth.*

But, when she looked across at Katie, she could see her friend was uncomfortable too. Not because of the Michael thing – that seemed to have gone away for the moment – but, if Beth wasn't mistaken, Katie had something else on her mind.

'Um. What's bothering you?' Beth asked gently.

Katie looked up sheepishly. 'I just wondered if Jake had been asking you for new trainers, fancy brands, anything like that...'

'Well, he did for the disco. And I messed up by not getting

the jeans, then trying to give him the sweatshirt instead. Thank heavens Josh came up trumps with those New York strides which really hit the spot.'

'But since then?'

'I think there was a T-shirt he was after... And actually yes, some expensive trainers, but I said a flat no to those. I suppose I might get him the T-shirt for Christmas. I've done nothing about it, though. Why?'

'Well, it's the kind of thing you get interested in, erm, when you want to impress someone, isn't it?'

'I suppose so.' Beth thought. Luckily for her, James had always seemed to tolerate her ratty jumpers, and indeed had worn similarly tired-out sweaters of his own. Harry was pretty much immune to fashion too, thank goodness. 'Are you saying that's what Jake's doing? God, is this about Allegra McKenzie? I was hoping that would fizzle out.'

Now Katie was definitely looking flustered. On the plus side, Michael now seemed a million miles from her thoughts. But Beth was actively worried about what was coming next.

'Spit it out, Katie. What on earth is going on?'

'I've been wondering whether to say anything,' said Katie, squirming in her seat. 'And in the end, I just thought to myself, would I want to know if it was Charlie? And the answer was a big yes.'

Beth thought quickly. In her view, Katie was too focused on wanting to know every single thing about her adored only son. Beth was generally happy just getting an overview. But then she considered the machinations of the awful Gregory King. If she'd been a bit more on the case, she could have seen that coming and headed it off.

'OK then. So you know something about Jake that you think you ought to share, but you're not sure about telling?' Beth said.

'Um, yes,' Katie mumbled. 'It might be a case of don't shoot the messenger, though. You might be quite angry with me for knowing before you.'

'I don't think so, Katie. If it's to do with Jake, and you really think I ought to know, then I'd say go for it. I might be upset or cross or whatever, but not with you.'

'OK then,' said Katie, taking a deep breath. 'The thing is, Jake wrote a poem to Allegra McKenzie and posted it to her, and now she's put a screenshot of it on her TikTok. And I'm afraid everyone's... well, they're laughing a bit.'

Beth sat back, reeling. Though she had just promised not to, her first instinct was to do some shouting and Katie was the only person within convenient yelling distance. She put a hand to her suddenly thumping chest and tried to steady herself. There were so many elements to this.

Jake, writing poetry? What the hell was that about? He had been shirking all academic input that wasn't strictly compulsory for his entire school career. And now he was sitting about writing odes to Allegra McKenzie's left eyebrow? A whole string of expletives rose to her lips, but she bit them down. And then the girl, putting poor Jake's outpourings onto her social media? The sheer cruelty of that smote her like a body blow. She'd been willing to give the girl the benefit of the doubt but now the verdict was in. Allegra McKenzie was every bit as horrible as her mother.

Poor, poor Jake. First love was no fun, even if it was reciprocated – there was so much to learn and negotiate, so many possibilities for misunderstandings and mistakes. And, if you picked the wrong person, as Jake had, then the potential for total humiliation was huge.

'Oh my God,' said Beth quietly. 'I thought he was a little out of sorts... but this is just ghastly. That girl! Do you think her mother put her up to it?'

'I wish we could give her that excuse,' said Katie in matter-of-fact tones. 'I think the truth is that she's just... not very nice.'

In Katie's lexicon, this was as harsh as saying Allegra was a dyed-in-the-wool witch, an opinion that Beth was now heartily signing up to.

'Poor Jake. He hasn't said a word,' said Beth. But now that she thought about it, had he been stomping around in a more miserable, gloomy way than usual? The trouble was, it was very hard to tell when a teenager – or almost-teenager – was depressed. All the slouching, sighing, moaning and groaning were already priced into the package. He was probably listening to really miserable music on his AirPods, but she had no way of knowing.

For the first time, it struck her how dangerously isolating devices were for troubled adolescents. They were now locked into their sorrow in a way she would only have been able to dream of at Jake's age. Her stilted and awkward first conversations with boys (few and far between, to be honest) had all taken place on the landline phone in the draughty hall, right next to the kitchen where her mother was transparently listening in. Any letters from lads to the house were scrutinised with all the energy of a prisoner's correspondence passing the censor. And the few meetings she'd had were surveyed by her big brother. At the time, it had all felt very irksome – and was probably the reason why she gave Jake a bit more privacy – but now she saw it was a safety net.

'I should have been there for him more. I should have noticed how upset he's been. Trouble is he's always a bit moody these days. I just put it down to the disco, or the homework, or his age, whatever. I had no idea anything like this had happened. Thanks for telling me, Katie.' After the white-hot anger, she now felt tearful. She smiled a little tremulously at her friend. 'Now I just have to decide what to do about it.'

'To be honest, Beth, I think you should just let Jake get on with it. He might assume you already know.'

'You don't think I should discuss it with him?'

'Well, if you can bear it. But it's probably more important just to be there for him.'

But what did 'being there' mean? Beth was always there. How could she be *more* 'there', and show him she was? It was a conundrum that kept her mulling from the time Katie left to the moment Jake let himself in with his key.

As soon as she heard the familiar sound, she did her best to assemble a cheery carefree smile, which she beamed right at him as he ambled into the kitchen. He stopped dead, took one look at her, and said, 'Someone's told you, haven't they?'

She dropped the grin instantly and rushed to her feet and gave her beloved boy a big hug. It was like trying to embrace an unwieldy parcel, as he stood awkwardly, his huge backpack still weighing him down, but even though he didn't exactly reciprocate, after a few seconds she felt the slightest unbending in his posture. He might be too old, now – and too sad – to hug her back, but she knew her love and sympathy were being transmitted somehow into his trampled heart, and hopefully giving him a little bit of comfort.

'Don't say anything, though, will you, Mum? I don't want to talk about it.' Jake's voice was muffled as he bent to speak into her shoulder.

'Of course not. Not if you don't want to. I completely understand. But I just wanted to say... I am here, if you need me,' said Beth, patting his back reassuringly. And then she couldn't help herself. 'As for Allegra, she's a complete...'

Jake pulled away. 'Yeah, that's what I didn't want to get into,' he said, with a crooked smile that was an inch from tears. He filched an apple from the bowl on the table and then shambled up the stairs to his room.

Beth sat back down and sighed. That girl! *That family*. They really were beyond the pale. Beth wasn't a fan of murder, but suddenly a good old-fashioned mob-style machine-gunning was seeming like a great option. She was quite relieved when her phone shrilled into her thoughts.

'Beth? Hi, it's Julie-Ann.'

Aha. Julie-Ann, Josh's girlfriend, who was turning out to be not so much of a mouse after all. With an effort, Beth put aside Jake's cares and focused on the call. 'How's it going? I never got the update from you after your chat with the SOCO team in the village. Anything to report?'

'You won't believe it when you hear this,' the girl said.

FORTY-ONE

Beth had no hesitation in summoning Julie-Ann to the house. It would make it less awkward for Jake (and Beth) if she was there for supper, and it was as good a place as any for a proper debriefing.

Once Beth had done the honours with the cups of tea, and set a pan of water to boil for yet more pasta, she settled down to hear the full story.

'Well, I was quite nervous at first, I wasn't sure if they'd talk to me at all,' said Julie-Ann, brushing a tendril of hair off her face.

'Yes, why on earth would bored police officers doing quite a dull job want to talk to an extremely pretty girl?' said Beth.

'Exactly.' Julie-Ann gripped her mug earnestly with both hands. 'But they were really friendly. At first they didn't really tell me anything but, after a while, they sort of forgot I was there and just started discussing the case.'

'Excellent,' said Beth, getting up, finding four dinner plates and arranging them round the table. Harry might not be back in time to eat – but there was always hope. 'So what did you hear?'

'Well, you know everyone is saying the poor lady was strangled?'

Beth nodded absently. There were only three sets of cutlery in the drawer; she'd have to wash up a fourth.

'She wasn't.'

Beth dropped the knives and forks with a clang. 'What?'

'No,' Julie-Ann said, with a shy pleasure at being in the know for a change. 'She was actually poisoned.'

'Really? You're kidding,' said Beth, wondering why Chris Campbell hadn't said a word to her. But it was that confidentiality business again, she supposed. Although he had spent a lot of time telling her about boiling up nicotine... 'And... do you know what the poison was?' She held her breath.

'They were going to send lots of samples away for testing. I was quite glad they'd removed the, erm, er...'

'The body, you mean?'

'Yes, exactly. So they were really just doing a fingertip search and photographing any finds when I was there, there was nothing, you know, horrible. But they said there was no sign of bruising on her neck, no ligature, no really obvious cause of death. It looked like a heart attack. She was pretty old, maybe in her thirties even, but they thought she still looked quite healthy considering, apart from being dead. So they thought the attack might have been brought on by a toxin. That means poison, right?'

Beth nodded absently, digesting the news of Bella Harrington's apparent great age. She compared it with her own tally of thirty-whatsit years, and wondered exactly how old Julie-Ann was. Too young for Josh, that was now for sure.

'So it was some sort of poison,' she said, slowly and thoughtfully. 'A poison causing a heart attack. I wonder how that story about strangulation got out? It was Nina who told me that initially...'

Julie-Ann shrugged. 'This does seem like quite a gossipy place,' she said.

Beth laughed. That was the understatement of the year. Just then, she heard the rattle of a key in the lock. 'Oh, it's Harry,' she said with a beaming smile.

* * *

It was lovely to sit round the table together in uncomplicated harmony, thought Beth, smiling fondly over her wine glass at Jake, now much more relaxed. Harry was chatting kindly to Julie-Ann, and Julie-Ann herself had blossomed from the silent, shy girl Josh had left on her hands a couple of days ago. Beth was dying to bring up the poisoning question with Harry, and also discuss the whole Nina situation, but she knew that would instantly destroy the moment. He'd feel honour-bound to remind her, yet again, of all the issues that constrained him. He'd also be furious with the SOCO team for blabbing and beside himself at what Chris Campbell had told her. Julie-Ann would then feel guilty for spilling secrets, and Jake would be fed up with the whole lot of them – especially, no doubt, his mother. Beth had no choice but to bide her time.

As they'd eaten up all the dregs of ice cream when Josh had been round, there was nothing for pudding except ancient frozen pains au chocolat which Beth had bought long ago and forgotten about. She served them up with a carton of richly yellow ready-made custard, of the sort that would have Katie running to the nearest Waitrose for crème anglaise, and would have Nina's poor little Wilf licking his lips. Needless to say, it was delicious.

It wasn't until they were in bed, much later, that Beth sleepily asked one of the questions that had been on her mind all night.

'Does the Met still consider poisoning to be a woman's crime, you know, like people did back in the day?'

Beth could feel Harry's hesitation, as he fought both sleep and the desire to avoid any shop talk at all costs. But, even though he obviously doubted her motives for asking such a question, she wasn't surprised when he eventually answered thoughtfully.

'To some extent. It's premeditated. That could suggest particular cunning – or just the knowledge that you aren't going to win in a fight. The majority of women don't have the physical strength to subdue someone face to face, unless that person is quite a lot smaller and weaker than them. A child, say.'

Beth shuddered. After a moment, she spoke again. 'But could a woman ever strangle another woman, for instance?'

'Are you asking for a friend? I thought you were getting on pretty well with Julie-Ann,' Harry said with a chuckle.

Beth nudged him with her elbow. 'I think she's great. No, I'm just... interested.'

'Hmm. Well, the answer is that it depends on both women, their relative size and so on. But generally speaking a woman's grip is at least forty per cent weaker than a man's. So strangulation is going to be hard work for a woman, even on another woman's smaller neck. It depends a bit on hand size and a lot on grip strength. If you have big hands and never have any trouble opening pickle jars, then you might be fine. Otherwise, there's a good chance that whoever you are trying to throttle would get away, and maybe kill you instead. Let's just say it's an incredibly rare crime for women.'

'And Harry?'

'Mmm?' he said sleepily.

'You don't think Nina did anything bad, do you?'

'Don't be silly, Beth,' he said.

It wasn't the kind of bedtime chat that most people would enjoy. But Beth nestled under the duvet that night with statistics and crime scene tape and white puffa jackets jostling happily in her dreams. She hadn't interrogated Harry in depth about Nina's guilt, but those few words had been reassuring enough. If he'd been just about to arrest one of her best friends, she was pretty sure he'd simply have refused to answer at all.

She drifted off to sleep quite contentedly, pleased at the thought that the solution to these perplexing deaths might – just might – be getting closer by the hour.

FORTY-TWO

All Beth's smugness evaporated in a moment the next morning, though, when she got a one-line text from Nina at breakfast. It read, cryptically, *Horse pedal Wilf.*

At first, Beth smiled as she tried to decode the message. But then her face fell a mile. Nina's texting was as quirky as her speech, but there was only one translation that seemed to fit, and she didn't like the sound of it at all. She made a quick call to one of Nina's neighbours, Bob, and her worst fears were confirmed. With just a brief word to Harry and Jake, she dashed out of the house, for once able to ignore Colin's pleading gaze without a backward glance. Wilf was very ill, and had been admitted to King's College Hospital.

It wasn't until she had found Wilf's ward – in itself no mean feat in the labyrinth of corridors – that she caught her breath, though seeing his little white face on the pillow did nothing to allay her terror. Nina was by his bed, visibly twitching with anxiety.

They hadn't been on the easiest terms since Beth had found out about Nina's fling with Len, not to mention Wilf's parentage, but there is no leveller like a sick child. Beth kissed Wilf's clammy forehead, wrapped her arms around her friend, and then dragged up another chair. Wilf seemed to be dipping in and out of sleep so Beth asked in a low voice, 'What the hell happened?'

Nina shook her head from side to side in weary self-disgust. 'It was all my stupid fault. Got a present in the post, some chocs. There was no note or nothing. I just assumed it was from my aunt, you know, Katrina's mum.'

Beth nodded, and Nina continued. 'Sometimes she sends me and Wilf a little something. I let him have one last night, after brushing his teef. I knew it was a really bad idea but he was whinging on and, what with one thing and another, I just haven't been feeling up to it lately,' she said, glancing away.

Beth slid an arm round Nina and hugged her again. 'I'm not surprised. I'm sorry, a lot of that is on me. I didn't react well to the whole, erm, Len thing,' she said, with an eye on Wilf. His long eyelashes were fanned out on his cheeks now and his chest was moving up and down peacefully.

'It was just one chocolate – one!' wailed Nina. 'And at first he went straight off to sleep... but then, in the night, I heard something. He'd only fallen out of bed. When I went in, I saw he'd been throwing up. His little face was all red. He was heaving, like he couldn't breathe. God, it was scary, Beth. It was awful.'

'Did you call an ambulance?'

'No time for that, I just woke up my neighbour, Bob, you know, the bloke whose dog Rosie died a while back. He's a sweetheart. He took us straight here.'

'Yes, he's the one I rang just now. He was brilliant.'

Nina's block of flats was legendary for its fantastic community spirit, and seemed to have done her proud this time. 'They said if it had been five minutes later, he'd have gone into full cardiac arrest.'

'But what on earth happened? What caused this?'

Something about Beth's urgent tone woke Wilf from his slumbers and his eyelids fluttered.

'Shh, babe,' said Nina, smoothing his forehead as he drifted off again.

When he was safely asleep once more, Beth looked over at Nina and raised her eyebrows.

'All right, I'll tell you,' said Nina beadily. 'But on one condition.'

'What's that?' said Beth, equally cautiously.

'That you tell your bloke I didn't blimmin well do it!'

'He knows that! Don't fret. I talked to him last night – well, after a fashion – and he's definitely not going to arrest you. Don't worry.'

'Thank Bob for that!' said Nina, now wreathed in smiles. 'Well, listen to this, then, babes.'

* * *

On the way out of King's, realising they had next to no food in the house after all her unaccustomed entertaining over the past few days, Beth decided to pop into the hospital shop. It was such a relief that Wilf was out of imminent danger, and her mind was so busy with everything that Nina had just said, that Beth spent much longer than she would normally have done, browsing the shelves. There was nothing here that she could possibly cook for supper, it was all trashy magazines, boxes of Milk Tray and get well soon cards, but she had a good mooch anyway. Then she realised there was someone slightly familiar at the till, talking to the shop manager, and waving some cellophane bags around. It was a grey-haired lady, who was talking fast but getting nowhere.

She stepped closer, and realised it was Harriet French. At that moment, the woman turned.

'Oh! The girl from the salon,' Harriet French said, her face flushed.

'Erm, yes. Oh, those look nice,' Beth said, gesturing at the bags with their pretty bows and labels saying *Jardins Francais.*

'Thank you! You see?' Harriet French said triumphantly over her shoulder at the manager. 'Someone appreciates my pot pourri.'

'I saw it in Tomlinson's the other day,' said Beth slowly. 'Love the packaging. And the labels. *Jardins Francais*, that means...'

'French Gardens. Yes, exactly,' said Harriet French eagerly. 'Honestly, it's the perfect hospital gift, isn't it? But try telling them.' She gestured contemptuously at the poor manager.

Beth confined herself to a wide smile. 'So, what's in it?'

'My special mixture? It's all my most beautiful summer blooms, captured for an all-year-round scent explosion,' said Harriet, obviously quoting from her own promo material. 'It's a heady, floral yet intensely woody scent that's really unique. That's because, as well as roses, lavender and jasmine, it has a little nicotiana in it... my secret ingredient.'

'Ah,' said Beth, and her smile dropped.

FORTY-THREE

'I can't believe we're doing this,' said Katie, her black hat pulled down low over her shining blonde hair.

'I know, but at least this time we knew in advance there's a big meeting going on here, so it would be easy to get in,' said Beth, playing her phone torch over the line of doors in front of them. They were back in the council buildings, and had got as far as the corridor where Len Broughton's office was located. 'Of course, there's one thing we didn't think of when we left Teddy at home this time.'

'What's that?' said Katie, stopping in her tracks.

'How to get in if it's locked,' said Beth, stopping in front of the door that, despite Teddy's recent attentions, showed no signs of damage.

'Rats!' said Katie. 'I can't believe we didn't think of that.' She looked disconsolate.

'Well, let's give it a try,' said Beth, putting a hand on the doorknob anyway, just for form's sake. There was no trace of any fresh crime scene tape, so could the police have lost interest? To her amazement, it gave. They were in.

Their delight turned rapidly back to dejection, though, when they saw the state of the office. The shelves had been swept clean, the desk drawers were hanging open as if to demonstrate how empty they were. There was no sign of the laptop, or of any of Len's other possessions. Even the air smelt different, less stale, with no tang of old pipe tobacco to remind them of his smoking addiction.

'What on earth do we do now?' said Katie.

Beth swung round in the echoing space, racking her brains. She was just about to say they ought to call it a day and get home, when she spotted a door. 'Wait a minute, is this a coat cupboard?'

It was – and inside was a small tower of boxes. 'Ta-dah,' she couldn't resist saying. Within minutes, they had got what they came for. Beth handed the item to Katie, and it was her turn to shove the evidence up her jumper. This time, instead of trying to saunter out undetected, when they got downstairs in the lift they headed straight for the meeting room, and were treated to the ten last minutes of an epically dull meeting about speed cameras, at which members of the Wyatt's Estate were cross-questioning council officials about the exact angle the devices would be fixed at, in case they encroached on the privacy of the ancient and beautiful gardens of Wyatt's Museum of Art, and the allotments over the road.

Beth and Katie were sitting right at the back, and Katie's head was nodding by the time the last person got up to speak. But something about the voice of the latecomer woke her right up.

'Wait a second! Isn't that...?'

'Shh, yes, yes it is. But let's try and act like nothing's wrong,' Beth hissed urgently.

'OK,' said Katie doubtfully, eyes fixed now on the speaker as though they were going to vanish in a puff of smoke.

The meeting broke up a few minutes later, and a stream of people started coming towards them.

'Right, now's our chance,' said Beth, nudging Katie, who was closest to the aisle. They both got out of their seats and started edging along, to join the crowd steadily making for the exit.

'It's working so far,' said Katie brightly to Beth, just as they passed a guard. Indeed, there was only the security gate to get through now, then the revolving door, and they'd be out in the outside world again...

But then, just as Beth had been dreading since they'd first set foot in the building, a familiar voice called out. 'Hey, you. Yes, you, Beth Haldane. Stop right there.'

Immediately, Beth went rigid, then cursed herself for doing so. If she'd just pretended she hadn't heard, or it wasn't her, then maybe she could have got away with this. She tried walking onwards, twice as fast, but out of the corner of her eye she could see one of the security guards moving towards her, slowly at first but then gaining pace.

This was like one of her nightmares, where nameless people were chasing her. Only this time, she knew full well the identity of her pursuer. There was no guard near the revolving doors, though. Could she and Katie squeeze through in time? In a dream, she would easily finish the race and then her enemy would vaporise. In real life, however, the person following her would just continue to do so even outside the council building. Could she really keep on running?

Beth took a decision, and put her hand on Katie's arm. 'I've got to stay and face the music. But you can get away. I'll see you tomorrow,' she said breathlessly.

'Don't be silly, Beth. We're in this together,' said Katie, her eyes wild. She turned round bravely, but Beth waved her off frantically, and allowed herself to be led away.

This was something she had to do. Something that had been looming ever since she'd sat in the church of St Matthew with Wendy, at Len Broughton's funeral, and seen – amongst the crowd – a certain person trashing her mother's wreath – and converting it to pot pourri.

FORTY-FOUR

Rough hands shoved Beth into a small stockroom just off the main reception area, and the door closed. Now she was finally facing the person she'd been dreading bumping into all night. The last speaker at the meeting, a woman with a strong interest in matters of privacy, and the Dulwich allotments – the one and only Mrs Len Broughton.

'So,' said Margery Brinkwell. 'We meet again.'

'Looks like it,' said Beth, aiming for casual rather than scared out of her wits. No need for the woman to know she was already reduced to a quivering wreck by the very thought of this confrontation.

'It's been quite a while since you first asked me your silly little questions,' said Margery, twirling one of her long dangly diamond earrings.

'Yes. A lot's changed since then,' said Beth. She must have sounded a little more confident, because Margery Brinkwell immediately went to stand with her back against the door – the only exit from the room – and crossed her arms.

'I don't know what you think has happened. As far as I can see, you're still an idiot, and an idiot's daughter.'

'Leave my mother out of this,' said Beth, bridling. She didn't mind the woman berating her – after years of Belinda McKenzie's jibes, she was used to it – but Wendy wasn't here to defend herself. And her only crime was loving not wisely but too well. 'I don't know what you hope to gain by shutting me in here, Margery. You can't keep me here forever, you know. You'll be wanting to go home yourself.'

Or, at least, Beth very much hoped she would. The truth was that Margery didn't have much to go home to these days. Len was no longer around, the secret of her marriage was out, and no doubt all the women he had conned were making their disgruntlement plain, and coming to her to get their money back. Margery was not in a good place. And that was if you didn't factor in the whole double murder thing.

In fact, you could see from her face that Margery had got to the end of her tether some considerable time ago. She had the snarling features of someone with very little left to lose, and the jolly dangly earrings cut a discordant note against the frankly doolally look in her glassy eyes.

'It's up to you, really, Beth. You can make this easy... or you can make it very, very hard on yourself,' said Margery, her voice low and insistent. She was advancing towards Beth now, the space between them in the small room shrinking as rapidly as a Dulwich yummy mummy on a New Year fad diet. Beth instinctively started backing away, only to find herself pressed up against a metal bookshelf. There was nowhere else to go.

She cast around frantically for weapons. There were a few mops, but they were right over by the door and she couldn't get to them. There was a vacuum cleaner by the wall, but what was she going to do, hoover the woman into submission? Beth started berating herself. When would she ever learn not to act on impulse? Tackling killers was definitely stuff best left to the actual police. She had enough scars by now to provide proof of this horrible fact. What on earth had she thought she was doing?

It was too late to change things now, though. This was the situation she was in, and she was not going to give up without a struggle. All right, the woman in front of her was bigger, stronger, and definitely bonkers enough to try anything. But Beth had got herself out of tight situations before. Her body was flooded with adrenaline, right down to her fingertips. She could feel it jolting through her system. She couldn't do the flight bit; her only chance was to fight.

'What do you think you are going to do, then, Margery?' Beth said, bursting into speech, hoping her tone sounded taunting and not terrified. 'It's not quite as easy as killing Len, is it? I don't have any convenient addictions for you to exploit, like his pipe. And I'm not going to eat one of your chocolates, like him or Bella Harrington or little Wilf, either. So you're a bit stuck, aren't you?'

Beth glared at Margery, feeling her terror dissipating, anger taking its place. This woman had led the people of Dulwich a merry dance. She had broken Wendy's heart (well, with Len's help, to be fair), she had killed the entirely innocent Bella Harrington. She had nearly poisoned poor Wilf, a sweet boy who had never done anyone any harm. She was an evil, cruel woman. No wonder even a reprobate like Len wouldn't admit to being married to her.

'You've forgotten one thing, Beth Haldane,' said Margery, as she came closer still. She was really infringing Beth's personal space now, and looked like she had no intention of stopping. Beth could see, in blinding close-up, the red veins crazing her bulging eyes, and the flecks of spittle on either side of her pinched mouth. The woman was as nutty as a Mariella's café praline slice, that was for sure. 'You're very, very small and insignificant.'

Beth knew this to be humiliatingly true, if one was just confining oneself to height terms. But she was so much more than a tiddly tally of inches. She drew herself up and said loudly and clearly, 'If I'm so insignificant, how come you're doing all this? You could let me go if I don't mean anything,' said Beth, trying to keep the desperation out of her voice, but unable to stop picturing the scene at home. Jake, lovelorn and a bit lost in the new world of hormones engulfing him, would be wondering where she'd got to. Colin would certainly be tapping a paw, waiting for his walkies. And Magpie might, just might, be feeling a bit peckish and asking herself where her bowl-filling minion was. Harry probably wouldn't be home yet, but he'd miss her when he got there, of that she was sure.

'Let you go? You must be joking,' said Margery, with a savage laugh. 'I just mean you're a shrimp, and it will be the work of a moment to prise those flapping jaws open and get you to swallow one of my lovely morsels.'

True to her word, Margery advanced even further, and Beth was treated to a waft of Jo Malone's Pomegranate Noir fragrance, a scent she'd never much liked even when it wasn't being worn by a homicidal maniac. Suddenly one of the woman's hands was gripping the side of her head, while the fingers of the other rushed at her, trying to yank her mouth open. Beth could see a plastic bag full of chocolates bulging out of her pocket. Poisoned, deadly chocolates, no doubt tainted with the same huge dose of boiled-up nicotine that had seen off Len and Bella, and nearly done for Wilf too.

She didn't have a moment to lose. With a lightning movement, Beth ducked to the left, while with her right hand she searched blindly along the metal shelves pressing so painfully into her back. If she was right, and this was the room where all the ground floor cleaning equipment was dumped, there was going to be something useful here somewhere... suddenly she was flooded with relief. She felt a familiar, reassuring shape. Exactly what she was looking for! Then she shot her arm forward – and gave Margery Brinkwell four or five liberal squirts of Flash bleach spray, right in the face.

'Not such a shrimp now, am I?' Beth yelled. 'And who says cleaning is a waste of time?'

FORTY-FIVE

Before Beth had a moment to feel too awful about burning Margery Brinkwell's face off, the door of the oppressive little room flew open, and Katie, two security guards and Harry burst in.

'She needs medical treatment,' Beth babbled immediately. 'I had no choice, she was trying to get me to swallow one of her poisoned chocolates. You need to flush out her eyes.'

Harry reached her in a stride, and pulled her into his arms. 'Don't worry about that woman, I'll make sure she gets seen to.' He jerked his head at Narinda Khan, who had just popped her head round the door. 'Take her away. And Katie, you'd better get home to your family.'

Katie didn't need telling twice. She gave Beth a quick hug and made for the door.

'But how come you knew we were here?' Beth mumbled into Harry's familiar, beloved, navy blue peacoat.

'Simple. I'm a detective. Plus Katie rang me from the carpark. And then, ahem, I used the "find my phone" function on your mobile,' Harry said, chuckling.

Beth felt the warm reverberation of his laugh deep in his

chest, and tightened her embrace. On a normal day, she might have complained about him tracking her. But it felt so very good to be safe, and in his embrace. 'Does that mean you had an inkling something was up?'

'Apart from there being a murderer loose on my patch? Yes. I didn't tell you, but after it turned out Bella Harrington also had unusually high levels of nicotine in her blood, and wasn't a smoker, it was clear her "heart attack" was something else. And the reason I was back really late last night when Julie-Ann was round was because, well, we exhumed Len Broughton.'

Beth gasped. 'You could have told me!'

'Actually, I shouldn't even be telling you now. But the second post-mortem findings strongly suggested he was poisoned in the same way, with a very high concentration of cotinine. That's metabolised nicotine, which fortunately lingers a lot longer in a dead body than nicotine does. Although I think it's understandable we missed the toxicity the first time, as he was such a dedicated pipe smoker.'

Beth wisely didn't reply, just enjoying their hug. But she did wonder how different things might have been, if Harry had been more suspicious from the start. Bella would still be around, and Wilf wouldn't have had his near-death experience.

Margery Brinkwell was a wily, determined woman, though, and as Beth knew full well, it was hard to outwit someone so hell-bent on their course. If things had been different – if Margery hadn't gone so decisively to the dark side – Beth could even have admired her. But as it was, she shuddered at her narrow escape.

'We'd better get you home right away,' said Harry, misinterpreting her shiver.

'Yes please,' she said, gazing up at him. She knew there'd be a lot of statements to be taken, police interviews to endure and hoops to jump through, but for now, she was just yearning to be at home, with her son, her pets – and her man.

* * *

The first frost was on the ground when Beth met Katie in the park a few days later. Both had their dogs in tow. Beth had persuaded Katie to give Teddy a few walks herself, as well as using Sophie the dog-walker. 'So that he wouldn't get out of practice at proper walkies with his real mistress.' Katie, always trying to do the right thing by her family, hadn't needed much convincing that this was a good idea. They both enjoyed the space and freedom to discuss the Len business properly, and of course Margery Brinkwell's final comeuppance.

To Beth's relief, the woman's eyes were fine – Narinda Khan had taken her off straight away to the nearest loo and seemed to have taken great pleasure in dousing her from head to toe in plenty of ice-cold water.

'There are a few things I still don't understand,' said Katie. 'Even though we've talked about it a lot. I mean, how did Margery Brinkwell know so much about poisons anyway?'

'She started her career as a nurse, I think she was virtually running King's by the time she left. She would have seen a lot there. My guess is someone came in with nicotine poisoning and that's how she got the idea. Chris Campbell – the pathologist, you know – said even eating one cigarette could kill a small person. So boiling up loads and then steeping Len's tobacco in the result would be lethal. All she had to do then was wait for it to dry out again, repack it in one of those pouches, and send it to his office.'

'But how did she know Len would die that night?'

'Oh, I don't think she did. It was a bit like Russian roulette. She was just waiting and waiting. But I think she also sent him those nicotine-poisoned chocolates we found in his office the second time – that box you smuggled out under your jumper. She must have been getting impatient. Even so, she had no idea when it would happen. He could have had the chocolates there for weeks, before he decided to scoff a few.

'If she'd had an inkling when he'd die,' Beth went on, 'I bet she would have arranged a proper watertight alibi. As it was, that was a weak spot. She was at home alone. But that's why she was so convincing when I first talked to her. She was able to convince herself she hadn't really done it – it was his smoking that literally killed him, or his greed in eating the chocolates.'

'Do you know why she even wanted to kill Len in the first place?'

Beth gave Katie a look, and she had to laugh. 'Yes, I suppose that's a silly question,' Katie admitted. 'He was running around with everyone in town, he was a gambler, he was a swindler... who wouldn't want to get shot of him? But she could have just divorced him.'

'Good point. But my guess is that she was worried if she started proceedings, then the news would somehow get out. She liked keeping the marriage a secret, and again you can see why. It would have been humiliating if it had been public. Solicitors round here aren't always that discreet,' said Beth, thinking of another tricky case she'd worked on. 'I wonder if it was my mother believing she was engaged to Len that sent Margery over the edge. If, as Mum says, Len popped the question right outside his house, Margery could even have been lurking somewhere, listening. Maybe that did it.'

'And then I suppose she got rid of Bella Harrington because she knew too much.'

'I was thinking that possibly Bella clocked the tobacco pouch arriving at the office, and thought it was a bit odd... maybe she started putting two and two together. She'd probably caught on about the way her boss was swindling people, too.' And, thought Beth, Bella would almost certainly have known about Wilf.

'And then Margery asked her to meet up at the LTN planters and fed her a chocolate?'

'Yes. It must have been laced much more strongly with nicotine than the others, to kill her so quickly. Or maybe they met somewhere else, and Bella then keeled over in the flowerbeds on her way home. I guess we'll never know – unless Margery decides to speak up.'

'Do you think Harry will get her to trial?'

Beth kicked at a stone on the path. 'It's not up to him at this point – he just turns everything over to the Crown Prosecution Service and they decide whether they can get a judgement against her. But I'd say she might actually be mentally fit to stand.'

'You really think she's sane?' asked Katie, looking horrified at the very idea.

'There was a lot of premeditation, a lot of cunning... hard to be that organised if you're unstable. And the way she tried to kill poor Wilf too, it was so evil. Though I think that was probably aimed at Nina, in case she realised who had swiped her phone to decoy Bella to the meeting. Nina thought it was at a Len's Ladies meeting, but Margery didn't go to those. She must have pinched it in one of the coffee shops, right under Nina's nose. Then she dumped it back on her doorstep. Margery would have known all about Nina, and Wilf. It was probably one of the secrets that helped drive her to kill. Len really had a lot to answer for.'

'How is Wilf, do you know?'

'He's absolutely fine,' said Beth, with a relieved smile. 'Jake went over there yesterday and they spent the afternoon gaming. And Nina and I had a proper chat, too. Cleared the air. It's all Gucci now, as she would say.'

They walked in silence for a minute or two, Beth admiring the silhouettes of the trees, now bare of leaves and poking into a crisp bright blue Dulwich sky. Then Katie piped up again.

'At the beginning, you seemed so sure it couldn't possibly be Margery. Why was that?' Katie had her head on one side.

Beth sighed. 'That was entirely my fault. I'm afraid it was simply because my mother was so sure it *was* her. You know Wendy and I never agree on anything. That completely clouded my judgement. It was a really useful lesson. Plus for ages I thought the killer was Harriet French.'

'But you said Mrs Hill confirmed nicotiana only flowers in summer?'

'That's right, but Harriet makes pot pourri with the petals, so she has them around all year... I thought she might be boiling them up. There's one type of nicotiana which has a really high concentration of nicotine.'

'Weird that it smells so nice, while cigarettes are so stinky. So what made you decide it wasn't her?'

'Well, her motive wasn't as strong as Margery's. Even if the polyamory thing isn't true, she seemed quite happy about her relationship with Len. And it wasn't clear she even knew Bella, or Wilf for that matter. Whereas as Len's wife, Margery would know Bella was his secretary and Wilf was his son. And I reckon the poison from dried nicotiana leaves would be weaker than fresh nicotine, anyway.'

'How is Wendy?' Katie asked. 'Has it helped her, getting some sort of closure like this? Though I'm sure she'd hate that word.'

'She does. But yes, I think it has been useful. We got it all sorted in time for her blessed Bridge tournament, so she was thrilled about that. She said it meant she could compete without thinking people were talking about her. And you know what she really loved?'

'No, what?' Katie asked.

'It was when I told her that Len was using her birthday as his computer password. It was as though I'd given her the biggest bouquet of flowers ever. She was just smiling from ear to ear. She really did love him, you know. That was so clever of you, to suggest it.'

Katie smiled and pressed Beth's arm gratefully. 'What about the money? Did he rip her off as well?'

'Not nearly as much as the others. She had a lucky escape there. And actually she's adamant that he didn't have a gambling problem anyway. You know how she can swear black is white. She's as bad as Harriet French in some ways. I've given up trying to get her to face the truth.'

'Very wise,' said Katie kindly, before continuing a little gingerly. 'I know it's hard, because you loved your dad so much, but... do you think she'll start dating again properly now?'

'God, I really hope not,' said Beth. 'Imagine who she might pick next!' They both burst out laughing. 'Can you think of anything worse? But at least she's stopped crying now. And I suppose it's shown me I ought to listen to her more.'

'Does that mean you and Wendy are going to be in total accord from now on?' Katie said with a smile.

'I doubt it.' Beth's tone was wry. 'I don't think I could do that big an about-turn in my thinking at this late stage.'

'Late stage? We're only in our thirties,' Katie said in mock-outrage.

'I know, I know. But tell that to Julie-Ann, she thinks anyone over twenty-five has at least one and a half feet in the grave. Apart from Josh, maybe. If anything, though, this whole Len business has shown me that my mother isn't always wrong... and I'm not always right.'

'That's a toughie,' said Katie, turning to Beth and giving her a hug. This was a mistake. Naughty Teddy had a sixth sense for when Katie's thoughts were elsewhere. Now he made a break for freedom. He scampered off, ears flapping like silken streamers, bouncing happily over the green grass – until he came to a long-legged, long-haired blonde vision on the path ahead, who was walking several Irish wolfhounds.

Beth spotted what was going on, and set off at a speed previously unknown to her. By the time she got close to the little group, the girl with the wolfhounds was red in the face, sweating and swearing fluently, her enviably lithe limbs splattered in mud and worse, while Teddy was jumping about unrepentantly and making unmistakable overtures to the smaller of the hounds, who looked terrified at this persistent suitor. Just as Katie came running up, the girl with the dogs got pulled right over into the mud, and then was dragged through a puddle for several yards by the excitable pack of hounds.

'Oh, hi, Katie,' said Beth, her phone in her hand and a big smile on her face. 'Poor Allegra, looks like she's taken a bit of a tumble.'

'Er, yes she has,' said Katie, looking at Beth sharply. 'What exactly are you doing?'

Beth was staring fixedly at her phone, transparently unsure whether to proceed with something or not. 'Oh, just making a decision...' With that, she jabbed a finger at the screen and then put the mobile away. 'Isn't it terrible, the sort of things people will upload to social media these days?'

FORTY-SIX

Walking to school the next morning, Jake was surprised when Charlie slapped him on the back as he got to their usual meeting point.

'Seen this, mate?' he said, waving his mobile.

Jake shook his head and focused on the little screen. Then he leant in closer. A shaky video showed a scarlet-cheeked blonde being dragged through the mud by several large dogs... for a second, he really felt for her. But she did look quite ridiculous. He met Charlie's eye. It was the first time he'd cracked a huge smile in ages.

He probably wouldn't mention Allegra's downfall to his mum, though. She was always banging on to him about being nice, and the importance of treating girls with respect, and he totally got it, he really did. And he tried, even though that thing Leggy had done to him was pretty mean. Still, what his mother didn't know wouldn't worry her, would it?

He wondered fleetingly who might have filmed the whole slapstick episode, then dismissed the thought. There were some mysteries which really didn't need to be solved. He grinned up at Charlie, and they sauntered off to school. Today was going to be a very good day in Dulwich.

A LETTER FROM ALICE

Thank you so much for choosing to read my book. I love writing about Beth Haldane and I hope you've enjoyed finding out what she got up to this time. If you'd like to know what happens to Beth next, please sign up at the email link below. Your email address will never be shared and you can unsubscribe at any time.

www.bookouture.com/alice-castle

If you enjoyed the story, I would be very grateful if you could write a review. I'd love to hear what you think. I always read reviews and I take careful account of what people say. My aim is always to make the books a better read! Leaving a review also helps new readers to discover my books for the first time.

I'm also on Twitter, Facebook and Goodreads, often sharing pictures of cats that look like Magpie. Do get in touch if that's your sort of thing. Thanks so much again, and I really hope to see you soon for Beth's next adventure. Happy reading!

Alice Castle

Alicecastleauthor.com

facebook.com/Alicecastleauthor

twitter.com/AliceMCastle

Printed in Great Britain
by Amazon

23019596R10169